THE WIREGRASS WITNESS

JOE CARGILE

SEVERN RIVER
PUBLISHING

Severn River Publishing
www.SevernRiverBooks.com

ISBN: 978-1-64875-421-0 (Paperback)

ALSO BY JOE CARGILE

Blake County Legal Thrillers

Legacy on Trial

In Defense of Charlotte

The Wiregrass Witness

The Burden of Power

To find out more about Joe Cargile and his books, visit

severnriverbooks.com/authors/joe-cargile

1

Blake County, Georgia
October 10, 2016

The call rang out from somewhere deep in the darkness—*Bingo! Bingo!*

He drifted toward the sound, listening for others to echo the alert. He recognized it. The sound of the voice. It was hard to miss. It was the same one he'd heard all night, chirping at him since the first snap of the game. Since they'd all been kids, really.

The call sounded again. This time louder, closer.

He tried to move his feet in the direction of the sound. He had good feet. A sort of natural gift, or so he'd been told. Whether planted, shuffling, or on the run, he was an athlete who knew how to use his feet. Something was wrong with them tonight, though. They wouldn't budge.

Again—*Bingo! Bingo!*

He struggled once more to move, but he couldn't. He felt pinned down. As if sandbags lay on top of his chest. That, or his mind had been detached from the rest of his body. Either way, he only had one play, and that was to do what he did best. Not panic. Colt Hudson never panicked.

Then he heard it—*Eyes up, Hudson.*

Colt opened his eyes and saw a familiar face. He'd just seen it on the field a few minutes ago. At least, he thought he had. They'd jawed at one another for most of the game. A back-and-forth perfected through years of squaring off against each other. First on the rec-league fields, then under the lights of high school stadiums. Now, Colt's childhood friend leaned over his left shoulder, breathing down on him with a look of concern.

"Deacon?" Colt asked, his throat dry. His voice sounded cracked and weak in his own ears. He wasn't sure he could trust it. "What in the—"

"I'm right here, Colt," Deacon answered, leaning closer. "Damn boy, thank God you're alive. We weren't sure you'd come back to us."

"Back from where?"

Deacon Campbell stood back up to his full height of six-five and offered Colt a wide smile. He'd been an all-state linebacker the season before, and he was well on his way to another first-team selection come fall's end. He'd become known for his speed and size. The constant encouragement for his teammates. The smart pre-snap adjustments. He had the tools that would take him to the next level, and maybe even the level after that. More than anything, though, Deacon Campbell had been born a leader, and a damn good friend.

"You just checked out on us there for a minute. Had me all worried."

Colt considered his friend's words for a moment. They weren't the kind that came easy to young men.

"Where am I?" Colt managed. "And...what the hell happened to me?"

A lamp came on nearby and the added light confirmed Colt's suspicions. He was in a hospital room, that much he knew. As he turned his head to take in the surroundings, pain shot down his neck. The sudden bout of agony surprised him. Colt closed his eyes as screws seemed to grind into his skull. He took in a deep breath, trying to collect himself. Everything had started to throb at once and both eyes would soon be brimming with tears if he wasn't careful. He shut them in an attempt to stave off the inevitable.

"They call this a hospital," Deacon replied, his tone lighter. "You know, where babies are born and folks come to die."

Colt didn't want to open his eyes. He didn't want to move at all because he feared the pain might escalate if he so much as breathed in again. He couldn't help himself, though. He smiled at his friend's comment, then lifted a finger. The middle one.

"Hudson hospitality," Deacon said with a laugh. "A guy comes down to the hospital to see an old friend in need and gets this bum treatment. It really seems to me that—"

"It's still rivalry weekend, brother. You know how it is—no truce until next week."

Deacon paused before responding. "This the first time you been awake?"

"I don't know," Colt said as he opened his eyes again. He stared at the ceiling for a moment, thinking. Something was off. "I think so."

Deacon crossed his arms. The T-shirt he wore had the sleeves cut off and looked a size too small. The cocky linebacker stood there silent for a moment—a bad sign because Deacon Campbell wasn't known for his restraint. He was known more for the endless string of insults he hurled at his opponents after each hit. Always done in a creative, single-wide jargon that made him one of the most memorable players in high school football.

"So, you don't know if anyone has been in here to try to talk to you?"

"Like I said, man, I can't even remember the last time I was awake in here. You could tell me that some doctor just came in here with a drill to bore out one of my temples. I'd probably believe you."

Deacon smiled. "Take a beat, my brother. Try hard to remember if you've talked to anyone. Anyone at all."

Colt felt the first twinge of frustration. It mixed in with the confusion that already consumed him. "Deacon, what is going on? I need you to talk to me."

Colt watched his friend's face for a reaction. He noticed the eyes as they flicked to a corner of the room. Colt wanted to look over in that same direction, but he didn't want to risk another shot of pain to his skull and neck.

"Nobody from the Blake County Sheriff's Office has been in here?" Deacon asked. "Nobody from BPD?"

"I need one of these nurses or doctors to get in here," Colt said as he made no attempt to hide his impatience. He started to fumble around the bed for a remote of some sort. There had to be a way to get the attention of the nurse who was on call. "I know it's Friday night and all, but I need someone to get in here and tell me what the—"

Another voice interjected, one that Colt recognized right off. "It's

Monday, son, so you'd better get your head right before you speak to anybody. You hear me?"

Colt gritted his teeth at the sound of his father's voice as it polluted the otherwise sterile room. He felt the man's presence now, almost suffocating him. That's how it'd always been with Liam Hudson.

"I'm just fine without your advice," Colt said as his hand found the remote. He started to lift it up from under the thin sheet. "How about you just—"

"Oh, that's right," his father hissed as he placed a hand around Colt's right forearm. The one lifting the remote to call the nurse. "You're a big boy now, aren't you?"

"Mr. Hudson," Deacon started. "I don't think Colt meant that—"

"No, Deacon, my little Colt here doesn't need a thing from his family or friends. Big-time quarterback with a scholarship to college now. Bright future ahead of him somewhere far away from Blakeston."

More pain greeted Colt as he turned to his father. "Get your hand off of me."

Liam just smiled back. The man had thick mitts for hands and the callouses on each had been earned through decades of hard work. Colt knew his father stopped going to school as soon as the county quit calling about him cutting classes. That didn't mean the man stopped learning, though. No, after some thirty years in the trade, his father knew exactly how to break another man down to the studs, especially his only son.

"You don't know the first thing about the cluster you're in," Liam said, squeezing his son's ulna and radius together as he spoke. He liked to grab Colt's throwing arm when he cussed him, usually threatening to break it in one swift motion. "You think I'd be here at your side if you'd just bumped your sweet little head on the ground at the homecoming game?"

Colt considered the logic in his father's question. He was about to offer his own set of harsh words when the door to the hospital room opened. A nurse in blue scrubs entered, pushing a cart in front of her. She looked surprised to see everyone crowded around the bed. The lights on. The patient sitting up.

"He's awake," Deacon blurted out. "I was just about to come find someone and—"

"That's right," Colt's father added, squeezing the forearm once more before he released it. He stepped away from the side of the bed. "Been awake for maybe a minute or two. That's pretty good news, right?"

Colt watched the nurse's eyes as she seemed to evaluate the men who flanked her patient. They appeared to linger on Colt's father a moment longer. His oil-smudged work shirt. The words *Hudson Auto* stenciled on one half of his chest. *Liam,* on the other.

"It's great news," the nurse replied as she moved from behind her cart. She made her way toward the bed, the side that Liam had just occupied. Colt watched her as she took in information from the nearby monitors. Calm and collected. Just another day at the office.

"How are things looking?" Colt asked.

"That depends on quite a lot," the nurse said as she picked up Colt's arm. The same one that had been in a vise-grip only moments ago. She turned the arm over, no doubt noticing the red marks on the skin. "I'll need to get some information from you first."

Colt nodded.

"First, Colt, my name is Anne, and I've been checking in on you since they brought you into the hospital on Friday night. You're in our intensive care unit right now, the ICU."

The statement didn't strike Colt as one that required a response, so he just listened and watched as the woman continued to inspect the different tubes running from the nearby machines. She moved methodically, as if following her own carefully memorized checklist.

"You've taken a series of severe hits to the head," she said, her voice both informative and reassuring. "I imagine your body is experiencing significant pain, but we've been most focused on your brain since the EMTs brought you in. That three-pound organ in your skull is the most complex part of your body. We're going to make sure we take good care of it."

"We can't have you losing the little bit of sense you have left," Liam added with a snort. "Wouldn't that be a damn shame to—"

"That's not helpful, Mr. Hudson," the nurse snapped. "If you're going to interfere with my evaluation, then please step out of the room."

Colt noticed his father raise an eyebrow as he accepted the warning.

Liam didn't handle women in positions of authority well. Still, he showed the nurse his open palms and took another step back in mock retreat.

"Thank you, ma'am," Colt said. "For taking good care of me, that is."

Anne turned her attention back to her patient. "Of course. Now, can you try and tell me what you remember from Friday night?"

Colt focused as he tried to recall the last play of Friday night's homecoming football game—Blake County vs. Sumter County. The two high schools touted undefeated records before the regional showdown, but Colt couldn't remember who ended up walking off the field with their first loss of the season. He looked from the nurse's face to Deacon's, then his father's. They all had their eyes locked on his.

"We had a game against Sumter," Colt said, nodding in Deacon's direction as he spoke. "Deacon's squad."

"Do you remember where the game was played?" Anne asked.

"Right here in Blakeston."

"Good," the nurse said as she started to write something on a clipboard. One she'd pulled from the nearby cart. "What else do you remember?"

He recalled flashes of memories. Fans cheering in the stands. The sound of the band playing the school's fight song. Whistles blowing and coaches yelling from the sidelines. He thought for a long moment as he tried to conjure up details from the game itself. Specific plays. The coin toss. A touchdown celebration.

"I remember throwing an interception in the third quarter," Colt finally said. "I let the ball sail high on my receiver, CJ. I called an audible, a mesh concept that we'd had some success with early in the season."

Deacon discreetly held a thumbs up for Colt to see.

"I remember the calls from their defensive secondary," Colt said as he felt his way through the memory. "They all yelled out—"

"Bingo," Deacon quietly added with a smile. "My boys always call out Bingo when they make a big play on the—"

"Let's not help him," Anne said, cutting Deacon off in a stern tone. "I want to hear Colt's version only."

Colt thought for another moment before pushing forward with his narrative. He could see the play as it unfolded. He couldn't remember how it ended, though. The memory felt more like a dream than something he'd experienced. A dream that just seemed to slip away.

Colt started again. "Their free safety picked me off. A real gangly guy. Wore an even-numbered jersey. Twenty, maybe?"

The nurse turned to Deacon for confirmation. He nodded to her.

"The guy held the ball out, showboating as he turned up field to follow a string of blue jerseys. I remember sprinting toward the opposite sideline because I thought I might be able to catch him near the boundary. I hopped over their weak-side linebacker as he lunged at my feet, then I made it to within four, maybe five yards of the sideline."

The room went quiet for a moment as Colt tried to remember what happened next. The reel in his mind seemed to freeze at that point in the memory. All he could see was an image of the Sumter County player, just out of arm's reach.

"Do you remember getting hit during that play?" the nurse finally asked. "I wasn't there, but I believe it was a shot to the back of your head and neck. I'm told it was a scary moment."

Colt started to shake his head, sending another dose of pain for his skull to deal with. This time, the pain came with something new, too, a faint ringing in the right ear. A timbre that he'd not heard before.

"I guess that must be when they stopped the game for an ambulance to bring me here," Colt said. "Because I really can't remember much after that."

Anne paused a moment. Her pen scratched on the clipboard.

"Maybe my boy here needs just a little bit of rest," Liam said in his best attempt at fatherly concern. It sounded unnatural. "We all know he's not going anywhere. At least not anytime soon."

Colt caught his father's eye just before the nurse looked up from her notes.

"No, we'd like to be able to measure where he is right now," she said in a tone that left little room for debate. "Now, Colt, do you remember trying to get up after that hit on the interception?"

"No, ma'am."

He was trying, but there wasn't anything there, not really. Only flashes of memories. Faces of people in his life. Coach Weeks. Deacon. A few of his teammates. And Natalie, of course.

"You don't remember being helped back to the sideline?"

"Like I said, I don't really remember."

"Keep trying."

Colt's thoughts drifted to Natalie. Her blue eyes. The freckles across her nose. Her long blonde hair that she twirled into big curls. Her smile as he'd lean over to kiss her on the field after a win.

After a win, he thought. *They'd won the game.*

"There are pieces of memories, but that's all," Colt said after another long moment. "I can remember Coach Weeks talking to me while I was on the ground. I can see Deacon's face through his facemask as he came over to pat me on the shoulder."

Talking about it helped. He remembered more and more now.

"I can see CJ and Connor as they helped get me up, supporting me as I walked off the field. I think I can maybe even remember us winning the game?"

"Y'all sure won alright," Deacon huffed, his arms still crossed. "Even with that hit you took to the head. You still got back out there and played."

The nurse started to lift a hand, but Deacon pushed on.

"You threw another touchdown in the fourth quarter, Colt. Are you telling me you don't remember that?"

"No," Colt said as he shook his head. "I think I can remember everyone pouring onto the field after the game, but the memory is all distorted. It's as if I watched it happen from the sidelines, or the bleachers even."

"Well, you sure as hell were out on that field because—"

"And I remember seeing Natalie," Colt added. "She ran over and kissed me after the game."

"Okay," the nurse said after a short pause. "What else do you—"

"Does she know I'm awake yet?"

"Let's try to focus on what you remember first."

Colt ignored the nurse's prodding. He looked over at Deacon. "She'd probably appreciate an update. You mind letting her know?"

Colt absorbed the sudden stillness in the room. The expression on his friend's face as he looked away.

"Deacon?"

His best friend—the kid with the never-back-down philosophy baked into his DNA—ran a hand through his hair. He shook his head, wiping something from his eyes.

Colt pleaded. "Talk to me."

"She didn't make it," he said in a quiet voice. "She's gone."

Colt went back to the memories. The flashes. There wasn't anything there to help.

"Deacon, where is she?"

2

The man knocked twice on the door.

Another one in a white coat—Dr. Beck—had done the same some forty-five minutes earlier. Right before he delivered the only good news of the day.

This man was different, though. Not the type that brought good news. No white coat, either.

"Colt Hudson?" the man asked, already lifting a badge from inside his jacket. He held the gold-plated emblem up for a moment before continuing, "I'm Trevor Meredith, an investigator with the Blake County Sheriff's Office."

Pre-game coverage for Monday Night Football played on the hospital room's television. Colt absorbed the appearance of the investigator. The badge. The slim folder tucked under one arm. The sport coat and jeans.

Great.

Colt's eyes returned to the television. Lisa Salters appeared on the small screen. He liked Lisa. Colt listened as she provided a concise, last-minute injury update on the beleaguered offenses that the Cardinals and Jets planned to trot out for the night's lackluster event.

"You may not have heard me over the noise of that TV," the investigator said. A real tough guy. "I'm looking for Colt—"

"That's me," Colt finally said as he started to turn the volume up on the television. He kept his eyes on the screen. "What can I do for you?"

"You mind if I come in?"

Colt had lived his whole life in Blake County. Given his father's business, he knew most of the deputies, police officers, and troopers that worked the area. Although he didn't know a lot about Trevor Meredith's role with the BCSO, he knew for a fact that this was no wellness check.

"Grab a seat," Colt said. "I'd stand to shake your hand and all but—"

"I get it, Colt," Meredith said with a laugh that sounded fake. "Even though you can't stand yet, you're still lucky to be alive."

Colt didn't respond.

"Anyways, how're you feeling?" Meredith asked, still standing beside the bed. "I mean, all things considered."

Colt muted the television as it went to commercial, then responded. "Like I've been hit by a truck. At least, that's what they're telling me happened."

"Well, like I said, you're lucky. That accident was something else."

Colt grimaced at the mention of the *accident*. A piece of reality that he was still getting used to. In fact, Dr. Beck had been the first person willing to give Colt the facts. Everyone else wanted to tip-toe around what happened. Not Dr. Beck, though. He did what every good doctor was supposed to do. He leveled his eyes with his patient and gave it to him straight.

It wasn't the hit on the football field that put him in the hospital. No, there'd been a car accident—the cross-by-the-roadside kind—and Dr. Beck told Colt what he knew about the scene of the wreck. Something Colt wasn't sure the good doctor always did for his patients. Then, after delivering the details, Dr. Beck provided Colt with a positive outlook as far as his injuries were concerned. No internal bleeding. No broken bones. No torn ligaments. *Lucky.*

Natalie hadn't been so lucky.

"Grab a seat," Colt said, motioning toward a chair. "You're making me nervous just standing there."

Meredith obliged. As he sat, he placed the thin folder in his lap and looked over at the television. Both watched as the kicker for the Jets—Nick

Folk—placed the ball on the tee and stepped off the opening kickoff. Colt mashed the volume on the remote and set it to low.

"Has anyone been in here to talk to you about the accident?"

"Nobody from your office."

Both watched as the kick sailed through the air and into the end-zone. As the teams jogged onto the field for the opening series, the commentators ran through the starting offense for the Arizona Cardinals.

"I can't believe Palmer is still playing," Meredith said in an attempt at small talk. "He has to be at least—"

"You come here just to watch the game with me?"

"No," Meredith said quickly, then shifted to a more business-like tone. "I need to ask you a few questions about the wreck."

Although the investigator sat only feet away, Colt felt comfortable. He knew pain medication could have that effect, though, so he reminded himself not to say something stupid. His dad would have his hide if he did.

"Did one of your guys take my cell phone?" Colt asked. "I can't seem to find it."

"Yes," Meredith replied. "A BCSO deputy that responded to the scene of the wreck inventoried it. It's in evidence—along with some of the other items found in the car."

Other items, Colt thought, trying to remember what else was in there.

"I need it back," Colt said. "I want to call Natalie's family. Mr. and Mrs. Abrams haven't heard from me yet."

Investigator Meredith wasn't much older than Colt. Six or seven years ahead in school. Donned the green and gold jersey for Blake County High. Another kid from Blake County. A quarterback, just like Colt.

"I'm not so sure they want to talk to you right now."

"Yeah?" Colt asked. "I'm not all that sure I want to talk to you either. Here we are, though."

Meredith didn't respond. Colt knew that the young investigator was supposed to tell him something important. That Colt didn't have to talk to law enforcement about anything. That it was his constitutional right not to. *Yada, yada, yada.*

"I can give you the number for Natalie's parents. You should be able to call them from the hospital."

The offer floated in the air for a moment. It was an olive branch of sorts. Colt thought about it as he watched the game. He waited until the broadcast cut to commercial again.

"I still want my phone back," Colt finally said with some hesitation. "But write the number down on a piece of paper."

Meredith smirked as he pulled a pen from his jacket. He did as he was asked and scribbled a number on a slip of paper. He placed it on a nearby table that still had the dinner tray waiting to be collected.

"There you are."

"Tell me what you know about the wreck," Colt quickly said before Meredith could ask him a question. "Was the other driver drunk or something?"

"Maybe," he replied. "We're still not sure. It was a hit-and-run, so we're still looking for the driver of the truck."

"That other vehicle was drivable?"

"Not even close," Meredith said as he shook his head, "but we're still investigating that side of things. The driver probably got out and ran from the scene on foot. We'll find the guy."

Colt stayed on the offensive. "Well, tell me how it happened. What do you know?"

"I'm supposed to be the one that asks the questions."

"Come on, man. I'm in the dark here."

Meredith nodded. "The preliminary report that I saw has you running a stop sign. Right out there at the intersection where Five Forks Road crosses old 27. The truck that hit you on the passenger-side had to of been doing close to fifty-five."

"Bullshit," Colt said. "I wouldn't have run that stop sign out there."

"You asked."

"I just know that road," Colt added, quietly. "I know that intersection. I wouldn't have—"

Meredith interrupted him. "I was at the game, Colt. One of the better games I've seen you play."

"I'll be sure to watch the film."

"You took some shots out there. Coach Weeks shouldn't have put you back in that game. The whole town knows that now."

The football players at Blake County High School had the privilege of being coached by a legend. Twenty-nine years as the head coach. Sixteen regional championships under his reign. Four state championship titles. Coach Melvin Weeks more than deserved his respect. And because of that, no one questioned the man's decisions.

Colt smiled. "When you were the starting quarterback, Trevor, how many games did Weeks pull you out of?"

"Zero."

Colt nodded. He knew from the doctor's assessment earlier that he'd suffered a series of concussions on Friday night. The first one or two most likely occurred during the game. Another one or two certainly followed in the wreck. The combination produced a sort of post-traumatic, retrograde amnesia that Dr. Beck hoped would resolve itself with time.

"That's what I thought."

Meredith leaned in closer. "That's not what this is about, though."

An orderly slowed in front of the door to the hospital room. He offered a greeting as he stepped inside to collect the half-touched dinner tray. As he did, he stopped to take in a few seconds of the game on TV. The quarterback for the Cardinals—Carson Palmer—dropped a beautiful pass in the hands of his receiver for a 58-yard touchdown.

"Reminds me of your touchdown pass in the fourth quarter of Friday night's game," the man said with a smile. "Haven't seen a game end like that in years."

Colt didn't know what to say. He just watched the man place the tray on his cart and start back down the hallway.

"I'm here to talk to you about the night of the wreck," Meredith said once another moment passed. "It's about the—"

"We've been talking about it. Besides, aren't you supposed to read me my rights or something?"

"You've been asking most of the questions," Meredith replied. "I can if you want me to. I know your family has a lawyer. You want to call him?"

"That's my dad's lawyer," Colt replied. "And he's a prick."

The investigator nodded. He probably agreed.

"You already know that I don't remember much," Colt continued. "It was an accident. What more do you need to hear from me?"

"It's about what was in your trunk."

The trunk, Colt thought. He ran through a list of what he could remember was in there. *Half a case of Coors, gym clothes, a box of condoms, maybe some old fireworks.*

"What about it?"

Meredith answered the question with a question of his own. "Did you let anyone else drive your car on Friday?"

"No."

"Did you leave your keys with anyone during the game?"

"Nope. They would've been in my locker."

Colt waited as the investigator seemed to consider his next move. As a young quarterback, Colt knew that diligent preparation was the key to success. Conditioning. Lifting. Watching game tape and studying the other team. It all came down to preparation, and Meredith seemed prepared.

"So, no one else would have had access to the trunk of your car?"

Colt shook his head, confused. "No one."

The investigator nodded. He seemed to hesitate, then said: "Are you sure you don't want to speak with a lawyer?"

The question took Colt by surprise. In fact, the question sounded more like a suggestion. Colt didn't care, though. He didn't want to speak with an attorney. He wanted to speak with Natalie's family. That's what he was focused on.

"No," Colt replied. "I'm good."

"Are you sure?"

Colt laughed. "Damn, Trevor, you sure are thorough. Just ask your questions."

"Was everything that was in the trunk of your vehicle on Friday night your property?"

Colt paused a second. He felt a sensation in his gut that he only felt right before throwing a big interception. That ill-advised throw that was the product of poor preparation. That one mistake that shifted the course of an entire game.

"Everything was my property."

"Well, there were two and a half pounds of methamphetamine in your trunk, Colt. I need to know where you were planning to take it to."

Bingo.

3

Colt crossed his arms and glared at the investigator.

"You don't have very many options," Meredith said, fixing his eyes on Colt's. "Not many at all."

Colt knew it was already past time to shut up, so he just sat there and thought about the information he'd heard from the investigator's mouth. *Two and a half pounds.* It didn't take a lawyer and a fat retainer fee to explain that two and a half pounds was the kind of weight that meant serious time.

"I see it going two ways for you, bud."

Bud.

Colt ignored the investigator and looked back up at the television screen. He watched as both teams started to jog off the field. It was halftime now.

"And this is why," Meredith said, opening the file in his lap. He removed a picture from the folder and placed it in front of Colt. "I'm a visual guy, so I'll use pictures to help explain your little predicament."

Colt took in the image of the mangled vehicles. His red Mustang looked like a half-crushed Coke can. The other vehicle, a mint green Toyota, reminded him of a rolled-up tube of toothpaste. The picture did little to jog his memory, which surprised him.

"As you mentioned earlier, this was an accident," Meredith said in a matter-of-fact tone. He pointed at the image in Colt's lap. "You lost your girlfriend in that wreck. A family lost a daughter, and a sister. The whole town will view this for what it is—a tragedy."

The investigator placed another photo in Colt's lap. This one showed part of Natalie's face in it. He could make out blood and glass and debris in the picture. It made him sick to look at it.

"It shouldn't have happened," Meredith continued. "But early reports suggest Natalie had some alcohol in her system. And if I were a gambling man—which my old girlfriend will tell you I am, Colt—I'd bet that the tests they did here at the hospital showed some alcohol in your system, too."

Colt just stared back at him.

"See, this is your first problem because vehicular homicide is no joke, and the district attorney's office is going to be getting some heat on this one. That means if alcohol was in your system, the DA must go for the felony. With time."

Colt knew his post-game routine well. Coach's speech. Showers. Protein shakes. Head out. He never took a sip of alcohol until he reached the after-party. He also never—*ever*—drove with a hint of alcohol in his system. With a college scholarship already inked up at Vanderbilt, he knew the stakes.

"You might be thinking you know you didn't have any alcohol in your system. That makes this tragedy a misdemeanor. Maybe even one that the DA would kick based on the circumstances. Maybe."

Colt nodded.

"That doesn't take care of your second problem. The real problem."

Colt gritted his teeth. "I didn't put it in there and you have to—"

"I don't have to do anything," Meredith replied, "because you're cooked, Colt."

"It's not mine, Trevor. You know that."

"No, I don't, and it doesn't matter."

Colt started to look over at the door to his hospital room. It had to be well past visiting hours.

"Before you think about reaching out to your daddy's lawyer," Meredith added. "I'm going to make something clear. You have a take-it-or-leave-it proposition to consider right now."

The investigator pointed up at the screen on the wall. Both teams were re-taking the field and getting ready to start the second half.

"You'll have until Arizona kicks off to make a decision and—"

"Cut the shit and tell me," Colt said. "What are my options?"

"Option one: You lawyer up and fight both your vehicular homicide charge and the slam-dunk trafficking charge. You lose on both charges. You lose on one. Either way, you aren't walking out of a courtroom with a win on both counts."

"Listening."

"Option two: You agree to serve as a confidential informant. Apparently, you, me, and everyone else knows where those drugs came from and—"

"I'll stop you right there and tell you it's not happening."

"Ever?"

The kicker for the Cardinals—Chandler Cantanzaro—started to line up for the opening kick of the second half. Trevor Meredith patted Colt on the forearm and stood to watch the kickoff. The commentators lauded both teams for the hard-fought performance in the first half.

"That's right," Colt said. "Not in this lifetime."

"You've always been a great second-half player," Meredith said with a smile. He collected the photographs and returned them to his folder. "But there's no coming back from this one, bud."

The kick sailed through the end-zone. The investigator left.

4

Muscogee County, Georgia
Seven years later

Tim Dawson drove north on US 27. His newly issued Dodge Charger—one that was unmarked and packing a 6.4-liter Hemi V-8—rumbled as the speedometer crested eighty-five.

Oh, speeding privileges, he thought. *How I've missed you.*

He checked the time on his wristwatch, slowing now as he crossed into the outskirts of Columbus, Georgia. He'd taken what was usually a two-hour trip up from Blakeston and whittled it down to almost ninety minutes. A feat that was nearly impossible given the string of sleepy speed-trap towns along the route. All the regulars on the roads of the Wiregrass Region knew you had to watch your speed on 27. All except those that carried a badge.

Tim's cell phone rang through the car's speakers. He glanced at the name that appeared on the center console's screen, then answered it.

"Morning, Mags."

"Good morning to you," his wife replied in her I-just-woke-up voice. "You snuck out the door early on me. I didn't even hear you leave."

He could picture her in bed, still under the covers, rolled to one side with her phone pressed to her ear. "Yeah, I couldn't sleep," he said. "Figured I'd get a head start on the day."

"Any first-day jitters?"

Tim slowed the Dodge some more as he spotted his turn. "Nah, not really."

"Liar," she replied after a short pause. "You'll do great, though. Don't worry."

"I know you're not accusing an upstanding member of law enforcement of being untruthful."

"Not yet," she chided. "It's still early in the day."

"Early bird gets the worm."

"Not a good-luck breakfast, though. With my worm and eggs, anything is possible for you to—"

"See, that'd require you to be up before seven," he said, smiling at the thought. The talented Maggie Reynolds was a lot of things, just not a morning person. "How about we grab dinner instead?"

"It's a date," she replied. "It'll be just like old times."

He noted the first direct mention of their past, their origin story. They'd not talked about it much since his decision to accept the new job.

"Those were good times."

They'd been an unlikely pair back when they met. Maggie Reynolds, the fiery public defender with a reputation founded on sensational wins in the courtroom. Tim Dawson, a rising star in the eyes of those involved at the Georgia Bureau of Investigation. Both successful. Both driven. Both on separate paths.

"We're still having good times," Maggie replied. "Wouldn't you agree?"

Tim certainly agreed. Although his marriage to Maggie came with its challenges—*What marriage didn't?*—the bad never outweighed the good. Their differences fueled them. Made them better partners. And Tim felt confident that even with his new job, the irresistible force that bound them, that attractive phenomenon that continued to this day, would remain.

"Great times," Tim said. "With more to come, I hope."

"Definitely."

Tim smiled as he pulled his vehicle up to a guard shack. A chain-link gate blocked the entranceway to a large complex, one surrounded by metal and razor wire. He nodded through his window to a uniformed guard who sat slumped inside the shack.

"I need to run," Tim told Maggie. "I just pulled up to Rutledge."

"Rutledge?"

"That's right. I'm up here in Muscogee County."

She gave a small laugh on the other side of the line. "I know where Rutledge State Prison is, Commander Dawson. You might be a little bit lost, though. You're supposed to be going to work with the narcotics squad in Blake County."

"I need to run, Mags. I'll see you later tonight."

"Good luck today."

Tim ended the call as the guard stepped out of the shack. The Mike Biggs look-a-like stretched his back out before slowly making his way toward the vehicle. Tim rolled his driver-side window down and handed the man his BCSO credentials. The guard looked at them, then leaned down to look closer inside the vehicle.

"Morning, Commander Dawson," the big man said, handing the crisp ID card back through the window. "Y'all keeping everybody straight down there in Blake County?"

"We're trying to," Tim replied. "We know you always need some new residents. We'll keep sending them your way."

"Hold on, now, we already have plenty to deal with."

"I may be able to take one off your hands, then."

"One less knucklehead to worry about," the man said with a smile. "That sounds fine to me."

"I bet."

"All right, who're you here to see this morning?"

Tim gave the man the inmate's name, then pulled through the gate.

5

When Colt heard his name called, he didn't turn away from the bathroom mirror. Hot water flowed from the faucet in front of him. A luxury of sorts, at least one he didn't enjoy on a weekly basis. Colt felt the warmth rising from the sink as he rubbed shaving cream on his face. He slowly massaged the white foam over his stubble, careful along the left side of his jaw—a tender spot that still showed some swelling from a disagreement.

"Yo, Hudson!" a guard called from the bathroom's doorway. "There's a request in for you up at visitation. They need you up there now."

Colt held the cheap razor under the water as he listened for more information. Hearing none, he started to shave. He couldn't remember the last time he'd received a visitor. Most of the inmates at Rutledge—the Rut, as it was known among its residents—had at least a visitor a month. A lawyer. A family member. An old girlfriend. Not Colt, though. He never saw the need to file any appeals, and he didn't have much in the way of love or family waiting for him on the outside.

"Come on, Hudson," the guard said, feigning some frustration. "Quit jacking around. Don't make me come in there and get your—"

"Give me a second," Colt finally said, splashing the warm water on his face to remove the rest of the shaving cream. He eyed his face in the mirror.

One he hated. That of a twenty-four-year-old convicted felon with at least a few more years to go. "I'll head that way on my own."

"I have to walk you over there."

Colt pulled his shirt on and turned around to face the guard. "Why?"

"Cause I'm telling you so. That's why."

"I know that," Colt replied with a smile. He knew the guard wasn't going to be angry with him. It was standard protocol to trade light remarks with the gatekeepers at the Rut, expected even. "I haven't had someone come see me in a while. I thought the visitation area was still just down the main hall. They change the procedure?"

"Nothing has changed," the guard replied. "Your meeting is in the main building. Over there in the private rooms."

"Well, well," Colt said with a raised eyebrow. "Y'all get me something special for my birthday?"

The guard shook his head as he held a set of handcuffs out. "Turn around."

"That's not what I meant."

"Come on, let's go," he replied with a laugh of his own. "I'll walk you over there."

Jack T. Rutledge State Prison allowed its inmates to visit in private when meeting with their lawyers. The attorney-client conference rooms allowed the inmates to freely discuss their appeals and habeas petitions without the fear of others listening in. Tim knew from discussions with Maggie—a dyed-in-the-wool courtroom brawler—that there were two kinds of criminal defense lawyers in the world. Those that specialized in trial work, and those that handled the appeals. Tim knew that his wife preferred the former, and once told him that she believed the well-articulated appeals made to those robed intellectuals—the judges and justices seated at varying levels of the appellate process—were mostly just Hail-Mary attempts from desperate men and women. Tim tended to agree. For that reason, the private attorney-client conference rooms at prisons also doubled as the perfect setting for investigators who needed to interview inmates about active cases. Every investigator knew that once the appeals ran out, those same desperate inmates started to look for other ways to get back home.

A small speaker on the wall beeped twice, then a woman's voice poured into the room. "We're sorry about the wait, Commander Dawson. The inmate is on his way up."

"It's not a problem," Tim said in the general direction of the speaker. "I know I came without an appointment this morning."

"You're fine, sweetie. Shouldn't be but another few minutes."

Tim sat at a small table in the center of the room. In front of him the old file that the BCSO compiled for Colt Hudson's case lay open. He'd already read through it three or four times. The details read like a DARE Officer's dream fact-pattern. A nasty hit-and-run car wreck the night of a homecoming football game. A teenage girl killed in the crash. Two and a half pounds of crystal meth in the trunk. A bad case that eventually ended in a young man being sent off to prison.

He flipped to the last page in the thick file. It was the final disposition form—the official outcome of the prosecution in the case. Tim noted the judge's signature at the bottom of the form. Judge John Balk, Blake County Superior Court. Balk had accepted the defendant's plea of *Guilty* as to one count of trafficking in methamphetamine and handed down a pre-negotiated sentence. A term that totaled twenty years—with the first ten to be served in prison.

A long time.

The metal door to the visitation room opened. In stepped two men. A correctional officer and an inmate.

"Where do you want him?" the guard asked, looking to Tim for direction. "And you want to keep him cuffed?"

"Right here," Tim said as he stood, pointing to the chair opposite his. "Take the handcuffs off, please."

"Yes, sir."

"Colt," Tim said, extending a hand across the table. "I'm Commander Tim Dawson. I'm with the Blake County Sheriff's Office."

"It's a pleasure," Colt replied as he rubbed his wrists. He stepped closer to the table, then took Tim's hand to shake it. "Been a long time since I've seen anyone from your office."

"I imagine it has. Grab a seat, Colt."

"Yes, sir."

Tim returned to his own chair, silently evaluating the young man who now sat across from him. He remembered when Colt Hudson played for Blake County High School back in 2016. Most of the recruiting services that covered high school prospects at that time rated the kid as a three-star quarterback. 6-foot-1. 185 pounds. Growth potential to add another inch or two in height, and another twenty to twenty-five pounds in size. Above average athleticism. Adequate mobility. Strong arm talent with an exceptional deep ball. One of a kind as far as his ability to perform under duress.

"How tall are you now, Colt?"

"Close to 6-foot-3."

"Weight?"

"Haven't had to go into medical for a while, so I'm not too sure. Probably somewhere north of two hundred."

Tim nodded. He'd already noticed the black-and-blue mark across Colt's jawline. The long hair. The tattoos down his arms.

"You affiliated?" Tim asked. "And be straight with me."

Colt looked over his shoulder at the guard in the corner of the room. "Is that what this is about?"

"Answer the man," the guard grunted.

"Is that what this is about?" Colt repeated, turning back to face Tim. "Bloods, GDs, and Ghostface—"

"No," Tim replied, cutting him off. "I just need to know who I'm dealing with."

Colt crossed his arms.

"Are you?" Tim asked again.

"No, sir," Colt responded after a long pause. He let out a sigh that told Tim what he needed to know. "I've managed to survive on my own."

Tim nodded again. He knew it was possible. Although enlisting in a prison gang was considered a good decision for those that sought status and protection, not all inmates were forced to join a clique. Those that didn't just had to be capable of reckoning with a gang's main form of influ-ence—violence.

"You mind if I step out?" the guard finally asked from his spot in the corner. "We're short-staffed today."

"That's fine," Tim replied. "Besides, I need to talk to Mr. Hudson here in private."

———

Colt's jaw hurt each time he opened it to speak. He knew it wasn't broken. Still, it clicked in his ears each time he tried to move it around to loosen it up. A reminder of where he was, as if he didn't have enough of those already.

"What do you need from me?" Colt asked. "I assume you're here because you need something."

The investigator leaned back in his chair and crossed his arms. Colt considered the man's relaxed demeanor. The appearance that he was paying careful attention to everything. He looked patient, and Colt had learned to respect that quality in a man. Even fear it at times.

"You tired of dodging right-hooks in here?" the man asked. "I see it looks like somebody caught you on the chin."

Colt nearly winced as he smiled. "This is nothing. A sucker punch from some new kid that didn't know how things worked."

"You show him?"

Be polite, Colt reminded himself, *and keep your mouth shut. This stiff will go away just like the others.*

"Yes, sir."

"No slack, right?"

"Not in here."

The man nodded. "Still, it has to get tiring, am I right?"

Colt shrugged. It was a dumb question. As he waited for another, he tried to place the lawman. A Black guy, maybe somewhere around forty. No uniform. The look of a former athlete with a good attitude. Not the bitter kind that joined law enforcement after their glory days just to bust some skulls.

"Do you mind if I see your badge or some ID?" Colt asked.

"Sure," the man replied as he reached into his jacket. He placed both his badge and a plastic card on the table. "Have a look."

Colt didn't touch the items in front of him. He just leaned over the edge of the table and took in the information. *ID is brand-spanking new,* he thought. *But why do I recognize this guy's name? I know he wasn't with the BCSO back in the day.* Colt stared at them a moment longer, thinking.

"I'll give you a piece of paper and a pen if you need to write that information down," the investigator added. "I don't mind."

"No, sir. It's okay. Thank you, Mr. Dawson."

"Just call me Tim."

The cool cop.

Colt nodded. "Sure thing, Tim."

The investigator collected both the badge and ID, then slid a bulky folder across the table.

"What's this?" Colt asked.

"When was the last time you looked at your case file?"

Colt crossed his arms and frowned across the table. He didn't want to look at the file. He didn't want to read the reports. It'd been bad enough the first time. The photos of the wrecked vehicles. The shots of Natalie pressed up against the airbags. Dried blood and glass in her cotton-colored hair. The drug lab results. The toxicology reports. A God-awful mess, all of it.

"I went over it with my lawyer at some point," Colt finally said. "Back before I told the judge I was guilty."

"When was that?"

"You don't have that information in the file?" Colt replied, knowing the man did.

"I can open it up and we can look," Tim said as he reached for the flap on the folder. "I'm sure that—"

"No," Colt said with a hand up. "It's all right."

"Okay." Tim leaned back in his chair again. "When was the last time you saw the file, then?"

"Well," Colt said, carefully choosing his words, "the wreck happened in the fall of 2016, but I didn't take the offer for another couple of years."

"You mean the plea offer?"

"Yes, sir," Colt replied, looking up at the ceiling as he spoke. He hadn't thought much about those days recently. A good thing, really, because he used to question the decision nearly every minute of every day. "My lawyer ran the clock on the case as long as he could. I don't know if you were around Blake County at that time, but there'd been some big murder cases knocking around the court system. The first was during the fall of 2016. A big politician from Blakeston—Senator Bill Collins—lost his son and the guy that did it was—"

"I remember the Lee Acker case," Tim said. "I'm not here for that. I'm here to talk about your case."

"All right," Colt said. "Well, when the new DA finally got around to my case, he made the offer."

"They made you other offers though, right?"

Colt shrugged again. "All offers went to my lawyer."

"Okay."

Colt remembered all those conversations with his lawyer. His dad's lawyer, really. They discussed the offers and dismissed them. Offers that required Colt's cooperation in an investigation that targeted his family's business. Offers that Colt couldn't take. So, the lawyer put together the best deal he could, then told Colt to take it and run. That if he didn't, he'd be convicted at trial and sent away for at least twenty years in prison. Maybe more.

"Who was your lawyer?" Tim asked.

"The family lawyer," Colt replied, lowering his eyes from the ceiling. "Abe Coleman."

Abe Coleman stood at no more than 5-foot-7, but he had a reputation for being one of the most dangerous lawyers in the area. A bulldozer that rarely had to go to court because he demolished cases by bribing witnesses, hiding evidence, and striking creative deals in the back rooms of courthouses. Abe drank hard, gambled plenty, and still had a mind as sharp as the teeth on a cottonmouth.

"Honest Abe," Tim said with a smile. "I've dealt with him a time or two."

Colt nodded. "It was a good deal."

"Okay, so you pleaded guilty and—"

"They sent me up the road about a month later."

Tim stared across the table. "So, you've been here at Rutledge for how long?"

"Almost five years."

"With at least two or three more to go until they send you out on parole?"

"That's what they tell me."

"So, that brings me back to my first question," Tim said, tapping his fingers slowly on the table that sat between them. "When was the last time you looked at this file?"

"At least five years ago."

Tim stopped the tapping. "Okay, well, I haven't been with the BCSO long. In fact, I just started as the commander of the narcotics squad."

Big whoop.

Tim continued. "And I saw that someone added a set of photographs to your file just recently."

"Okay."

"Do you want to see them?"

Colt stared across the table at the investigator. He worked to keep his face from reporting any reaction to the question. A stupid question.

Hell yeah he wanted to see them.

6

Tim pulled the case file back to his side of the table and opened the front flap. The BCSO investigator that initially handled the case—a younger guy by the name of Trevor Meredith—hadn't spent a lot of time on the investigation itself. In his defense, he didn't really have to. There'd been a car wreck with a fatality, and it'd been the on-scene EMTs that noticed the drugs in the trunk. Not because they searched it. No, they didn't have to. Colt Hudson's Coke-red Mustang sat cracked open on the roadside for all to see.

"The homecoming game was the night of this wreck, right?" Tim said, flipping through the paperwork in the file. "Blake County against—"

"Against Sumter," Colt replied.

Tim nodded as he kept paging through the file. The accident report, medical records, lab reports, and photographs made up the bulk of the documents inside. There'd also been an interview conducted by the investigator at the hospital—a piece of the investigation that ended up being the only defensible aspect of the case. A more seasoned investigator would have known better than to interrogate a criminal suspect without first providing a Miranda warning. Especially one that was confined to a hospital bed, under a large amount of pain medication, and still recovering from recent head trauma. It'd been a rookie mistake, and one that allowed Abe Coleman to broker a deal his client could stomach.

"I requested the film from your last game and watched the whole thing. You were one heck of a player, Colt. A real field general from the quarter-back position."

Colt didn't respond. Tim figured the compliment probably did nothing for the young man. Those days were gone.

"Okay," Tim said as he pulled a manila envelope from the back of the casefile. "Here we are. I'll let you see the photographs, but I don't have any copies for you. The originals will need to stay with the file."

"Sure."

Tim unfastened a string at the top of the envelope. He pulled several glossy 8x10s from inside. They felt heavy in his hands.

"Do you remember where you warmed up the night of that game against Sumter?" Tim asked.

"Same place as always. The south end-zone."

Tim slid a stack of eight photographs across the table. He carefully separated them one-by-one, as if administering a simple photo array to an eyewitness. A technique he'd employed hundreds of times in his cases over the years. Always looking for a physical reaction from the individual. Words didn't matter much. Body language told all.

"These are all photographs of you going through your pre-game warmups the night of October 7, 2016—the night of the wreck."

Tim leaned back in his chair and watched the young man in front of him. The images had probably been taken by a student photographer on the field. A person that Tim hoped he would be able to locate. They showed Colt Hudson, wearing number nine, throwing to a group of his receivers positioned somewhere outside the frame of the photographs. Off to the side, stood the back-up quarterback and an assistant coach. Green grass and crisp white lines made up the foreground of the photos and the freshly painted end-zone covered most of the ground behind number nine. At the top of each photo, a chain-link fence stood tall. A fence that stretched the length of the entire south end-zone.

Colt almost looked like he wanted to smile. "It's wild to see these pictures after all these years," he said, picking them up one at a time. "The school paper used to send students down to the field to take photos like these before the games. Every now and then, the photographers slipped the good ones into my locker."

Tim let the moment sit with the young man for a few seconds more, then dove into the task at hand. "Where'd you usually park for your home football games?"

Tim watched Colt. He wanted him to see what he saw. He didn't want to have to point it out.

"We usually all got to the fieldhouse early on gamedays," Colt replied. "Everybody usually parked right along the fence that backed the south end-zone." Colt placed a finger on one of the photos. "See, there's my Mustang right there—the tricked-out red one."

Tim nodded and watched as Colt's eyes searched for it in the other photos. The young man's expression didn't change much when he saw it, but it changed just enough for Tim to catch it.

The body doesn't lie.

Tim leaned forward, placing his elbows on the table. "What do you see?"

Colt picked another one of the photographs up and studied it. Tim knew the image well. The interior dome light looked to be on inside the same Mustang that Colt pointed to earlier. Two men stood on both sides of the vehicle. While they looked on at the field from the other side of the fence, someone at the rear of the Mustang had the trunk popped open.

"I don't see anything," Colt finally said.

"Yes, you do."

Colt placed the photograph back down on the table and crossed his arms. "What do you want me to tell you that would matter today? My case is closed. Been closed for a long while."

Tim pointed at the photo. "I want you to tell me why these two men we see here—both dead men, I'll add—are standing beside your car the night of this—"

"Like I said, what do you expect me to—"

"I know who they are," Tim said as he pushed the conversation forward. Andrew Karras and Nick Moralis had been a couple of small-time hustlers from Detroit. Somehow, the two gyros ended up getting into business with

Liam Hudson. A decision that probably cost Karras and Moralis their lives. "I'm willing to bet you know who they are, or were, too."

"Were?"

"They're dead, Colt. Both of them. A ranger back in Blake County found them down by the river. A shallow grave near the Kelley property."

Colt seemed to consider this information. "Even if I did know these guys, why would it matter?"

"Because it would mean—"

"Wait, are you trying to pin some kind of murder rap on me?" Colt asked, raising his voice for the first time. "This is unbelievable because—"

Tim lifted both hands and showed Colt his palms. "I'm not trying to pin anything on you, Colt. I'm trying to help you. You just need to listen to me."

"Right."

"You're smart enough to know what these photos mean. You didn't put those drugs in the car the night of that wreck. You might not have even known they were in your trunk."

"I told the judge I was guilty, didn't I?" Colt shot back. "Move on, *Tim*. This case is closed."

"It doesn't have to be."

Colt stood from his chair.

Tim now raised his voice for the first time. "Sit down, Colt. We're not done here."

Colt didn't say anything for a long moment. He simply stood there, staring back at the BCSO's newest narcotics squad commander. Tim could tell the young man was thinking, and that was good enough. Tim almost had him. He just needed to wait it out.

"Sit down," Tim said, again.

"I'll stand," Colt muttered as he looked away. "Let's finish up. I'm ready to go back to—"

"To your cell?" Tim laughed.

"Nowhere else for me to go."

"How'd you like to go back home?"

Colt laughed this time as he returned his eyes to Tim's. His mind looked to still be turning. "Sure, let's go right now."

"I'm serious. I can get you back home to Blake County."

Tim let the words hang in the air. Colt didn't react. He didn't look away. A good sign.

"So, the judge is just going to re-open my case over some old photos?"

"No," Tim replied. "That might be possible, but it'd take a long time. Too long in my opinion."

Colt leaned down to the table and picked one of the photographs back up. He stared at it a moment more. Tim could tell the image angered the young man.

"All right," Colt finally said. "What do you have in mind?"

7

Blake County, Georgia
Back in the Day

Hudson Auto opened its garage doors to the people of Blake County in 1986. Liam Hudson, then a twenty-two-year-old aspiring stock-car driver, started the business because he needed something legitimate to do with his money. A good problem for a guy that never finished high school. Still, the things that Liam excelled at—driving fast cars, brawling, and dope—didn't prepare him for the difficult task of laundering his money in a manner that didn't draw the attention of good old Uncle Sam.

So, when young Liam Hudson bought the four acres at the edge of Blakeston's city limits for his business, he simply paid cash. When he built a brand-new auto repair shop, one with four bays and a handsome office, he paid cash. And when he poached the two best mechanics from the local Jiffy Lube and hired on the best-looking woman he could find to answer the phones—a twenty-three-year-old named Sandy with strawberry hair and a perfect set—he paid them all in cash, of course, then took Sandy out to dinner.

As far as Liam Hudson was concerned, he had the world by the balls. Reaganomics was in high-gear and efforts in the War on Drugs were being directed at Blacker, more urban areas of the country. Liam's garage prospered during the day, and he moved his more lucrative product at night. With plenty of cash flowing in the door, Liam quickly earned a reputation for being a rather capable businessman. He ran a clean garage, built relationships with other small business owners, and said all the right things at the local bank. He paid his people well and stressed a customer-first approach. He even mounted respectable marketing campaigns in the area, with commercials that advertised Hudson Auto as a one-stop-shop. One that offered an auto owner *everything* they could ever need.

All seemed to be going well until a sternly typed letter on official government letterhead arrived. The IRS had some questions about Hudson Auto, and Liam understood then that he needed professional advice. Simple tune-ups paid the bills, but the most profitable aspect of Liam's business was as dark as the country boy's long hair. He had no intention of stopping. He just needed someone that could help him explain his earnings to the government, carefully.

Enter Harold J. Bates, CPA.

Liam met his good friend, confederate, and CPA—Harry—in the summer of 1988. The two found themselves at the same Fourth of July party, waiting in a long line to use the downstairs bathroom at their mutual friend's house. The large house, one that sat obnoxiously among the other modest river houses that lined the Chattahoochee River, had plenty more bathrooms upstairs, and Harry knew the way.

"I have to take a piss," the guy later known as Harry said as he turned to the young man behind him, Liam. "And knock a rail or two down, you in?"

Liam didn't respond. The guy had to be somewhere into his mid-thirties —*old*—and he looked out of place at the party full of people in their early twenties. He was dressed like a frat boy, too. One turned country clubber. Beers in both hands, popped collar, and what looked like a sloppily rolled joint tucked behind his right ear. The guy turned away from Liam and started speaking with two young women in front of him. A Prince track blared from the speakers down the hall, masking their conversation. The girls both laughed as they appeared to listen.

"Party is upstairs!" the guy hollered as he pulled one of the women from the line. The other followed. "Everybody is welcome," he added, slapping Liam on the shoulder as he started toward the staircase at the end of the hall. The unusual character sang along with the poppy chorus and threw an arm around one of the girls.

Liam noticed that most in the line for the bathroom looked amused at the sight of the older guy. He was a square, obviously. One clearly still trying to hang onto his edge. Still, Liam watched for another moment as the guy laughed easily with his new friends, unbothered by what others thought of him. Liam liked that quality in others. He stepped out of the line that wasn't moving and followed.

Once upstairs, the four-pack of partygoers—Liam Hudson, Harry Bates, and the two women—found the largest of the bathrooms on the second level. The overornamented powder room, with its chandelier hanging from the ceiling and fake gold accents shoved into every element of design, felt like it was close to the size of a racquetball court.

Game on.

"The head's in there," the guy said, pointing to a pocket door on the opposite side of the room. He shoved several items aside on the bathroom counter and tossed a bag of powder onto the granite surface. "Go on in there and tinkle. I'll line us up a few."

Liam nodded, then stepped into the toilet area. He pulled the door behind him. Music thumped from the party downstairs and laughter from the blondes could be heard through the door. As Liam's stream hit the water, he enjoyed the few moments of solitude.

"You're up," the guy said as Liam stepped back out to the group. He motioned toward the counter with a rolled-up bill in his hand. He offered his best impression of Arnold Schwarzenegger in *The Terminator*. "Those are live rounds right here. Approach. With. Caution."

The blondes both had their hair up now. They laughed at the lame comment, bobbing in unison as they waited for their second go at the stash. Liam knew their panties would be off before the end of the night. Coke had that effect on the fairer sex.

ot know you?” Liam asked as he accepted the bill. He stepped to
the edge of the bathroom counter and eyed one of the gator tails
before him.

“Name’s Harry,” the guy replied. “Harry Bates.”

“You from around here, Harry?”

“Nah,” Harry replied, sounding a little too nonchalant. If that was possible. “I’m from California.”

“California, huh?”

“That’s right,” Harry replied. “You been out to the West Coast before?”

Liam didn’t answer. He just winked at one of the girls as he leaned down to the counter. The sharp bite of the powder hit his senses as he inhaled. He allowed the blow a moment to do its job, then wiped the remnants of coke from the counter and rubbed it on his gums. As he stood up, the shorter of the two blondes, a curly-haired chick that couldn’t weigh more than a buck-ten stepped close.

“This stuff is gnarly, Harry from California.”

Harry nodded. He didn’t point out Liam’s mock California accent. He also didn’t ask Liam for his name.

“Slopes are open,” Liam said as he kept on with the accent. “Who’s up?”

“Me,” the small chick replied, her curls bouncing from the energy. Liam could already tell that she looked talkative—*pass*. “I’m Rebecca by the way.”

“All right, Becky,” Liam replied. “Harry and I’ll line us all up a few more if you and your friend here go downstairs and get us a couple more cans of Budweiser.”

She nodded, eager to please.

“Go on,” Liam said as he motioned with the bill. It functioned almost like a talisman. “Harry and I’ll be here.”

The girls left and Harry turned to Liam with a smile. “You trying to run the betties off?”

“Nah, Harry. It’s just important we lay the rules out early. They do what *we* tell them. Not the other way around.”

Harry nodded as he stepped back to the counter. He dumped half the bag out and started breaking up the coke efficiently, businesslike.

“How do I know you, Harry?” Liam asked.

“Hell if I know,” Harry said as he ripped another rail off the granite. He smiled as he came back up for air. The guy had a mischievous glint to his eyes. Liam liked that about him. "I know who you are, though."

"Yeah?"

"Damn straight," he replied. He still didn't offer any other information. "Anyways, which one of these girls you want?"

Liam wasn't concerned with the women. He could pull tail anytime, anywhere. "You can have them both, Harry. Tell me what you do for a living?"

The girls burst back through the door to the bathroom. They'd made a lightning-fast trip downstairs.

"The party is back!" they shouted, laughing as they handed out the beers. Both started toward the counter.

"I'm just a paper-pusher," Harry said, continuing the conversation. He placed his hand on the rear of the blonde closest to him and handed her the hundred-dollar bill. She leaned over the counter to work on the blow. "Nothing real exciting."

"What kind of paper you pushing?"

"The green kind," Harry said with a smile. "And as much as I can get of it. I just have to make sure the government gets their cut first."

The curly-haired blonde, Rebecca, was back on Liam's hip. She danced along to the music that rumbled from below them. The edges of her bikini top brushed against his bare arm.

"You must be a lawyer," Rebecca added, trying to get involved in the conversation. She kept with her dancing as she spoke. "I'm actually going to law school this fall. I'll be at—"

"I'm not some lawyer," Harry replied with a grin toward Liam. "I'm just your friendly, neighborhood tax man."

"Gag me with a spoon!" Rebecca shot back, laughing to her friend. The party favors had removed the soon-to-be-law-student's filter. "I could never do all that crap with—"

Harry pointed toward the exit. "The door is over there, sweetie. All that crap is what's putting this powder up your nose."

"No, that's not what I—"

"My new accountant friend here has a point," Liam added, halting the young woman's backpedaling. "I think you'll need to apologize to him, nicely."

Rebecca looked at Liam for a few seconds, then turned to Harry. She offered him a sweet apology as she started toward the counter again.

"I don't know, Becky," Liam said as he patted her on the bottom. "There's a nice big bedroom through that door there. I think you should walk to the other side of it with Harry and tell him you're sorry in private. You might even need to take your friend here with you."

Harry grinned at the suggestion. The girls exchanged a glance with one another, then shrugged a response that told Liam they could be persuaded.

"Go on," Liam encouraged. "I'll take care of everything in here. There'll even be a couple more lines waiting for you girls when you get back."

A Bon Jovi track started on the stereo downstairs. Its synthesized instrumentals cut clearly through the floor below them. The girls nudged Harry toward the door.

"I owe you," Harry said as he was being pulled along. "Big time!"

"I'll come see you next week," Liam replied with a nod. "I have a few questions for you."

"Don't you need my information to—"

"I'll find you."

Harry didn't argue. "Catch you later."

Liam watched the three as they disappeared into the dark room, giggling. He turned back to the counter, all covered in white smudges from his product. Liam eyed the half-empty bag nearby. He recognized the taste of it. It was premium stuff from the latest batch his boys carried up from South Florida. A small portion of the top-shelf blow that his crew distributed all over the Wiregrass Region.

It's time to expand, Liam thought as he looked up at his reflection in the bathroom mirror. He still looked like a country boy. A mechanic with a little cash in his pocket. *Not for long though,* he thought as he poured another small mound onto the counter and started to chop it up. He had big plans for his operation. He just needed a little help from a professional crook. *All those money boys are crooks anyway.*

Liam leaned down and popped another bump. His eyes returned to his reflection in the mirror. He wanted to grow his influence, his business, his reach. He wanted more politicians in his pocket. More friends that owed him favors. More deputies on the take.

More.

Laughter sounded from the other side of the door. Liam listened a moment, then turned to make his exit. He'd go talk to Harry Bates next week and feel him out. He had a sense about people, and Liam's gut told him that this was his guy.

With more trips to South Florida, along with a jaunt or two over the border, Liam planned to double the money coming through the door. He just needed somewhere—*someone, really*—to help clean the bills. They'd reinvest the profits into more legitimate businesses and into the pockets of those that held elected office.

In Liam's business, politicians made for smart investments, and he already had someone in mind—an up-and-comer with ties to Blake County. A political animal who appeared ready for a lifetime of campaigns for higher offices. Another friend—*like Harry, maybe*—that Liam could rely on for a long time.

First, though, Liam needed the clean money.

Lots of it.

8

Blake County, Georgia
Present Day

Colt Hudson sat in the main holding area at the front of the county jail. He waited at the end of a metal bench, seated alongside close to a dozen other inmates. The open area—a cinder-block room with hard fluorescent lighting—bustled with activity. Colt took it all in, noting the tell-tale signs of a court day.

Corrections officers barked commands at inmates as they organized the jail's court calendar. Heavy metal doors slammed as deputies came in and out of the room, shuffling the accused from the holding area to a courtroom on the other side of the thick walls. Lawyers, most in bad suits, pulled their clients aside to discuss last-minute strategy, along with final offers from the prosecution.

Place hasn't changed much, Colt thought as he spotted a familiar face or two on the jail's staff. He waited for one of them to recognize him, but they didn't seem to make the connection. Not a courtesy nod. *Nothing.* Colt considered this as he waited. *Maybe the Hudson name doesn't carry weight anymore.*

A man complained to Colt's left. "I'm sick and tired of waiting," he said. "I'm supposed to be going home today."

Colt didn't respond.

The man continued. "This some bullshit, you know? Been in here six months. Six months on a lie. All because my girl went out and told on me for—"

"Shut up, Felix," another inmate spouted from further down the bench. "I'm just as ready for your sorry ass to go home. That way I don't have to listen to you bitch about that trick for another day."

"You shouldn't talk about your momma that way," the man called Felix replied. "Miss Oleta's so sweet and sexy and—"

"Keep my momma's name out of your mouth. Besides, she wouldn't even look twice at your Black ass. All busted and—"

"You must not know your momma like I do."

"Say it again," the other inmate said as he stood from the bench. "See what happens."

"Chill," Felix whined. "I'm just having fun. Got to do something with all this waiting."

Colt shook his head as he listened. He wanted to slap them, all of them, but especially the one with the cartoon-character name. They didn't know a thing about waiting, certainly not being tired of it. He'd spent the last five plus years in prison, and he'd learned plenty about how to wait. How to wait for the next disgusting meal. How to wait for the next chance to exercise on crap equipment. How to wait for the day to pass—only to start another day of waiting.

The waiting was close to over, though.

"You Hudson?" a big man called from behind a counter at the opposite side of the room. "Colt Hudson?"

Colt stood before he spoke. He clutched a single piece of paper in one hand. A plastic bottle of orange juice in the other.

"Yes, sir."

"You already missed breakfast," the man stated. "One of the run-arounds will make sure you get a tray for lunch."

Colt considered his response. For him, prison had been nothing more than a penalty box. A serious infraction that came with a timeclock counting down to his release. Most of the time, the guards served as nothing more than referees that controlled the clock. A clock that Colt assumed—at least up until a few days ago—still showed plenty of time left on it. Now that he was back sooner than expected, though, he wanted out of the box.

"I'm getting out today," Colt finally replied. "That's what I—"

"It'll be tomorrow, Hudson. Sheriff Clay told me to hold you here for twenty-four hours before releasing you back into the wild."

Colt shook his head as he started to lift the single piece of paper in his hand—the early-release paperwork he'd received from the prison. It was his only copy. "That can't be right because I have a sheet here that says I'm supposed to be getting out today."

"You want me to ask the sheriff if we need to restart your twenty-four hours?" The man asked this in a vindictive tone. One that Colt recognized from his journeys through the system. "It's not my butt that has to sleep in here tonight. Or tomorrow. Or the night after that for all I care."

A few of the other inmates on the bench—including Felix, *the crybaby* —started to laugh at the guard's comments. Their reaction to Colt's seemingly reasonable concern only encouraged the man to continue with his verbal assault.

Maybe there were a few people up here that still recognized my name.

"In fact," the guard said. He wore a broad grin, almost as wide as the waistband around his gut. "We've done some updating in here since you last visited us, Mr. Hudson. I'd hate to deprive you of the chance to take in the new facility."

Colt held his tongue.

"Come on, big shot. You don't have some clever response for me? Yeah, I still remember you. I remember you were supposed to go off to some smart college—what was it, Van-dur-bilt?"

The inmates all chuckled some more as the guard's public ridicule continued. Colt just nodded along, listening.

"I remember when your cocky ass was in here years ago. Your attorney was coming through here visiting you at all hours. Acting like he had some card up his sleeve to play. All your daddy's green bills hard at work to get you out of here."

Hard at work to keep me from turning state's evidence is more like it.

"All that sweet, sweet money," Felix added as if he'd contributed to the defense fund himself. "Those paid attorneys don't come cheap."

"All that money couldn't keep you out of prison though, could it?" the guard asked as he started to come around from behind the desk. "Your punk ass went up the road like the rest of—"

"Taylor!" another voice barked from somewhere outside of Colt's line of sight. "What the heck has gotten into you?"

Tim Dawson appeared from around the corner. His presence stopped the guard from making it to the other side of the counter. As the guard back peddled, Colt noticed that the man's eyes reflected the look that all cons learned to recognize—*respect*.

"I'm just—" the guard started.

"Harassing these guys is what you're doing," Tim said with an intensity that flipped the jailer's environment on its head. "I mean, they're all in chains over there. How much more insult do they need to take?"

"Colt Hudson over there was giving me some lip."

Tim looked over at Colt, then back at the guard. "Did he hurt your feelings, cupcake?"

"Hell no. He just told me when he was getting out, that's all."

"I spoke with Sheriff Clay this morning. He's getting out tomorrow morning at 9:00 a.m. Not a minute later, you hear me?"

"I just—"

"9:00 a.m."

"Yes, sir."

Tim turned to Colt and stared over at him a long moment. He had a harder look to him than the man who'd visited the Rut a few days ago. Colt wondered if it was all an act, or if he'd struck a dirty deal with another two-faced lawman.

"You report to your parole officer within twenty-four hours of release," he said. "You understand?"

"Yes, sir," Colt replied, still standing. "I'll be sure to."

Tim nodded, then turned to walk back out of the holding area.

"That's a bad dude right there," Felix said as he nudged Colt. "Better keep yourself straight, white boy."

Colt nodded as he watched the commander leave.

He planned to.

9

Liam Hudson sat at his desk in a ratty old swivel chair. On the surface in front of him, paperwork rose from an unremarkable desk. The stacks held the usual documents one might find in an auto repair shop. Invoices, manuals, purchase orders, loan applications, and so on. Paperwork. The bane of a small business owner's existence.

Liam saw it all as his responsibility, though. Aside from the man's relentless drive and appetite for violence, his attention to detail was one of the core attributes that made him successful. Liam understood the importance of doing the small things well, and he recognized that it was his responsibility to run a clean business. Not his CPA. Not his lawyer. Not his employees. *His.*

For that reason, Liam interviewed every employee before they were hired. He reviewed every bank deposit before it went out the door. And he reviewed almost every document that landed on his desk. The little things —the mundane tasks, the worn chair, his cheap desk—kept him grounded. They kept him from getting sloppy.

The phone on the desk beeped twice, then a sweet voice poured from the small speaker on the device: "Mr. Hudson, your eight o'clock is here to see you."

"Send them in."

"Yes, sir," the young woman on the other end replied. "And it's just Mr. Bates. I don't think Mr. Coleman is here yet. I'll be sure to let you know when he arrives, Mr. Hudson."

"I've told you that you can call me Liam," he replied. "I know you're using your manners, sweetie, but I don't mind. You can leave all that at the door with me. I'm sure my friend Harry out there doesn't mind either."

The young lady paused a moment. She'd been answering phones at Hudson Auto for the last couple of weeks. She was still in her—*well*—probationary phase. Liam thought she had potential, though. Plus, she was a certified knockout. Red hair. Gorgeous smile. A rack that turned heads like a monkey wrench.

"Okay," she finally responded. "Mr. Bates—I mean, Harry—is on his way into your office."

"I hear him already."

Like the tornado that he was, Harry Bates burst through the door to the office. He glanced around the dated space with the same look of disgust that he always displayed when entering his only client's office. Harry wore a brand-new seersucker suit, no tie, and a boater hat. What Harry liked was usually expensive, even obnoxious at times. He always drove the newest cars. Always lived in a stylish home. Always ate well. It was how he lived, and probably how he'd die.

"Is that *another* new girl you have answering your phones?" Harry asked as he closed the door. "She looks to be even better looking than the last one."

Liam offered a shrug from his seat. "It's a difficult position, Harry. I need the best up there."

"You have to quit firing the ones that won't bang you," Harry said as he plopped down in a worn leather chair. "These girls need a comfortable space to do that kind of work for their boss, and this office isn't cutting it for you."

Liam played along as he glanced around at his personal office space. He had little interest in maintaining an impressive office. His business—*businesses, really*—didn't require one. Harry knew that.

"You can leave too if you don't like it here."

"Let me send my decorator over," Harry said. "They'll at least get this place in the current century for you."

"You just stick to what you're good at," Liam replied with a grin. "Don't worry about my place here."

"Suit yourself," Harry said as he peered around the room. "All I'm saying is that—in my professional opinion—you've fully depreciated everything in this room, at least five times over."

Liam agreed. His office looked almost the same as it had when he opened the doors of Hudson Auto back in 1986. The only new additions that'd been made to the space over the years were two shiny safes that occupied one wall, and the photographs from his amateur dirt-racing career that he added every few months or so. The rest—the furniture, the paint on the walls, the finger-block parquet flooring—remained the same. That's the way he liked it, though. Everything within those walls had its place, even the people who walked through its door.

"Where's Abe?" Liam asked. "Didn't you tell him to be here?"

"I did," Harry replied with a sigh. "I haven't heard back from him."

Liam nodded. His lawyer was becoming more and more unreliable. A sign that he needed to consider other options. He pushed forward with the business of the morning.

"What do you have for me, Harry? What was so important that you couldn't tell me over the phone?"

"I heard from one of our boys at the jail that your son is apparently back in town."

Liam leaned back in his chair. He folded his hands across his chest as he absorbed the information. He could tell that his friend was watching him for a reaction.

"I thought he wasn't eligible for parole for another couple of years," Liam finally said, carefully choosing his words. "At least, that's what Abe told me last time we spoke about it."

Abe Coleman wasn't usually mistaken about those sorts of things. The old country lawyer had a reputation for bending the law, and for that reason, he always stayed current on its limitations.

"Abe knows what he's doing," Harry replied, "but the old boy is getting up there. He's been grinding the gears for years. It may finally be catching up to him."

Liam agreed, for the most part. They'd all been running wide open for a while now, but that's how he preferred it. He didn't have any interest in retiring. Liam planned to ride it out until he hit the wall in a blaze of glory.

"When will he be out?" Liam asked.

"Tomorrow, apparently."

"I imagine parole will send him here," Liam said, more to himself. "Which means the prodigal son returns..."

Harry smiled from his chair. The duct tape that held the seat cushion under him struggled as the large man repositioned himself. Harry had always been a little on the heavy side, but a steady diet of brown liquor and recreational drugs kept the pounds under control over the last forty years. Then, he'd suffered his first heart attack last year. A coronary event that hit the man hard on the night of his sixty-ninth birthday. If it weren't for the two strippers they'd paid to bed the birthday boy, Harry Bates would have died alone in his hotel room that night. It was nothing short of a providential miracle that the man was still alive.

"Life is short," Harry grunted. "The kid took a pinch like a man, Liam. He didn't say shit when they leaned on him, so I say you—"

"I'll welcome him home with open arms. There's no other way to do it."

"Good," Harry replied, obviously pleased. "We should get Abe's take on this whole situation, though."

Liam nodded. He'd survived in the trade for almost thirty years. Sure, there'd been investigations. A few close calls here and there. No one ever got close enough to touch him, though. No one inside his inner circle had ever been picked up. No one except his only son—Colt.

"Find Abe," Liam said. "I need his thoughts on this today."

"I'll drive by his house and see if—"

"And if I can't meet with him today," Liam added. "I need to start working on finding a new lawyer."

"I don't know if I'd recommend you make that change just yet," Harry said as he started to his feet. "There are a lot of moving parts to consider."

"I want to shop around. That's all."

"I have someone in mind if you want to take a meeting or two."

"Where is he out of?" Liam asked. "I'm not driving to Atlanta every time I need to see the guy—"

"It's actually she," Harry replied. "And her office is right here in Blakeston."

Liam paused a moment. "I know who you're talking about."

Harry grinned as he made his way for the door. He had that familiar glint to his eye. "She's one of the best."

"Close the door behind you."

Once Harry left, Liam leaned forward in his chair. *A change might be good,* he thought, pulling the top drawer of his desk open. He checked to make sure the envelope and documents still sat tucked away. Photos. Reports. Medicals. *All there.* He closed the drawer and locked it. Everything would stay there until he found someone he could talk to. Someone he trusted to handle the future.

10

Maggie Reynolds sat alone in the lobby of Blakeston National Bank. From a handsome leather chair—one that she'd been waiting in for almost twenty minutes—she watched as a number of the bank's employees trickled by. Most offered her a smile. Another complimented her shoes. One finally asked if she'd been helped already.

"I spoke with one of your co-workers before I sat down," Maggie replied, careful not to allow any frustration into her voice. "I have a meeting with Mr. Morgan. At 8:30, I believe."

Maggie recognized a decent poker face when she saw it, and the one on the young man offering his assistance certainly needed some work. He stood there, paused for what seemed like entirely too long—especially for such a simple response—and eventually assured her that he would check on the bank president's whereabouts. She watched him as he hurried off through one of the lobby's side doors, then reached for the cell phone in her purse to confirm the time for the appointment. As she pulled the device from the bag, it pinged—gently reminding her that she was scheduled to be in Blake County Superior Court within the hour.

Maggie unlocked the phone and typed a text message to her assistant: *Running behind. Probably won't make it by the office before the hearing. Bring file to the jail please.* She returned the phone to her purse, then leaned back in her chair. She closed her eyes and took a deep breath in, reminding herself not to get frustrated. *It wasn't personal.*

When she opened her eyes, she noticed one of the bank tellers watching her from behind the front counter. She was only one in a group of several young ladies, all huddled together in quiet conversation. Maggie could smell the coffee from their mugs. She could see the laid-back expressions on their faces. She could hear the authenticity in their laughter. It was Friday, and they all looked at ease with their place in the world.

"I'm so sorry to keep you waiting," started a voice from over her shoulder. Maggie turned to it and found a man in a pastel-colored polo hurrying in her direction. The man was not Todd Morgan. "Unfortunately, I'll be stepping in for Todd this morning. He's been tied up with something rather last minute."

"I understand," Maggie said as she stood from her seat. "I'm sure he has a lot on his plate."

"That he does," the man said, glancing at a gold watch on his wrist. "We all do."

"Yes, we certainly do."

The man lifted his eyes back up to Maggie's—literally had to lift them because Maggie, in her heels, stood two inches taller than the man. He seemed to straighten his back as he noticed this. "Have you been waiting long?" he asked.

"About twenty minutes or so, but it's—"

"Where are my manners?" the man spouted, clearly not pausing to listen to Maggie's response. "I'm Kent Talbot. I'm one of the senior VPs here."

Maggie glanced at the BNB insignia on the vice president's polo. The royal blue lettering contrasted nicely with the pink material. One she assumed the small man wore because it breathed nicely when he hit the course on Friday afternoons.

"Maggie Reynolds," she replied as she offered her hand. "We need to hurry, though. I'm due in court in about forty-five minutes."

"Of course," he said. "Follow me."

Kent held open one of the lobby's side doors and directed her down a hallway. Maggie thanked him as she entered a hardwood corridor lined with several oil paintings. Each depicted various scenes from the same sporting event. Dogs pointing to a covey full of quail. Horses carrying hunters under a canopy of tall pines. Sportsmen padding down clay-colored trails in search of their prey. The paintings were a nod to South Georgia's sport of privilege—bird hunting.

"How about coffee?" Kent asked as he scurried ahead of her to the next entryway. He opened a thick oak door that led them to a wood-paneled conference room. "We also have tea, water, Diet Coke—"

She smiled. "No, thank you."

"Are you sure?" he prodded. "I'll get you a water just in case."

Maggie made a mental note as she took her seat at the conference table. One of the last things she wanted was a partnership with a banker that felt the need to make pushy decisions for the female clientele.

It's not personal, Maggie reminded herself.

Kent hollered the order across the hallway, then turned back to Maggie to grab a seat on her same side of the conference table. The fifty-something VP leaned back in his chair with a smile. He crossed his legs, revealing sockless ankles above his loafers.

"Now," he began. "How's the law business treating you?"

"Good," she replied, rolling her chair back a few inches from his. "I've been settling back in nicely here in Blakeston."

"That's what I've heard," Kent replied with a chuckle. "I know my doctor friends are certainly terrified to see another trial lawyer set up shop right here in town. Especially one with a reputation such as yours."

While Maggie considered her response to the comment—one she wasn't quite sure was meant as a compliment—another BNB employee arrived with a cup of coffee and a cold bottle of water. Grateful for the interruption, Maggie changed the subject.

"I ran into Todd at a charity event two weeks ago and talked to him about some of the plans I have in mind for my practice. He seemed to understand the potential in high-level trial work and wanted BNB to get the first shot at my business. That's why he set the meeting."

"Right," Kent said, quickly. "That sounds like our new bank president. Todd, as you may know, came to us from a bank up in Atlanta and certainly brought some of their ideas with him. The board seems to like his thoughts on stepping outside of our usual partnerships, though. I guess in this economy, everyone is seeking out more non-traditional opportunities, right?"

Maggie wasn't sure if old Kent here was intentionally trying to bomb their meeting. It certainly felt like it, but his face told her that he was quite serious about what was actually coming out of his mouth.

"Non-traditional opportunities?" she asked.

"We just usually only extend the kind of credit you're looking for to business owners we've known for quite a while. People we've been working with for years." Kent sipped from his coffee and continued. "I mean, I get it, your kind of law practice has been around. It's lucrative, and we like that. It's just—"

"I understand," Maggie said, cutting him off. "My law firm is different than some of the other businesses here in town."

"Exactly."

"It's not as safe—as reliable—as the companies you usually work with."

Kent kept nodding, smiling.

"And I'm essentially an unknown compared to the guys you normally lend this kind of money to."

Kent stopped his nodding for a moment. He at least wasn't dumb enough to step on that land mine.

"I will say, the building that you purchased right downtown is coming along nicely. I know that it could serve as collateral in—"

"Did Todd brief you on what I'm looking for, Mr. Talbot?"

"He did."

"So, you know that I'm looking to partner with a bank that's willing to look beyond the traditional risk metrics?"

Kent coughed, politely. "It's just that in my time here at the bank, we've not worked with the lawyers that take the risky cases. It has nothing to do with you or—"

"Okay," Maggie said as she started to stand. "Then we don't need to dance around for another ten minutes for you to finally tell me that BNB isn't going to extend the kind of credit I'm looking for. I heard a very different tone from Todd, but he's obviously not here."

"Wait," Kent started. "Let's not get hysterical about this—"

Maggie shook her head—*unbelievable*. "Tell Todd that I'm taking my business to another bank."

"Maggie, please hold on. We can get Todd on the phone and—"

"Don't worry about it," she replied as she turned toward the door. "This obviously isn't a good fit for either of us."

"I'll tell Todd to call you," Kent said to her back. "He *will* call you."

Maggie didn't turn around. "No need."

"Let's try to get you and your husband back in on another day, then, just to—"

Maggie turned on the spot. "My husband is the commander of a narcotics unit with the sheriff's office. He doesn't have anything to do with my law practice. Todd and I scheduled this meeting to discuss the future of my business."

"Maggie, I just meant that we often take a more personal approach when dealing with our customers and their families." Kent sounded flustered as he said this. "It's how we do business and—"

"I need to run to court," Maggie said as she turned into the hallway. "Thank you for the water."

"We got off on the wrong foot," Kent called after her as she made her way toward the lobby. "It wasn't personal. We were just talking business."

No, she thought. *In Blake County, when it comes to money—it's always personal.*

11

Maggie passed through the metal detectors that guarded the county jail's small courtroom. A reporter followed behind her with his tripod in hand. He wore a faded T-shirt from a high school two counties over and spoke into his cell phone in an accent that sounded local. His dark-faded jeans, stacked bracelets, and vintage sneakers told everyone he wanted to be known as a bona-fide non-conformist. Of the creative type, of course.

"They called me thirty minutes ago," the reporter excitedly said into his phone. "I'm telling you, man, they have the guy here at the jail in Blakeston. We're the only ones on it."

The deputy working courtroom security nodded to Maggie with a smile, waving her through the sensors. He stopped the reporter, though, and motioned for the guy to pocket his cell phone. The phone went into a slim black backpack over the newsman's shoulder. A bag that the deputy demanded be searched.

"Have at it," the young man said. He looked over at Maggie and paused a moment, almost as if he recognized her.

Maggie noticed the glance, so she waited at the door to the courtroom. The young reporter struck her as a local kid who maybe grew up edgier than his peers. One who probably went away for journalism school in a big city but was settling now for a byline in the local paper.

"What're you over here for today?" Maggie asked in the direction of the reporter.

"I'm here for your case," he replied, not glancing back at her. "You're Maggie Reynolds, right?"

She nodded. "That's right."

The reporter kept his eyes on the deputy searching his bag. "I heard they're bringing John Deese into court this morning. Are you getting involved with that?"

"Not the criminal case," Maggie replied, although she wished like hell she was. "As you probably know, that's a State matter."

"Yeah?" the reporter asked as he looked back over at her. He grinned at the bulky file tucked under her arm.

"The prosecutors have what they need," Maggie clarified. "I'm only here to represent the interests of my client. A victim, I'll add."

"I know who your client is."

The deputy returned the backpack and tripod to the young reporter, then directed him toward the courtroom. Maggie didn't say anything else as she held the heavy door open for the local journalist, allowing him to easily maneuver his supplies inside. He thanked her and started toward one of the back corners of the room. She watched with a small amount of curiosity as the tight-lipped newsman walked away. Maggie always looked for creative ways to build leverage in her cases, and the media usually proved to be an effective tool. Maybe this young reporter could be just that—especially if he was willing to tell the story her way.

"Stay in line!" a voice hollered from the opposite side of the courtroom.

Maggie turned her attention to the front of the room. A row of inmates, all in orange jumpsuits, were being brought in through a metal side door. They shuffled along, careful not to trip on the chains at their feet. Maggie counted eight in the group. Four Blacks. Two Latinos. Two whites. She recognized only one, though.

"All the way to the end of the row!" the deputy called out. "Keep moving down. Keep it moving."

The inmates followed the commands until they fell into position. Once in place, they waited, shoulder-to-shoulder in a pitiful line for all to see at the front of the courtroom.

"Okay, boys, you can sit down now."

As the inmates sat, a few looked around the cinder-block courtroom. Maggie watched them—especially John Deese—as they took in the space. The jail courtroom was one she knew well from her time as a public defender, and it still looked and felt the same as she remembered. Torn and stained cloth covered several rows of pew-like benches that ran the length of the room. Fluorescent lighting hummed from the tattered ceiling above. And groups of family members huddled together on the back benches. Everyone—the inmates, the officers, the media, and especially the attorneys—they all waited for the judge.

Maggie stood at the back of the room for a moment, near the families of the accused. She was unsure exactly where she wanted to set up. Sure, she recognized several faces of those in the room that were in law enforcement. They all congregated near a table in the courtroom usually reserved for the prosecution. That wasn't her turf, though, and she didn't like how their energy seemed to juxtapose the depressing circumstances of the inmates and their families—the people she used to represent.

Don't worry about it, she told herself. *I'm still just finding my way.*

She decided to head toward the opposite side of the room, away from the BPD officers, the deputies with the BCSO, and the probation officers from the Department of Community Supervision. At first, they didn't seem to notice her as she made her way to the other side of the musty room. They were busy milling about, chatting with one another, laughing with a sort of gallows humor—the kind that was typical of those who worked in the sport of policing.

The lions in the den, Maggie thought as she glanced over at the group of badges. *So, what does that make me if I'm helping them?*

An investigator called over to Maggie, breaking her train of thought. "I heard you weren't slumming it in here anymore." He smiled a wide smile after he said this and cut across the room to stand beside her. "The new boss man has already put the word out on you. He told us, and I quote: *Maggie Reynolds isn't taking criminal defense cases anymore.*"

Maggie laughed. "Tell your boss man—my wonderful husband—that the courtrooms are open to the public." As she said this, she pointed over her shoulder at the back corner. "See Exhibit 'A' over there. That's called the press."

The BCSO investigator—an eight or nine-year narc by the name of Trevor Meredith—was only one of a dozen or so lawmen that now reported to her husband. Meredith offered her another good-natured smile, then looked over in the direction of the young reporter.

"Mr. Tight Jeans back in the corner is reporting on the process—not trying to mess it up."

"You know him?" Maggie asked, ignoring the jab.

"Yeah, that's Ben Moss. He's been working around here a year or so now."

"He a decent reporter?"

"I guess," Meredith said with a shrug. "Works the criminal beat, mostly. Not a heck of a lot to report on. I mean, all these people did it, right?"

Maggie smirked as she allowed her gaze to rest on one particular inmate in the room. Usually, she didn't mind getting into a little back-and-forth with cops about the presumption of innocence. Not today, though. Maggie's interests—for the first time in her career—rested squarely with those of the prosecution. Like them, she wanted John Deese put under the jail.

"It's hard to disagree with you today, Trevor."

Maggie felt like a turncoat, but she'd been rooting for the good guys for almost twelve months now. After what proved to be a grueling multi-agency manhunt, the BCSO now had their man in custody. Suspected in at least one high-profile murder in Blake County, John Deese had been on the run since the last case Maggie took before a jury. Her client—Charlotte Acker—walked free, but Acker wanted the prosecution to finish the job. She wanted the State—with a little help from Maggie—to make sure Deese never left the walls of a jail cell.

"I guess you're here for the fugitive's case, right?" Meredith asked. "The Deese guy."

She nodded. Deese was one of the only two white guys on the front row. Even with his back to her, she could see that he still looked tan from the small beach town they picked him up in. A *pueblito* outside of Lima, Peru.

"You know it," she said. "He'll be getting a nice little lawsuit from my client, too."

"Really?" Meredith asked. "No offense, but that sounds like the least of his problems."

Maggie understood the investigator's reasoning. To most people, a civil lawsuit didn't matter all that much when there was a murder charge in play. Deese wasn't most people, though.

"Anyhow," Maggie said. "You just here to see some fireworks?"

"No, not really," Meredith said as he shook his head. "I'm here on an old case I worked on some years back. This little punk by the name of Colt—"

"All rise!" called out the deputy at the front of the courtroom. The metal chains on the inmates clinked together, and the benches groaned as all those seated in the room began to stand. "This court is now in session, the Honorable Judge John Balk presiding."

12

Colt Hudson stood at the end of the line-up—right next to a blond-haired, middle-aged white guy who hadn't said two words to anyone. Colt had his head turned, surveying the depressing little space, when he heard the judge enter the courtroom. Everyone seated on the benches stood and Colt guessed there had to be at least thirty people in the room. It worried him to see the courtroom packed for a Friday morning garbage calendar, and Colt wondered why. He didn't need any unnecessary attention being placed on his early release from prison.

"Good morning, everyone," the judge said in a deep, baritone voice. "Please be seated."

Colt turned his attention back to the front of the room. The old jurist took his seat at the bench and started to flip through the stack of papers before him. Judge John Balk looked even larger than Colt remembered. His broad shoulders and large gut made the man in the black robe appear intimidating. The image of law and order.

"Now," Judge Balk said, "it appears we have a number of bond hearings to take up this morning, along with one matter that is set for arraignment."

Colt watched as the judge's eyes scanned the faces of the men in the line-up. He prayed the old judge wouldn't recognize him from years before.

Unlikely, Colt reminded himself. *A lot of time has already passed.*

The judge's eyes stopped on Colt's face, though. They rested on it for a moment, then went to the man's next to him. Colt turned around again just to make sure the judge wasn't looking at someone in the rows behind them, and that's when Colt spotted the investigator.

There you are, Trevor, Colt thought. *I knew you'd slink in here just to watch.*

Trevor Meredith leaned against the back wall of the courtroom. He acknowledged Colt's gaze from across the room, then leaned over to whisper something to a stunning brunette that stood to his left. Colt shifted his attention to the woman in the suit. He recognized her, too. He just couldn't remember from where.

"Is the district attorney's office ready to proceed with arraignment?" the judge asked.

Colt turned back around in his seat. He knew from his initial foray into the court process—almost seven years ago, *thanks to old Trevor*—that arraignment functioned as the beginning of a defendant's prosecution. A short hearing, from what he'd seen, that usually boiled down to three key parts. First, the defendant had to be informed of the charges that were in play. Next, they had to know what constitutional rights and guarantees they had available. And last, they were supposed to enter a plea on the record. For most defendants, that plea amounted to two words—*Not Guilty.*

A prosecutor from the DA's office stood. He buttoned the jacket of his dark suit and addressed the court. "We are, Your Honor."

"Mr. Hart, does the defendant have counsel involved?"

"Not that I'm aware of," Hart replied. He turned and looked over at the man seated next to Colt. "I believe the court may need to inquire about—"

"Mr. Deese," Balk said, interrupting the prosecutor before he offered a recommendation to the judge. "Do you intend to hire an attorney?"

The man stood. "I suppose I'll need to, Judge."

The deadpan reply from the blond-haired inmate spurred a few chuckles from those in attendance.

"Mr. Deese, please walk to the front of the room," the judge said, crossing his large arms across his chest. He waited as the man carefully made his way to the area directly in front of the bench. "You've been indicted in case number 22-CR-858—State of Georgia v. Johnathan A.

Deese. Now, I can read the charges to you, or you can waive a reading of the indictment itself and just enter your plea."

The room went silent for a moment as Deese appeared to consider his response. Colt pegged the man as the educated type. 5-foot-10. Decent shape. Clean-cut look and a country-club tan. A white-collar criminal, no doubt.

"Mr. Deese?"

"I don't believe I'm prepared to make that decision right now, Your Honor."

In Colt's time at the Rut, he met some interesting characters. Smart criminals. Dumb criminals. Even a few genuine wrong-place-wrong-time criminals. One thing he found, though, was that almost all the guys that were first-time offenders, they all seemed to believe they were smarter than the rest. That they could find a way out of their problem.

"Excuse me?" the judge asked.

Deese coughed into his hand. "I said, I don't believe I'm prepared—at least, not on this fine Friday morning—to make that kind of decision, Your Honor."

Several whispers spread through the small room as those in attendance seemed to recognize the stand-off that was taking place. Colt knew what it was, though. It was this guy's first time on the carpet.

"Well, do you need a lawyer, Mr. Deese?"

Another long pause. "Well, Your Honor, I don't believe I'm yet prepared to make that kind of—"

"I'll stop you right there," Judge Balk remarked. "I won't tolerate this foolishness. You can move forward with arraignment this morning, or I'll have counsel appointed to you. Which is it?"

Colt didn't know the man from Adam, but he already knew what the man planned to say in response to the judge's question. Colt leaned back in his seat as he waited for the judge to explode.

"I'll be honest, Judge. I'm not sure I'm prepared to make that kind of a decision this—"

"Get him out of here!" Judge Balk barked to the closest deputy. "I want this man in confinement. At least a little while longer so that he has plenty of time to think about his options."

The deputy responded quickly, grabbing Deese by the arm. "We'll make sure he's in solitary, Your Honor."

"I don't care where you put him. Just get him out of my courtroom."

Colt watched as they dragged the strange man from the area in front of the bench. He noticed as Deese appeared to stare toward the back wall of the courtroom. Colt turned and saw that the dark-haired stunner, the one standing next to Trevor Meredith, had a fierce look on her face as she watched him go.

Colt finally remembered who she was—*Well I'll be damned, that's Maggie Reynolds.*

13

Colt Hudson waited in a small holding cell, alone. After court that morning, a deputy explained to him that he would not be placed with those in general population. That they planned to release him the following morning. He'd heard the same thing earlier that day, though, and Colt wouldn't believe a word they said until they walked him out the door.

"Eyes up, Hudson," came a familiar voice from the other side of the cell door.

Colt stood when he heard the voice from his past.

A fist knocked twice on the metal door. "I said, eyes up, Hudson."

Colt stepped over the untouched dinner tray that lay on the floor and went to a small window on the cell's thick door. Through it, he could see the smiling face of an old friend.

"What in the hell, man?"

The door unlocked with a clang and in stepped Deacon Campbell. "I heard they brought you back," he said as he pulled Colt in for a bear hug. The beastly man-child from Colt's youth now looked to be close to thirty pounds heavier. Most of it muscle. "I had to come down here and see it for myself."

Deacon never visited Colt in prison. Not once. In the beginning, it'd bothered him, really pissed him off. They'd been close over the years, growing up alongside one another as competitors and teammates, and they'd been there for each other through some tough times. Colt now understood why his old buddy hadn't visited, though—his BCSO uniform said it loud and clear.

"Look at you," Colt said with a grin. "Your ass is Five-Oh, now."

Deacon nodded. His biceps and shoulders seemed to strain against the confines of his khaki-colored shirt. He looked unsure—an unusual look for the great Deacon Campbell—as he appeared to wait for the moment to sink in.

"Look," Deacon started. He looped both thumbs under the edges of his Kevlar vest. "I want you to know that I meant to come see you up at Rutledge. I just—"

"That's the past, Deacon. Don't worry about it."

"Yeah?"

Colt nodded, although he wasn't sure he believed it himself. He decided to change the subject. "You're still looking diesel, brother."

"You know it," Deacon replied. "The sheriff here—Charlie Clay—is in the weight room with us half the time, so it doesn't hurt to stay after it. I see you filled out, too."

"I had to," Colt replied, which was true. Prison didn't give him the option to go soft.

Again, Deacon appeared uneasy. "Man, I sure miss playing ball though. We had some days, right?"

Colt nodded his response. His friend's lack of self-awareness didn't surprise him, so he let it slide. Although Deacon never once visited him at the Rut, Colt tried his best to follow his friend's football career from prison. It'd been big news when a full-ride scholarship took his old friend down to Tallahassee, Florida, to play for the Seminoles. Deacon started two seasons at Florida State, until an offensive guard from Boston College pulled around and caught him wrong. The gruesome injury to the future-first-rounder's knee made the headlines in the college football world, then quickly left the national eye. Colt had tried to gather bits and pieces about his friend's attempts to rehab the knee. Most of what he found, though, suggested that the fierce linebacker lost a step with the injury. That once a return to the starting lineup became unlikely—partying became the priority.

"How's the knee?" Colt asked.

"Shit still hurts," Deacon replied. "It's all good, though."

It's all good? Colt thought, surprised by the comment. *A lot certainly has changed.*

"You here to bust me out or what?"

"Bust you out?" Deacon laughed as he looked at his watch. "Man, it's like eleven o'clock at night. From what I hear, you only have about ten hours left in this place."

"Ten hours too long."

Deacon shook his head. "How about I give you a ride out of here in the morning?"

"All right, bet."

"Where are they sending you, by the way?" Deacon asked. He sounded a little bit too much like a cop for Colt's liking. "Is the plan for you to go back out to your dad's place?"

Colt paused a moment as he considered his response. He thought back to the conversation he had with Tim Dawson in the private conference room at Rutledge. The lawman had been clear about the parameters of their agreement. No one was to know about their deal. Not friends. Not girl-friends. And especially not family.

"Yeah, you know how it is," Colt said. "I had to give them an address to be released to. That's what they keep on file at—"

A loud, hacking cough started in the hallway, and Deacon turned to look out the half-shut door. He signaled with his hand to someone outside.

"Who's out there?" Colt asked when his friend turned back to him.

Deacon paused a moment. "It's just Trevor. We rode up here to work on—"

"Man, I don't want to hear anything about that guy."

"All right," Deacon said. "Look, I'll be by in the morning."

"Fine."

Deacon started to turn, then asked: "Does your dad know you're back early?"

"I don't know," Colt replied. "Maybe he does. Maybe he doesn't. I don't really care, honestly."

Deacon nodded. "I get it."

"You seen him lately?"

"Nope," Deacon replied. "I don't see him around too much."

"I'm sure nothing's changed."

"You got that right," Deacon said. "Look, I need to run, Colt."

"All right."

Deacon slapped him on the back. "We're good, right?"

"Yeah, we're good. I appreciate you checking in, Deputy Campbell."

"Shit, not for long," his friend replied. "I'm rolling onto that narcotics squad next week."

"Yeah?"

Deacon looked proud. "Yeah, I got the nod a few days ago. They have a new guy running the shop. His name's Dawson."

"Congratulations, brother."

"All right, Colt, well I'm out of here."

"Your ass better not be late in the morning."

Colt watched his old friend smile as the cell door closed. A murmured conversation could be heard through the thick door as Deacon walked away with Meredith.

Colt shook his head as he turned back to the small cell. He stared at the depressing room and reminded himself that it was his last night as a caged man. He walked over to the bed and laid down. The thin mat felt familiar under his back. As he worked to get comfortable, he couldn't keep the wheels from spinning in his mind. Deacon, one of his oldest friends, carried a badge and took orders from the BCSO now. It didn't make sense.

Minutes passed as Colt tried to relax. For the first time in a while, his thoughts drifted back to one of his games in high school. He took a deep breath in as he tried to remember the smell of the grass stains on his jersey. The high after a big win on the road. The smiles on the faces of his coaches and teammates. And that look. The one on Natalie's face when he stepped off the bus and into the school's parking lot.

Maybe, Colt thought, *I'll find someone who looks at me like that again.*

Colt closed his eyes and tried to sleep.

Ten more hours.

As he started to drift off, he heard it—*bang, bang, bang!*

He opened his eyes and looked over at the door. After five long years up the road, he knew the sound. He'd heard it before.

Again—*bang, bang, bang!*

Colt didn't move as he waited for it. The sound that followed the pounding of a fist on metal. The sound that only came at night.

14

Tim Dawson stood at the kitchen stove scrambling eggs. He half-listened as one of the weekend morning shows played from the television in the living room. He could hear the clear voice of a reporter from one of the national outfits. The man sounded excited as he provided an update on the ongoing *safety crisis* in the American railroad industry. Tim couldn't see Maggie from where he stood, but he knew her eyes were glued to the television screen for this segment. She'd recently taken in four new cases involving injuries at railroad crossings and had since started keeping up with the industry like a true rail enthusiast.

"There was another big derailment over in St. Louis," she called to him from the couch in the living room. "U-P this time."

Tim cut the burner off. *U-P* stood for Union Pacific, one of the major railroad companies out west. "That's terrible," he called back to her. They'd taken to yelling back and forth at one another from different rooms. A sign that he and Maggie were only getting closer to the comfortable season of middle age. Tim scraped the eggs into a bowl and tossed the skillet in the sink, then headed toward the living room for what he could only assume would be more train talk.

"I'm telling you," Maggie said once she saw him enter the room, "the feds shouldn't have rolled back all those safety regulations." Maggie already had her laptop open, probably adding notes to one of her never-ending outlines. "Mark my words, these companies aren't going to step up without the government bringing the hammer down on them."

Tim plopped down beside her. "You do love the government bringing the hammer down," he said as he took a bite of his eggs. "It's kind of your thing now."

Maggie reached for the fork in his bowl. She scooped up some eggs and took a bite of her own. "I'm a lay-the-hammer-down-on-a-case-by-case-basis kind of girl."

"Especially when they're your cases."

"Exactly," she replied. "I mean, look at how much easier it'll be to sue John Deese now that he's in custody, and Charlotte didn't have to spend a dime to put him there. It really is amazing what you can do when all those government resources are at your disposal."

"That's what I've been telling you this whole time," Tim replied, grinning. He enjoyed being back on the public-good side of things. It allowed him to sit atop his high horse indignantly, while also painting his wife as nothing more than a tenacious rabblerouser. "Now, once you decide to stop blaming the government for all these small mishaps that happen from time to time, then we can really get on the same team."

Maggie looked ready to continue their game. "There are at least three train derailments every day, Mr. Dawson, and—"

"I've asked that you address me as Commander Dawson, ma'am."

"Not a chance," she laughed as she stood from the couch to argue her point from the living room rug. Her hair sat up in a messy bun, and she wore a short silk nightgown that showed off her toned runner's legs. "Now, with three derailments per day, that's nearly eleven hundred each year, so it's the NTSB and the FRA that are the ones that need to figure out what—"

Tim's cell phone started ringing on the coffee table. In an effort to act as much like an obnoxious crossing guard as possible, he lifted his hand to stop her momentum. "Let me get this call, counselor. That'll give you time to look up all these acronyms you keep throwing around."

"I see how it is," she replied. "Another government man who refuses to listen."

Tim winked at her, then picked up the phone. The Saturday morning call from his boss—Sheriff Charlie Clay—surprised him. "This is Tim," he said, pressing the phone to his ear. Tim listened as the sheriff skipped over the usual pleasantries and jumped right into it from the other end of the line. He sounded animated as he provided all the available facts. "Okay," Tim said after another moment. "I'm happy to assist as needed. I can be over there in about ten minutes."

Tim noticed that Maggie was watching him. He placed the phone back on the coffee table, then leaned back in his seat to take a deep breath in. The news from the sheriff was not at all what he expected to hear. It shocked him, really, and he knew Maggie would feel the same way.

"What did Charlie need?" she asked.

Tim considered whether he should keep the details from her until he confirmed everything himself. "Charlie asked me to come into the office," Tim said as he stood from the couch. "They have a situation on their hands over there."

"Is everything okay?"

"They have a death investigation going on in the jail," Tim said as he ran a hand through his hair. He'd have to forgo the shower and just head on in. "The sheriff asked me to come in and help them preserve the scene until the GBI arrives."

Maggie nodded. They both knew that whenever a death occurred in a county jail, it was considered best practice for the Georgia Bureau of Investigation to step in and handle the investigation. A startling number of deaths occurred in Georgia's jails and prisons each year, and the issue was finally getting the attention it deserved. The well-meaning attention, though, tended to put the microscope on all in-custody death investigations —especially those taking place in rural counties with limited resources.

"Did Charlie tell you who died?"

Tim nodded. He didn't know the guy all that well, but he knew his well-timed death would cause a stir in Blake County.

"Yeah," Tim replied. "And you'll hear all about it soon enough."

15

Colt Hudson stood close to the door of the holding cell. He pressed his ear against the cool metal door, trying to listen for details from the conversations taking place outside. He'd been awake for at least an hour or so when the commotion started. Nothing unusual, at first. After all, it wasn't uncommon for a short burst of energy to explode inside the walls of a jail. But when the sound of pounding boots erupted in the hallway, that's when Colt hopped to the small window on his cell's door to watch.

"Call it in!" a voice shouted as a man reached the door of the cell next to Colt's. "I said call it in, dammit!"

From the window, Colt could see a frantic corrections officer pull a radio to his mouth. He relayed the information before him, and a supervisor soon squawked back with commands. The guards shouted to one another to follow protocol. An admonition that quickly turned the tones of the men that gathered in the hallway to more muted, serious discussion. All Colt could gather from inside his cell was that there was a ten forty-four in progress—a suicide investigation.

Tim Dawson stepped into the main hallway of the county jail. He spotted
two deputies standing near the open doorway to one of the holding cells. A
yellow *X* of caution tape stretched across the entryway to the cell warning
all not to enter the scene.

"Who is the lead on this right now?" Tim asked.

An older deputy with a thin mustache responded first. "We don't know
yet, sir. I'm told the boys from Atlanta will be sending someone over for this
one."

"Well, until then, the sheriff wants me heading up this detail."

They both nodded their approval.

Tim turned to look at the dark cell. It'd been a while since he'd worked
a death case from law enforcement's point of view. The basics of scene
preservation still came to mind, though. "I don't want anyone else in this
hallway until someone from the GBI's local office is on scene. You
hear me?"

"You've got it."

Tim looked up and down the hallway. He counted six individual cells.
"Are all these holding cells clear?"

"That one's occupied," the second deputy said, pointing toward a beat-
up door that was a space over from the taped-off entryway.

Tim could make out half the face of the man inside the cell. They met
eyes through the window on the door. "You know who that inmate in there
is?" Tim said as he looked back at the deputies. He pulled a notepad and
pen from his pocket as if he were prepared to write the name down.

The thin-mustached deputy responded. "That's Liam Hudson's boy—
Colt." Tim noticed the deputy's tone sounded almost familial. "I think the
kid is supposed to be getting out today."

"He doesn't look like a kid to me," Tim replied, intentionally adding a
harshness to his tone. "If he has Blake County orange on behind that door,
that means he's doing time in here. That doesn't make him a kid in my
book."

"You're right," the deputy replied. "I just watched Colt grow up here
playing ball and—"

Tim raised a hand to stop the man from speaking. "I'm not concerned with all that. When the GBI gets here, they can decide what to do with young Hudson."

"Yes, sir."

Tim heard knocking on the glass. He turned to look at Colt's cell and saw him motioning for Tim to come over to the door.

"Nope," Tim said loudly for all to hear in the hallway. "You're staying in there until someone from the GBI decides whether they need to interview you. Sit tight, bud."

Colt knocked again on the glass and Tim walked a few steps closer. He leveled his eyes on Colt's, hoping his gaze could make it through the thick glass, and into the *kid's* thick skull. *I can't help you right now. You understand me?*

Colt stopped his knocking but stayed right up on the door. Tim hoped the message had been received.

"Nobody in or out!" Tim shouted as he turned to start back down the hallway. It felt good to be back, standing in the gap. "Once Mr. GBI graces us with his presence, I'll bring him back to check out the scene."

Tim Dawson watched from the sidewalk as a midnight blue, government-plated Tahoe pulled up to the curb of the county jail. Music blared from inside the vehicle, then abruptly shut off as a blonde stepped out of the driver-side door of the SUV. She wore jeans, boots, and a T-shirt with a list of concert dates down the front of it. As she approached, Tim could make out the words at the top of the shirt—*The Eras Tour.*

She offered him a professional smile. "Good morning, I'm Special Agent Cam Abrams with the GBI. I'm looking for Commander Tim Dawson."

Tim considered the appearance of the young agent standing before him. He knew that to be a special agent with the Georgia Bureau of Investigation, the GBI required that all their new recruits hold a bachelor's degree from a four-year college, and that they be at least twenty-one. They also had to be US citizens, meet basic vision requirements, and, among other things, not already be a criminal themselves. A rather low bar, in Tim's opinion.

"Morning," he said, sizing up the tall agent. She had a high ponytail that probably put her close to 5-foot-11. "That's me you're looking for."

Maybe I'm just getting older, Tim thought as he absorbed a firm hand-shake from the young woman, *but this girl doesn't look to be more than a day or two past her twenty-first birthday, if that.*

"Nice to meet you, Commander."

"Likewise," he replied. "Glad you could make it."

She nodded. "I hear y'all have a body for me."

"That's right, we've secured the area in the jail where they found him. A holding cell away from gen pop."

"Well, let's take a look."

"You planning to work this case alone?" Tim asked. He almost regretted the question as soon as he asked it.

"My parents already signed off on my permission slip," she replied with a smirk. "Now, let's get on with this field trip."

"That came out wrong. I meant that—"

"Don't worry about it." She said this without a hint of animosity in her voice. "My boss told me you're a former agent. Said I might learn a thing or two from you."

Tim noted her egoless response to the unfair assumption he'd made about her experience. Not an easy thing to do sometimes as a young agent. Put another rookie agent in that same spot—*say a new guy, especially*—and they might scoop that comment up and add it to the growing bag of chips on their shoulder.

"That all he told you?" Tim asked.

She laughed. "He also said for me not to bang any criminal defense attorneys while I was over here in Blakeston."

Tim smiled at the long-running joke that was often made at his expense. It wasn't the first time he'd heard it, nor would it be the last. All because years ago, the GBI's brass gave Tim the nod to lead a high-profile murder investigation in Blake County. The career-making case centered on two of the area's most distinguished citizens—Jake Collins and Lee Acker. While working the case up, Tim found himself in bed—*literally*—with

Maggie Reynolds, the criminal defense attorney making the case for the accused. The conflict created a problem for Tim's continued employment with the GBI and he left under a cloud of controversy.

"Fair enough," Tim said. "If you're going to jump in bed with the other side, though, make sure it's for the right reasons."

"Noted," she replied. "Your wife is incredible, by the way. I've been a Maggie Reynolds fangirl for years now."

"Did they let you watch the Lee Acker trial while you were in middle school?"

"Shut up."

"All right," Tim said, smiling. "Let's get you in there, Agent Abrams."

The door opened to Colt Hudson's cell.

"Come on out of there, Colt," a man's voice called from the hallway. "We need to talk to you."

Colt stepped out into the wide hallway. A group of seven or eight uniforms stood nearby, mostly doing nothing as far as he could tell. A gurney started to roll out of the cell next to his, and everyone seemed to give a wide berth to the pair of medical types charged with moving the body. As Colt watched the black bag roll by, he wondered who was inside, and why they decided the county jail was the right place to cash in early.

"Stand over there," a deputy said, pointing to an open space on the wall. Colt recognized the man as a regular at his dad's shop. A friend of the family. "There's an agent here who needs to talk to you, then we'll get you out of here."

Colt nodded his thanks, then crossed his arms as he leaned against the wall. A blonde in a pair of Ariats stepped out of the deceased's cell and Colt instinctively straightened his back at the sight of her. She looked taller now, probably close to six feet in those boots. He watched her as she pulled a cell phone from the rear pocket of her jeans. Her face looked the same as he remembered it—serious, much like her sister's—and it made his stomach hurt to see it again. She dialed a number on her phone, then turned in his direction.

"It's me," the agent said, speaking into the phone that was now pressed against her ear. "I'm not sure there's a lot more we're going to need to do here. Looks pretty standard. Guy used his sheet as a ligature. Probably hung himself sometime late last night."

Colt was still watching her when she noticed him standing in the hallway. She didn't smile.

"I'll keep you posted," she said, then ended the call.

They stared at one another from the short distance.

"Hey, Cam," Colt finally said. "What're you doing in here?"

"I should ask you the same thing," she replied. "I thought you weren't supposed to be out for another two or three years."

She took another few steps closer. Her glare felt cold as it zeroed in on him.

"Yeah," Colt said with some hesitation, "well, that ended up changing when—"

"You know what, I don't give a shit what you're about to say." She half-laughed, probably for the benefit of those around her. "I'll just reach out to the DA and get the truth from them."

Colt nodded as he took in the badge on Cam Abrams's hip. Unlike Deacon's decision, hers made perfect sense.

"Why are you just standing out here in the hallway?" she asked. "This is supposed to be a secure facility. Let's find a cell to put you in."

"I asked him to wait there, ma'am," the friendly deputy interjected from nearby. "I thought—"

Cam snapped at the deputy. "And why would you do that?"

He pointed to the door that was one space over from the crime-scene tape. "He was asleep in this holding cell last night. We figured you might want to interview him because he was probably the only one around when the guy did himself."

"Wonderful," Cam replied as she shook her head. "Death barely misses, *again*."

Colt waited for the awkward moment to pass. He wanted to make this as easy as possible on her. "Who was the guy that—?"

"I'll ask the questions," Cam snapped.

"Of course."

Colt noticed that the conversations no longer hummed from those nearby. They were, no doubt, listening to the skirmish between the inmate and the young agent. They'd all been young bulls themselves at one point in their careers, and they wanted to see how young Cam handled her own.

Push on, Cam, Colt thought. *I'm not going to fight you.*

She seemed to consider her options as she pulled a slim notebook from her pocket. Cam Abrams followed her older sister—Natalie Abrams—by eleven months. She'd been a year behind them in school, but Colt remembered the sisters being closer than most siblings. As the only two children to their parents, they were the focus in their tight-knit family. Colt couldn't imagine how hard it'd been for them after the wreck—after he took Natalie from them.

"Did you know John Deese?" Cam asked, tersely.

"I know I'm not supposed to be asking questions, but is that the name of the guy that died?"

Cam nodded. "That's right."

"I didn't know him. Hadn't heard his name until yesterday."

"How'd it come up yesterday?"

"I mean, it didn't really. I just sat next to him in court yesterday morning. That's all."

"Did he talk to you?"

Colt shook his head. "Not a word to me. The only time I heard him speak was to the judge."

"Okay," Cam said. "And last night, did you two do any talking between the cell walls or anything?"

"I didn't even know he was in there to be honest. I don't think he would've talked to me, though."

"Why's that?"

Colt shrugged. "I'm pretty sure he recognized the difference between us. I'm a soon-to-be ex-con. He was probably in here on some white-collar issue. Guys like that are criminals, too, but they don't talk to the riffraff like me."

"He had a murder charge hanging over his head," she said as she continued to look down at her pad, scribbling. "You didn't know that?"

"They've pretty much had me on lockdown the whole time I've been here. I haven't heard anything about anything, really."

"You didn't follow the trial of Charlotte Acker last year?"

"I was in prison, Cam."

"Answer the question."

Charlotte was a year behind Colt in school, the same year as Cam. A lifetime ago, he would've considered Charlotte a friend. "I followed her trial as best I could. I didn't put two and two together, though. He was involved in all that?"

"He was," she replied, clearly watching him for a reaction. "You seriously didn't know that?"

Colt tried his best to keep his facial expressions even. "No."

"Okay," she finally said after a long pause. Her eyes went back to her pad. "Well, did you hear anything at all last night that sounded strange?"

"Strange?"

"Yeah, strange. Out of place."

Colt thought about it for a second. Cam seemed to sense the hesitation in his response, so she looked back up from her pad.

"Not that I can recall," he finally said. "I slept pretty hard, though."

Cam's eyes narrowed. "Not that you can recall?"

"Not that I remember," he clarified. "I mean, I've heard a lot of strange stuff since I was sent off."

"I bet," she said, snapping her notepad shut. "I think I have what I need."

Colt looked at her another moment. It was good to see her. "Okay, well, if you need anything else, I'll be at my dad's place for the next few weeks."

"I'll have someone else interview you if we need anything else."

"I mean, that's not necessary if—"

"No," she shot back. "It is. I can tell my judgment is clouded."

Colt looked away from her. He didn't want a confrontation with a GBI agent in his last hour in jail.

"You want to know why, Colt?" she asked as she took a step closer to him. "Do you?"

He turned back to her. "If I could change what happened that night, Cam, I would. I'd switch places with her and—"

"There's the reason right there," she said with a nod. "It's the lying. I won't ever believe a word you say. Ever."

Cam didn't wait for a response. She just turned and walked away.

"Am I free to go?" he called after her.

"Get out of here."

16

Colt wiped the sweat from his brow as he crossed the parking lot of Hudson Auto. He wore a jail-issued T-shirt that stuck to his back like papier-mâché, plastered on by perspiration and the familiar South Georgia heat. Weather in Blake County could be unpredictable in the fall, especially during the latter part of October. While those in the states to the north talked of the first frosts of the year, residents in the southernmost parts of the Deep South simply hoped for relief from the tail-end to a long summer's blistering heat. Colt didn't mind, though. He could handle it. Especially now that his feet were back on the outside.

Finally.

As Colt made his way toward the office side of Hudson Auto, he noticed nine or ten vehicles waited on the side of the lot designated for customers. He heard the hum from the engines left running, keeping the air conditioners pumping cool air while the owners waited inside to settle-up. He considered the vehicles as he passed, noting the small changes to the body styles of the Big-Three's flagship models.

The Mustang came as a hatchback now? The Blazer was back? The new 300s looked slick.

He eyed the nicest vehicle on the lot. A newer model Range Rover. A mid-thirty-something mommy type sat in its driver's seat, toying with her cell phone. She looked up from her mindless scrolling, noticing him as he crossed in front of her Fuji-white SUV. Her large sunglasses—a set of killer eyes behind them, he guessed—rested on him as he passed. Colt smiled over at her, then heard the familiar *click* from the vehicle as she looked back down at her phone.

Assume away, Colt thought. *You don't know a thing about me.*

When Colt reached the exterior door to his father's office, he didn't knock. He knew several locks fortified the thick door from the inside and he felt their strength as he leaned on it hard, turning the knob. The locked door didn't budge. He looked up at the security camera over the door and noticed the red light blinking above the lens. Just above the camera, the old metal sign still hung tight to the building. In faded bronze letters, it read: *Hudson Auto's Family Office.*

Colt hammered his fist on the door. "Open up!"

He waited for a few seconds, then repeated the action. He felt a few droplets of his own sweat bounce from the door as he pounded the surface.

"Yes?" a voice finally started from a small intercom beside the door. "Can I help you?"

"It's Colt, let me in."

"Colt?" the female voice asked. She sounded confused.

He paused a moment as he considered his response. *This chick knows who I am, right?*

"I need in to see Liam."

"Do you have an appointment with Mr. Hudson?"

"An appointment with Mr. Hudson?" Colt scoffed. "Seriously? No, I don't have a freaking appointment."

The intercom went silent for a long moment. Colt waited with his arms crossed, all the while staring up at the small camera above the door. Someone had to be watching him.

"I'm sorry," the young woman began again. "Mr. Hudson isn't here right—"

"I'll wait for him, then. Let me in."

"No."

Colt hadn't eaten more than a few crackers in the last twenty-four hours. He was thirsty from the long hot walk. He just wanted to sit down, preferably in an air-conditioned room. It wasn't too much to ask.

"Where is he?" Colt asked. "Can't you call him?"

"He's not available," she replied, rather unhelpfully. "Look, Colt—it's Colt, right?"

"Yes," he replied. "Colt Hudson."

Another short pause. "Okay, well, I'll just make you an appointment."

"I'm his son, lady. At least let me in, and then we'll schedule an appointment with my—"

"I'm sorry, sir, but you're not going to be able to come inside."

Colt muttered chosen profanities, more to himself, as he turned away from the door and started along the side of the building. The voice started again from the intercom, but he ignored it, shaking his head as he stomped along. *Unbelievable.* After waiting for Deacon for almost an hour on the curb outside the county jail—*some friend Deputy Dickhead was*—he'd been forced to walk the five miles to their shop on the outskirts of town. A walk of shame through a town he once stood on top of as a young man about town. Now, Colt didn't have a vehicle, a cell phone, or a dime to his name. He was floundering, just like most other guys fresh out of prison. No family. No reliable friends. Nowhere to go, really.

Thanks a lot, Dad.

Colt made his way around to the other side of the building. There, he saw that the garage's large bay doors remained open. He could hear the old radio going. The drums on the classic rock station blended well with the compressors running the shop's pneumatic tools. Colt recognized the familiar noise of the shop. He grew up around it, working alongside most of the mechanics that came and went over the years. The guys were as much his family as his father was. It was there he learned all about the world of fast cars, skanky women, and smoking and drinking. He learned about the great roadmen, and the history of racing. He heard more stories about love from the wrench-turners—each well versed in shotgun weddings and quickie divorces—than he ever did from Liam. It was the guys at the garage Colt looked forward to most in his return to Hudson Auto.

"Can someone tell me where Jimbo is?" Colt asked as he entered the garage. He didn't recognize the few faces crowded around the hood of a black CTS.

One of the men turned around and offered him a short response. It almost sounded routine. "Jimbo's not here anymore."

The news shocked Colt. Jim Hires—Jimbo, as the guys all called him—had been the manager of the garage for most of Colt's life. "Since when?"

The man shrugged. "Before my time, guy."

"All right," Colt said as he glanced around the garage, "where's Scott?"

"Cason?" the man asked. "Scott Cason's off today, but—"

"No," Colt said. He shook his head as he processed the fact that both Jimbo *and* Scott no longer worked there. "I mean Scott Barley."

"I don't know a Scott Barley."

"How about Cal?"

The man shook his head, then glanced down at his watch. "Look, it's almost five. The boys and I want to be able to close on time, so—"

"Don't worry about it."

The man wore the shop's standard coveralls. Blue with a red *Hudson Auto* patch on the chest. He held an oil rag in one hand and used it to wipe his forehead as he waited for Colt to say something more. His expression wasn't one of annoyance. It was simply one from a man intent on wrapping up a long workweek.

He pointed to a door on the opposite side of the garage. "You can head through that door there and it'll take you to our lobby. Our girl should still be at the desk until 5. She'll set you up an appointment for Monday."

Colt looked over at the door. He knew the hallway that it led to. One that would take him to the customer waiting area—not to Liam's personal office. His eyes lingered on that side of the garage for a moment as he noticed a familiar friend of his parked in the corner.

"I appreciate it," Colt replied, slowly. "I'll head over there and see if I can catch her before y'all close."

"That'll be fine," the man said with a nod. "We're not really supposed to have customers in the garage, though, so be careful walking through here."

Colt smiled. "I completely understand."

The man turned back to the Cadillac, leaning under the hood to return to his work. Colt thanked him again as he started across the garage. He walked slowly, taking in the familiar terrain. Hudson Auto's central working area was comprised of four large bays, each with a hydraulic lift. Large metal containers, all filled with almost every tool known to a mechanic, divided the four working areas of the shop. Several well-used computers had long since taken the place of repair manuals and each had been positioned around the shop to be easily accessible from a standing position. Their oil-smudged keyboards and large monitors were a testament to the role that electronics and technology now played in the life of the modern mechanic.

Liam must have cleaned shop, Colt thought as he made his way through the garage. *Maybe he is starting to feel the heat in his old age.*

Colt reached the opposite side of the garage and stopped to admire the two-wheeled beauty parked against the wall. He smiled as he spotted the key still hanging from the ignition. He looked over his shoulder to check on the few remaining employees in the garage. They paid him no mind as they worked away on the sedan. Colt turned back to the motorcycle. He stepped to it and slung his leg over the seat. A helmet hung on the wall, within arm's reach, and he grabbed it to strap on, quickly.

The engine started on the first try. The initial growl from the V-Twin filled the large garage, drowning out the startled cries from the mechanics nearby. He pulled the clutch in, revved the throttle, then shifted into first. He punched it, spinning the rear tire on the slick floor as he flew out of the open bay door.

Colt cut around the side of the building, back through the customer lot, back by the Range Rover still parked out front. He knew the security cameras outside the building would catch it all as he tore off on Liam's beloved bike. He hoped he saw it.

He may not come looking for me, but he'll at least come looking for his bike.

The wind felt incredible as it dried his sweat-stained shirt. Colt pointed the bike away from town and opened it up once he hit the county line road. For the first time in a long while, he felt free to run. He passed the last gas station before the Alabama-Georgia line and glanced down at the fuel light.

Good to go. The two-lane road ahead ran another mile and a half, then crossed the Chattahoochee into nowhere Alabama. Colt knew the stretch of road well, riding it most every Saturday night in trucks and cars loaded down with his high school friends. All headed to the banks of the Hooch to trespass on private land, build fires, and drink beer by the river.

A lifetime ago.

The twenty-four-year-old convicted felon couldn't shake the weight of his homecoming, though, even as the country road stretched out before him. *Open it up.* The one-time gunslinger of the gridiron—and small-town Rebel Without a Cause—had been at the top of the heap before he went away. Now, he faced a future as a pariah among the people he once considered friends. In prison, Colt didn't spend much time thinking about his reputation back home. Doing so didn't serve a purpose. Not in that environment, at least. Now, though, as he sped along the roads of Blake County, Colt knew that he'd be forced to confront his past. He had to. He owed it to himself. He just needed a spot to sit and think on it for a while.

Colt downshifted as a wide, sweeping curve approached. One that skirted the edges of a large hog farm. Even at fifty-five, with the October air rushing by his helmet and shoulders, Colt could smell the pens around the old barn. Mel Darden and his kin raised thousands of hogs each year, and their large family accounted for much of the farmland in western Blake County. Colt knew several kids that made up the Darden family tree. He knew their family's model. When one graduated from high school, they went to work in the family business, eventually buying more land to raise more hogs. They were hardworking, humble, and relatively ambitious by local standards. Colt searched for the edge of their farm to see if progress had been made in their war for more land.

Nope.

Colt spotted the sign. It still stood in the same spot beside the road. A subtle barrier that divided rural money from generational wealth. Rumor was that old man Darden had offered to buy pieces of the private hunting preserve for years. His kingdom of pork only stood to benefit from the additional acreage, and those that owned the land along the river rarely used their property for good. Colt knew—as did Mel Darden—that Kelley Hill Plantation wasn't for sale, though. It stood between the residents of Blake

County and the fresh waters of the river that the Creek named long ago, and everyone knew that if anybody wanted that land for their own—*they'd have to take it.*

Colt spotted the bridge ahead that crossed the river. He slowed the bike as he neared the clear boundary that'd been conditioned by parole—the Alabama-Georgia line. He cut off the two-lane road and rolled down to the only public boat launch positioned inside the fiefdom that was Kelley Hill Plantation. He parked the Italian-made machine on the Georgia side of the river and stepped off the bike. He could see from where he stood that the river was high. Trees along the banks dipped their branches into the wide tributary, offering their leaves to those that swam in the cool water. The clean air, along with the sounds of the water rushing by, nearly overloaded his senses. Spending years inside a cage—warranted or not—ruined a man, especially one raised under the skies of South Georgia.

Colt walked to the river's edge. He was alone for the first time in a long, long time. No traffic sped by over the bridge. No boats eased by on the river. It was just him, and the sunshine on his face. He almost prayed in that moment, given the beauty of it all. He couldn't find the words, though.

Grateful, still.

The sound of an engine approaching started slowly, invading the peaceful moment by the river. Colt heard the crunching of gravel under the vehicle's tires. The black-and-red Ducati leaned on its kickstand twenty yards back, too far to make a run for it if need be. Colt turned and glanced over his shoulder at the vehicle. He didn't recognize it, but at least it didn't bear the insignia of the BCSO.

Colt took a few steps toward the truck. He squinted to see the face behind the wheel. It took a moment, but he soon recognized it. It was the face of a man he'd not seen in five years.

17

Liam Hudson pulled into the parking lot of the old public boat launch. His two-wheeled beauty—an original 1993 Ducati M900—looked to be unharmed. A helmet, along with a ratty T-shirt, hung from her handlebars. As he pulled up to the rear of the bike, he took in the area around the gravel lot. No one else was around, except the young man at the river's edge.

How long had it been? he thought, gazing through the windshield at his only child. *Four, maybe five years. Too long.*

He shut the engine off on the vehicle—a worn-out Chevrolet 454 SS—and stepped out into the warm evening air. Liam nodded to his son from afar as he walked around to the front of the pickup. He pulled a cigarette from the pack in his chest pocket, then leaned against the truck's grill. At his back, he felt the comfort of the S&W wedged in his belt.

"I figured you kept a tracker on that Monster," Colt hollered from the edge of the riverbank, "so I knew you'd eventually come looking for her."

Liam placed the cigarette between his teeth and started a slow clap. He pulled on the stick, then spit on the gravel at his feet. The boy was smart. Hell, he'd always been smart. That was his problem.

"Here I am, Colt, what do you want?"

Colt started toward him. The young buck looked taller now, thicker. The muscles on his bare chest and arms were the wiry kind. Ones that a man built with hundreds of thousands of push-ups. The kind that came from time in the box.

"Let's start with what I'm owed."

"What you're owed?"

Colt nodded. "That's right, *Dad*. What I'm entitled to for my—"

Liam interrupted him. "See, that's the problem right there with your generation, Colt."

Colt stopped at the bike and lifted the T-shirt from the handlebars. He shook his head with that same smart-ass smirk. The one he always went to, even as a little kid.

"I'm listening," he said as he pulled the shirt over his head. "What's this problem that I—I mean, my entire generation has?"

"There's a list."

"I'm sure there is."

"What you don't understand—what you've never understood, really—is that you're not entitled to a thing in this world. Not a damn thing, son, because you—"

"Because you have to make it on your own, right?"

Liam nodded, tossing his cigarette to the ground. "That's right. Even take it, if you have to."

"By any means necessary?"

"Sure," Liam replied. "If the situation calls for it."

"Even if it means your own son gets hurt?"

Liam's eyes drifted over to the river as he considered his response. He listened as the Chattahoochee's familiar sound washed by. Like the water between its banks, the noise of a river never stopped. The momentum that was the river—the air, the water, its sounds—quieted, but never stopped. From some place high in the Blue Ridge Province, to the mouth of the Apalachicola Bay, the river eventually flowed through, around, and over all obstructions known to man. The dam to the river was like the cage to the man. It could hold it for a time, but eventually, it would break free, and wash everything away.

"Sometimes people get hurt in this business, Colt. You know that."

Liam pulled another cigarette from his pack. He cupped his hands around the flame, pulling at the soothing smoke. He watched his son's face, waiting.

"Consider what you owe me as the cost of doing business, then."

"I've paid enough for your fuck-up."

"I want what's mine, then. What's fair."

Liam snorted. "Fair."

"Yeah."

"I didn't call the sheriff on you for this little two-wheel joyride this evening. That fair enough for you?"

Colt shook his head. "You're going to send me off—*a second time*—just for taking a drive out to the river?"

"If I have to."

"You're a piece of shit, you know that?"

"Watch your mouth, son."

"Or what?" Colt shot back. He stood tall, arms at his sides. "You want to try to straighten me out?"

Another pull, then a long exhale. "I know you think you're bad now because you've been boxing punks up at Rutledge."

"You don't know anything. Hell, I haven't seen you in—"

"You don't think I had eyes up there?"

"Then you know that I handled my time just fine."

Liam flicked the cigarette down. "I know you didn't have to get cliqued up while you were in there. That no one once forced you to bitch-out like some of the others had to."

Colt looked away for a moment. Liam suspected his son knew the truth, though.

"Who do you think bought your protection?" Liam asked.

"I did."

"Nope, Colt. *I did*. The whites. The Blacks. The guards. Every month. Cash money in hand."

"Bullshit."

"I heard you could box, though." Liam said this with a hint of pride. The kind a daddy couldn't help but feel from time to time. His boy could handle himself, and that meant something to him. "The guards up there told me you had a nickname by year two."

Colt nodded back to him but didn't say anything. He then took a step to the side, looking up toward the entrance road to the boat launch. Liam didn't need to look. He knew that two more pickup trucks rolled toward them.

Colt Hudson eyed the two trucks now parked behind his father's old Chevy. As the men exited, Colt considered their faces one by one. *Four in all.* Three Latinos and a Hank Hill-looking white guy. Their scowls gave Colt the impression that these men believed they were hard. A bad sign.

"It concerns me to see you back so soon," Liam said, no longer leaning against the front of his 454. "See, I talked to our attorney over lunch today —you remember Abe, right?"

Colt nodded at the mention of the crooked lawyer.

Liam continued. "Abe mentioned you'd been released early. Something that he found, well, interesting, given the sentence the judge stuck you with."

The four wanna-be hardos stepped into position, flanking their boss on both sides. All except one looked to be out of shape.

"I can certainly tell you're pleased," Colt remarked, "seeing your friends and all are here to welcome me home."

"This isn't the time to be a smartass, son."

Colt grinned as he ran a hand through his hair. His own father had a reputation for being rather capable when it came to extracting information. Although Colt never once had to witness those heart-to-hearts Liam needed to have with rodents in his organization, he'd heard stories. Everyone had. Liam Hudson ran a tight ship. He had to from his seat at the helm of the largest domestic methamphetamine operation east of the Mississippi.

"I'm a first-time offender, *Dad*. I'm out a few years early. If you'd come up once to see me in the last few years, you'd know that—"

"I already told you I know just about everything that happened at that prison up there. If a crew jumped you, I heard about it. If you put some asshole in the infirmary, I heard about it. If you so much as farted wrong—"

"We get it, you heard about it," Colt said, winking at one of the men to his father's side. "Save the speech, okay?"

Liam took a step closer. "So, I know damn well they didn't grant you clemency, son, and this right here is your one chance to tell me why you're home early."

Colt expected this, at least some version of it. His father hadn't survived almost thirty years in his business on dumb luck. The man demanded loyalty from all he worked with, especially his own. He'd always been that way, ever since he started running marijuana and powder up from South Florida in the late eighties. Colt knew that his father's organization and influence had grown slowly over the years. Never engaging in flashy purchases at home. Never rubbing his success in the faces of the locals— especially not those in law enforcement that protected him. He was highly motivated, well financed, and responsible for most of the domestic dope that flooded the cities and jails in the Southeast. Everyone that surrounded his organization knew that when a loose end presented itself, Colt's father dealt with it, swiftly.

"If you know everything, why're you asking me?"

Liam spit on the ground in front of him. "I'm not screwing around here, Colt. Tell me what you did to get home. What did they offer you?"

Colt knew that the local narcotics squad's commander—Tim Dawson— based his offer to Colt on one core belief: No father could bring himself to commit the ultimate sin on his own son. He and Colt discussed this exact situation at length. It was the lawman's belief that a father demanding his son not snitch on the family business was one thing. Intra-family homicide was something completely different—*at least in places outside of Blake County.*

"I'm not doing this right now," Colt said as he started toward the motor-cycle. "I'll take this back to the shop, then I'll stay the hell out of your life. You won't have to worry about me being around."

Liam pointed to his only man that was still in decent shape. A short, stocky Latino started toward Colt from the other side of the bike. The young man wore a Kappa T-shirt and shorts that exposed the tree-trunk legs of a soccer player. Colt had at least five inches on the guy, but he knew a one-on-one between them could quickly turn to something much worse —a five-on-one.

"That's not an option, Colt."

Colt glanced over his shoulder. The river stood at his back, high from the recent storms. The water blocked the path that led south under the bridge. The only exit was a running trail that ran north along the bank— one that wove up into the hills of Kelley Hill Plantation. It'd been a while since he'd been for a nice long run in the woods.

"All right," Colt said with his palms up. "Give me a second here to think. I need to collect my thoughts."

Liam lifted a hand to stop the young man who hailed from somewhere South of the Border. Colt made eye contact with his father, trying to elicit any compassion in the man. He saw none.

"Let me hear it," Liam replied. "That's all we need, then I'll take you home."

The young footballer's feet stopped advancing in Colt's direction. Colt wiggled his toes inside the bargain-rack tennis shoes on his feet, then turned for the trail by the bank. He had twenty yards to cover if he wanted to make it to the first tree at the mouth of the trail—a distance he once had the ability to cover in around 2.2 seconds. The tendons in his legs felt strong and his feet didn't slip on the gravel as he flew toward the trail. He made it to the first tree and heard the loud shots of a semi-auto—*pop, pop, pop*. The sound of wood splintering from the trees behind him punctuated the shouts of the men. Colt had a head-start on them.

That's all he needed.

18

Small branches slapped his face as he flew down the path. He kept his eyes just above his feet, stepping high to avoid the exposed roots that criss-crossed the loamy trail. Colt knew the path ran straight along the edge of the river, until it cut up a steep embankment to one of Kelley Hill Plantation's service roads. A metal gate blocked the road, but Colt remembered it as one that he could hop easily. He pushed hard down the flat stretch of trail, knowing he would soon slow when the trail veered upward.

He heard the engines in the distance as the trucks roared to life in the boat launch's parking lot. Colt figured they'd head toward the main entrance to the hunting preserve and bribe the low-wage rent-a-cop to give them access to the service road. That gave Colt time to get deep into the woods or make his way back down toward the river. Either way, it'd keep his father and the other men guessing.

A voice yelled from somewhere behind him. "Stop running, Colt!"

Colt assumed it was the young footballer who decided to make chase. *Bring it on, amigo.* Colt started up the hill. With the steep grade, he began to feel the burning in his legs. It felt worse than expected. The years working out in the gym at the Rut had afforded him plenty of time to build muscle. Time to work on his agility. Time to work on his hand speed. Prison didn't give him space to run, though, and Colt knew that the time without endurance training would soon rear its ugly head.

Again, the voice called to him. This time shouting something in Spanish.

Colt yelled back one of the few Spanish phrases he'd learned in prison. "*Chíngate, cabrón!*"

The man laughed back in response. *From a close distance.* Colt slipped on the steep trail and caught himself. *Shit.* His legs groaned as he dug his toes into the earth and pushed further up the hill. The gate stood some thirty yards ahead. He'd risk a glance back at the young man that followed him when he hit the entrance to the service road.

"*Ojo, Colt!*" called the man, a playfulness in his voice. "*Cuidado!*"

Colt's lungs felt like they might burst. He reached the metal farm gate and grabbed the top of it with both hands. As he pulled up to hop over the five-foot rail, he glanced back to look for the young man on his heels. As he did, a fist was already on-line. The light brown knuckles caught Colt on the right side of his face, toppling him over the gate. Stunned, Colt fell to the ground. He looked up just as his aggressor came over the top rail with ease.

Eyes up, he told himself. *On your feet.*

Colt pushed up off the ground. He could barely breathe. Another fist caught him in the ear, spinning him back around toward the gate. He felt the man's arms grab his shoulders, but Colt pushed back off the sturdy gate and swung an arm around, wildly. The young man ducked the last-ditch attack and caught Colt in the ribs—*crack!* The blow sent pain through Colt's body and knocked the remaining air out of his lungs. He tried to push up off the dirt, but soon felt the bottom of a heel pressing into his back. The foot held him flat to the ground as he struggled to breathe.

It took them close to twenty minutes, but the trucks soon pulled down the service road. Colt Hudson leaned with his back against the gate, finally breathing with less effort. His left side ached. A cracked rib most likely.

"I see you met Paul," his father said as he stopped a few paces from the gate. He pulled the pack of cigarettes from his chest pocket, then motioned with it to Colt. "Looks to me like your glory days as an athlete are over. You want one?"

Colt shook his head. He pointed at the young man that bested him. "Wouldn't it be Pablo?"

Liam shrugged as he lit his Marlboro, then looked over at his guy. "Is your name actually Pablo?"

The man nodded. "It is, Mr. Hudson. *Pablo Francisco Palencia.*"

"Well, *lo siento,* I guess," Liam replied as he blew a stream of smoke out. "It's hard to keep up with all the different names you people have." With his cigarette, he turned and motioned to the only other white guy in the group. "Robert told me it was Paul."

The man called Robert didn't look too concerned with the mix-up. He stayed by his truck, stoic. A shotgun over his shoulder.

"Let's just get on with it, *Dad.*"

Liam turned back to him. "I was trying to, boy, but you ran off like a scared little—"

"You tried to shoot me."

"I shot at you," Liam replied. "There's a difference."

"Not to me."

"Well, boo-hoo."

Colt pushed up from the ground. His ribs signaled their protest to the movement with a sharp objection. "While I'm on the subject of complaints, you should know Pablo over there cracked a rib or two of mine."

"Well, these guys are mean, Colt. Do you want me to call them off?"

Colt waved a hand. "I can handle it."

"As interested as I may be in testing your theory, I don't have time for that. I came over here to give you your chance."

"My chance at what?"

"Your chance to tell me how you got home so soon," Liam said as he rubbed one of his temples. "Did your head get thicker since I last saw you?"

"I told you already. I don't want to talk about it."

Liam smiled. "And I told you that wasn't an option, son."

"Okay?"

"You must just be hellbent on testing that theory of yours."

"I must be."

Liam motioned to Pablo and another one of his countrymen to grab
Colt. They did so, quickly. Colt threw an elbow but caught a short jab to his
injured ribcage in return. He headbutted one of the men as he fell forward.
The shot stunned the man, but then his partner shoved Colt to the ground.
The duo proceeded to kick at Colt like a ratty *fútbol* back home. Colt
covered his face with his hands and tried to roll into a ball. The shots kept
coming, though. The men muttered *güero, puta, mamón,* and other carefully
chosen descriptions as they worked.

"All right, *hombres!*" Liam finally exclaimed. "Knock it off."

The men kept kicking—*whap, whap, whap!*

"He said knock it off!" shouted another voice. A shotgun blast from
somewhere near the truck followed it. "No *más* kicking."

Colt heard the shoes of the men scuffing along the ground as they
stepped away. *Thank you, God*, Colt thought. He felt tears start to well in his
eyes. He knew Tim Dawson couldn't help him now. It'd been a stupid plan.
They'd underestimated the ruthlessness that was Liam Hudson. Colt
suspected his father would as soon kill his own son right there and bury the
body in the woods. *God knows there are others buried out here.*

"Okay," Colt gasped, spitting blood out onto the dirt in front of his face.
"I'll tell you."

"What's that?" Liam shouted.

"I said I'll tell you," Colt stammered. "I'll—"

Liam leaned down close to his face. The man didn't have a trace of
sweat on his forehead. Not a wrinkle of regret, either. "Start talking."

Colt rolled over on his back. All around him, tall pine trees reached up
toward the October sky above. Colt held a hand up for his father to help
him off the ground. After a long moment, Liam took it, slowly helping his
son to his feet. Colt ambled over to the gate. He wheezed as he leaned
against it, feeling like a boxer trying to survive a ten-count. *Screw the plan.*

Colt kept his voice low. "I need you to promise me something."

"I'm not in the mood to negotiate, son."

"I need you to promise you won't kill me," Colt said, this time louder.
"Please."

Colt still leaned against the gate, looking down at the steep trail that led down to the river. He heard his father behind him. The man took in a deep breath as he seemed to think about it.

"What'd you do?"

"I can fix it," Colt said as he turned around. The truth could kill him, but so could a lie. "We can—*you* can use it."

"What'd you do?" Liam asked, again.

"Promise me."

Liam stared at him for a long while. Colt wondered what his father saw when he looked at his son. Beaten. Bloody. Back against the wall.

"You have some balls," he finally said. "That's how I've always known you were mine."

Colt nodded, then looked away for a moment. He didn't have any other option than to tell the man the truth. Dawson would just have to send him back to prison.

"Hand me that pack of Marlboros."

"Yeah?" Liam replied with a grin. His first of the day. "Okay, big man."

Colt took the pack from his father. He held it in his hands for a moment. As a kid, he'd stolen smokes from the packs his dad and the other guys left around the shop. He and Deacon smoked them together for a time, but they soon decided to make a pact to play in the NFL one day. They vowed to keep each other straight. To keep each other on the path.

Not anymore.

Colt placed a cigarette between his lips. As he did, he felt the cuts along the edge of his mouth—the blood barely dried. Liam tossed over a lighter.

"Thanks."

Liam nodded back. "What do you know, Colt?"

Colt sparked the flame. He knew there was no turning back once he started with the story. Still, he planned to tell it.

All of it.

19

Maggie Reynolds sat in her office with the door closed. She rubbed her temples as a clip from one of the local news stations played at a low volume on her desktop computer. Ben Moss, the young reporter she spoke to the Friday before, walked his viewers through the latest updates on an investigation taking place at the county jail. He appeared surprisingly camera-ready in his slim-fit sport coat. No tie.

"I met this morning with a representative from the Blake County Sheriff's Office," Moss began, speaking straight into the camera in a clear, radio-quality voice. "I've been able to confirm that investigators from the Georgia Bureau of Investigation were summoned to the county jail over the weekend to investigate the death of a man who was being held there in pre-trial custody. The accused—a Mr. John Deese—faced a four-count indictment that stemmed from his potential involvement in last year's brutal killing of Blakeston native, Lucy Kelley Collins."

The reporter stood on the perimeter of the county jail. His positioning allowed viewers to take in the entire scene behind him. The aging facility, complete with chain-link fencing, concertina wire, and thick walls to house its inmates, provided the local correspondent with an intimidating backdrop.

Moss continued, holding up a document as he spoke. "This indictment, naming John Deese as the lone defendant, was returned earlier this year by a Blake County grand jury. The counts range from felony obstruction of justice—to malice murder. I'm told by the prosecutors involved that additional charges were being weighed prior to this weekend's developments."

The young man turned and pointed to the facility behind him. The camera zeroed in on a secure side entrance to the jail—the sally port.

"John Deese arrived at the county jail this past Thursday night. Federal authorities delivered the wanted man to Sheriff Charlie Clay and his deputies through this side entrance here. Although it has not yet been confirmed by the BCSO, it was previously reported that John Deese had been the target of an international manhunt. One that ended in South America several weeks ago, leading to negotiations that surrounded the accused's extradition back to the US. Prosecutors planned for him to stand trial for the murder right here in Blake County."

The camera pulled back, allowing Moss's face to return to the screen. He looked into the camera, ready to deliver the meat of the story. Maggie kept her eyes on the screen. The young reporter exhibited many of the key qualities that made for a talented on-camera newsman. Command of the subject matter. Concise delivery. Excellent hair.

"Those close to the investigation into John Deese's death indicated to me that the apparent suicide—that is the coroner's preliminary opinion as to the cause of death—occurred late Friday night. The night-shift personnel working the county jail didn't discover the body until sometime early Saturday morning. Officials have assured me that the BCSO began their investigation as soon as the body was discovered and are continuing to evaluate their own protocols surrounding self-harm prevention."

Maggie shook her head as she listened to the reporter. She'd been closer than anyone to the initial news about the investigation. When Tim left their house early Saturday morning to hustle over to the county jail, he didn't even give her a hint about what was going down. This ticked her off. She'd spent the rest of that day prepping the lawsuit against Deese. *Wasted energy*. Now, some forty-eight hours later, she finally had the chance to hear the story from Ben Moss.

"The original theory surrounding the murder of Lucy Kelley Collins centered on another Blakeston native—Charlotte Acker. The testimony presented at Acker's trial, though, along with other information obtained in the wake of the dismissal of all charges against her, led prosecutors to develop a theory that targeted John Deese and several other potential co-conspirators."

Maggie listened closely as the reporter touched on the last case she tried before a jury. One that ended with the right result for her client but left plenty of unfinished business for the district attorney's office.

"I've reached out to the Blake County District Attorney's Office for comment. They refused to provide any information as to whether their investigators made attempts to interview Deese prior to his death. They did confirm, however, that they still planned to pursue those that may have acted in concert with Mr. Deese to carry out the killing."

Maggie almost snorted as she heard this. She assumed that John Deese took any information about his accomplices with him to the grave. Without that testimony, the prosecutors would have no real shot at presenting a strong case. At least, not against the one person who needed to be held accountable.

"We've reached out to Senator Bill Collins—the victim's widower—for comment on this matter. Senator Collins employed John Deese in his office for close to fifteen years. Those supporting the senator's office in Washington haven't returned our calls or provided a comment to share with our viewers."

The segment ended, and Maggie closed out the browser window on her computer. She leaned back in her desk chair, mulling over the news she'd just received. She and Tim had spent the last seven years working together on cases. He served as her law firm's primary investigator. He interviewed witnesses, took photographs, ran down leads, and reported back to her on almost everything he discovered. Tim served as more than just her husband during those years. He understood what motivated her. Respected her and her business. And always followed her directions as far as ethical obligations to the clients. She'd always respected his adherence to that duty of confidentiality. Now, though, he had a different responsibility as a member of law enforcement. *So, why was it so maddening that he hadn't shared the news with her about Deese's death?*

A knock sounded on Maggie's office door. She turned to it and called out: "Come in."

Maggie's assistant half-opened the door and popped her head inside. "Sorry to bother you, but there are two men here that asked to speak with you."

Maggie sighed, then offered a smile to her only employee. "I didn't think I had any appointments this morning."

"You don't," she replied. "They know they don't have an appointment. They just asked if you had time to speak with them."

Maggie nodded. As a solo practitioner in a small town, it wasn't unusual for her to receive the occasional drop-in appointment. The sign out front read: *Reynolds Law, Trial Lawyer.* Nothing more. Nothing less.

"Okay, well—"

"I know you had the morning blocked off, so I can run them off if I need to."

She had in fact blocked her calendar off for the morning. Maggie planned to put the finishing touches on *Acker v. Deese, et al.* A lawsuit that her client hoped would lead them to some answers to their questions. *No reason for that now.*

"No," Maggie replied, glancing down at her watch. She needed to work, and the firm needed the money. "I can probably meet with them. Did they tell you what they wanted to talk about?"

"They didn't really say too much. They just asked for you."

Maggie rolled her eyes. Walk-in consultations usually amounted to little. Mainly because the clients often had little themselves. As a trial lawyer, she wanted to work exclusively on the big cases. Small-town problems always seemed to find their way into her law office's lobby, though. No-hassle divorces on the cheap. Small business owners on the brink of bankruptcy. Repeat offenders facing yet another batch of criminal charges. All serious legal issues that still required time, money, and a lawyer willing to take the case.

"They didn't tell you anything?" Maggie prodded.

"It sounded like they wanted to talk to you about a business issue."

"Did you get their names?"

"I did," she said as she looked down at a piece of paper in her hand. "Liam Hudson and Harry Bates."

Maggie decided to take the meeting in the building's main conference room. When she entered, she found two men seated on the same side of the large room's conference table. Both stood to greet her.

"Good morning," one of them offered with a wide smile. The man wore a summer suit. Orange tie. He tested the seams on the seersucker jacket as he reached across the table to shake Maggie's hand. "I'm Harry Bates."

The other man, slightly shorter, younger, and in much better shape, also extended his hand across the oak table. He wore jeans and a short-sleeved button down. "And I'm Liam Hudson, ma'am. I appreciate you agreeing to see us."

"Gentlemen," she said with a cautious smile. She recognized them now. "It's not a problem, and nice to meet you both. I'm Maggie Reynolds."

The men nodded and they all took their seats. Neither appeared to have brought anything for the meeting. Unusual for clients that wanted to talk about a business matter. Most small-town business owners—*something these men weren't, really*—didn't have the resources to hire an in-house lawyer, so they only walked into a law office when a problem arose. Problems always came with paperwork.

"Did my receptionist offer you coffee?" Maggie asked.

The man called Harry continued to smile at her. "She did, Maggie. I believe the young lady is bringing it now."

"Good, well, I want to be up front with you both by saying that—"

"This is a beautiful building," Harry said, making a show of gazing around the conference room. "I'd heard you bought the place earlier this year, but I wasn't sure what the condition looked like on the inside. The original listing online never showed any pictures of the interior."

"Usually a bad sign, right?"

"Right," Harry winked. "Have you had to put some work into her?"

Maggie nodded. That she had, along with plenty of cash. "The place is a money pit."

The men laughed. *It was just money. One could always make more.*

"Harry here fancies himself as an architectural connoisseur of sorts," Liam said as he patted a hand on his friend's back. "Don't let him try to buy the place out from under you."

"Did you get a good deal on it?" Harry quickly added, obviously prying.

The two-story office building that surrounded them—a 5,500-square-foot structure wedged between two downtown staples, Stack's Sandwich Shop and Gallinari's Pizza—sat just two blocks from the Blake County Courthouse. Part of the town's historic district, the old building fronted one of downtown Blakeston's oldest streets. During Maggie's first years in Blakeston, back when she served as a meagerly paid public defender, she often walked the downtown's brick streets, admiring the old buildings that needed work. She dreamed of one day buying one and making it her own.

"We negotiated hard," Maggie finally said. "These old buildings seem to hold their value."

"Now you know why," Harry said with a sigh. "The owners have to put so much damn money into the upkeep, they can't afford to sell them for a fair price."

Maggie couldn't help but laugh along with the man. He was right. Although she was well on her way in the dream renovation process, the project had exceeded her original budget months ago. She purchased the unique looking building—a blue Moderne style structure that always looked out of place in the city's historic downtown—with the settlement proceeds from an awful wrongful-death action she'd filed on behalf of a local family. Her clients—Eli and Maya Jones—decided to forgo a nasty jury trial and accept a handsome offer for the loss of their mother and brother in a car wreck.

"I think I paid a fair price."

"Good," Harry replied. "Fair is fair."

The door to the conference room opened and Maggie's assistant slash receptionist entered with coffee. Both men thanked her, sneaking glances at the young twenty-something's behind as she left.

"Well," Harry said after sipping from his coffee cup, "we know we came without an appointment, and can only assume that you're very busy, so we'll get down to it."

Maggie nodded. She knew that one of the men seated before her had a reputation for running a rather nefarious operation. Sure, he ran legitimate businesses, but most suspected that those ventures only served as fronts for the activity that fell well outside the bounds of the law. She could listen, though. She didn't plan to take any drug cases because of her husband's new role with the BCSO, but that didn't mean she couldn't potentially counsel the man on other matters. Tim certainly planned to keep things from her in his work—*she planned to do the same.*

Harry continued. "I handle most of Mr. Hudson's bookkeeping and tax related matters for his businesses. For the last twenty plus years or so, Abe Coleman has worked on most legal matters."

"I know Abe well. He's a solid lawyer."

"Right, well, businesses are always evolving, as you know, and I believe it'd be prudent for my client here to consider bringing a new voice into the discussions that come up from time to time, especially around certain legal matters."

Maggie absorbed this. No lawyer in South Georgia could argue that Abe Coleman didn't know his way around a courthouse. The lawyer embodied the old guard's view as far as what it meant to be a hard-nosed criminal defense man. Countless jury trials. Good-old-boy relationships with most of the sheriffs in the area. Questionable tactics when it came to witness preparation. Excluding the opinions of prosecutors in the area, most lawyers considered the man to be a living legend.

"Is Abe retiring?" Maggie asked, knowing damn well the man would never do so. Most in the local bar suspected he would simply die on his way to court one day.

"We think that might be coming."

Maggie acted as if she was considering the prospect of this happening. "Well, gentlemen, you should know I've been focusing my practice on civil work, mostly. I believe Abe still maintains a rather robust criminal defense practice."

Harry started to speak again. "Sure, and—"

"I'm only looking for a different perspective on certain legal matters," Liam said, quietly taking control over the direction of the conversation. "A consultant of sorts."

Maggie shifted her eyes to Liam's. "Okay, well—"

"I'm not asking for you to step in on anything right now, Maggie. I'd just like to pay you a retainer of sorts so that you'll be available to answer my questions in the future—confidentially, of course."

"About your business?"

Liam nodded. "That's correct. My auto repair shop is based right here in Blakeston, but I have customers in Alabama, the Carolinas, Kentucky— most of the Southeast, really."

"You ship auto parts to these customers?"

"That's right," he said. "We deliver mostly through individuals that we've contracted with over the years."

"And these—auto parts—are sourced locally?"

"Yes, ma'am. Everything's American made."

Maggie took in a deep breath, considering the proposal. She didn't plan to represent any clients in Blake County for criminal defense matters. Maybe a few DUIs here and there, but no one on drug-related issues. No one on the narcotics squad's radar."

"I'm not sure I'm the right person for this role as a—"

"Consultant," Harry quickly added from his seat.

"Right," Maggie said. "Consultant."

"We want it to be clear that Abe is still our guy," Harry said. "Still Mr. Hudson's primary lawyer. You might just serve as a sounding board on certain legal matters. A second opinion, if you will."

"I don't want to assume anything, gentlemen, nor do I wish to cast aspersions on my colleague, Mr. Coleman. I can't assist in anything that might break the law, though. My bar license doesn't permit me to do so, and I don't believe that's the role of a legal advocate."

"Sure," Liam said, nodding his head. "And I'm not asking for that kind of advice."

Maggie doubted this. "Obviously, a concern has come up that you want one of these second opinions on."

"That's correct."

"Tell me about it," Maggie said, clasping both hands in front of her. "That'll give me a preview into what kind of advice you're looking for someone to consult with you on."

Liam turned to his sidekick. "Harry, how about you step out for a minute?"

"Sure," he said as he started from his seat. His big frame took a moment to get vertical, then he made his way for the conference room's door. "I'll go admire the renovation work in this beautiful building."

The door closed and a short silence fell over the room. The two considered each other as they waited for the other to move the discussion along.

"What I tell you in this consultation remains confidential, right?" Liam asked.

Maggie nodded. The consultation—the initial phase of the attorney-client relationship—received nearly impenetrable protection from the courts. All communication from the potential client to their potential attorney, remained confidential. The privilege afforded to these early discussions was one that could not be waived, unless the potential client allowed for the attorney to do so.

"That's right."

Very limited exceptions applied to the broad shield that protected communications between lawyers and clients. An imminent threat to someone that the client wished harm on. The concealment of a person whose life was in danger. Instances where the lawyer assisted in criminal or fraudulent activity. In those situations, a lawyer might divulge what was said in confidence. Might even be compelled to, depending on the circumstances. Almost anything else, though, the lawyer couldn't share without permission to do so.

"Okay."

Liam looked around the room before he spoke again.

"Do you have any recording devices in here?" he asked.

"No."

"You're sure?"

Maggie smiled politely. "If my office has been tapped by some agency, I have bigger problems to worry about."

"Right."

Maggie wondered if the man suspected his own lawyer—Abe—could no longer be trusted. A fact that would surprise her.

"What's on your mind, Mr. Hudson?"

"It's my son," he finally said. "He's back from prison."

"Okay."

"Paroled at the end of last week."

Liam stared across the table at her. His eyes seemed to be watching her, closely. She didn't break his gaze.

"That's a good thing, right?"

"Maybe," he said as he finally looked away from her gaze. "I'm not sure yet. Time will tell."

As she heard this, Maggie thought of a Chinese proverb she learned about in college. The one about the farmer who lost his horse. She didn't necessarily peg Liam Hudson as a Taoist, though.

"Why's that?" she asked.

"Because he wasn't supposed to be out for another couple of years. His sentence wasn't up yet."

"Well," she said, "the parole process can be complicated at times. I've had cases that—"

"Not in this case," he said, leaning forward with his forearms resting on the table. "Some people pulled some serious strings to get him out early."

Maggie recognized the fact that not one word had been mentioned yet about Liam's *business problems*.

"People in your industry?" she asked.

He shook his head. "I know the parole board isn't above taking a little cash under the table, but that's not how this came to be."

"Who brought him home, then?"

"Someone here in law enforcement. Someone local."

Maggie smiled. "And who told you that?"

"My son did."

20

Colt Hudson sat in the passenger seat of the van. He watched the horizon as the early morning sun rose, casting beams of light across the open farm- land that whirred by. It was the first sunrise he'd seen in years. A moment he took in as the soft rays tinted the rural landscape a golden hue. The cows grazing in the pastures. The haze blanketing the row crops. The stands of tall pine trees. The rays seemed to warm everything they touched. *Beautiful.*

"I can't believe this shit," said the man behind the wheel of the van. Sean Caverns—one of Liam's delivery guys—steered with one hand and used his other to shove a Kool between his teeth. He turned up the dial on the radio, drowning out the noise from the rough backroads that ran below the tires. Hosts from a morning show with one of the local radio stations started in on another prank call to an unsuspecting victim. "These people answering their phones are freaking morons, right?"

Colt kept staring out the window of the van. It was his first day working with Sean. His first day working for Liam. A trip from Blake County up to Fulton County—*The A*—to drop a wholesale order with a group of buyers. Colt offered to make the five-hour drive alone, but his old man insisted Sean do the driving.

"I mean, if some asshole calls my cell phone at seven in the morning to prank me," Sean said in his already annoying accent, some blend between New York and South Florida, "I'm tracking that—"

Colt interrupted him just to keep him from continuing to talk. "Just don't pick up on a number you don't recognize, Sean. Problem solved."

The wheelman took another drag on his cigarette, then looked over at his passenger. Sean Caverns went by *Caveman* among those that were friends. Dumb as a box of rocks with a temper like a neanderthal. Colt didn't yet know the guy like that, but he'd been warned by his father not to piss Caveman off.

"I don't save any contacts in my phone," Sean said, an added gruffness to his voice now. "I have to pick up on the numbers I don't know."

"Just save the numbers for the people you do know. Then there is no need to pick up on the others."

Sean tapped his head with an index finger. "I keep all the numbers I need right up here."

"I thought you just said you have to pick up on—"

"I'm not repeating myself. That's my process and I'm not changing it."

"Suit yourself."

Sean rolled the window down and tossed his cigarette out onto State Route 22. He seemed to stew a moment before starting again. "Look, I saw this documentary on TV once—a real-life story about this guy living up in some shithole town in Montana."

"That's what documentaries are."

"Documentaries aren't all about Montana."

"No," Colt replied, shaking his head. "All documentaries are about real life, though. They're like the movie version of non-fiction books."

Sean drummed the steering wheel with his fingers, thinking. "I don't know if that's true, Colt. Look at Apollo 13. Titanic. Remember the Titans. That movie about Facebook."

"Those aren't documentaries. Those are movies based on true events."

"Right, so they're real-life stories."

Colt rubbed his forehead. Caveman logic. *Make it stop.*

"Am I not right?" Sean prodded.

"Just tell me what you were going to tell me."

"All right, well, the documentary followed these investigators as they interviewed and questioned people about some murder that happened in southern Montana. When they interviewed the main guy, he let them look through his cell phone during their little sit-down. The man didn't have any contacts in his phone, so the detectives couldn't question him about who it was he was calling the night of the crime. They ended up having to let him go. Genius, right?"

"The cops can still figure out what numbers you call. They don't necessarily need to have the name of the contact in your cell phone."

"I'm not sure they can, Colt. The cops can't prove you know the person you've been calling if you don't have a name with the number. Especially with a burner. You should start doing the same."

"I don't have a phone."

"Your pops will give you one. It comes with the job."

"What about health insurance?"

"What about what?"

"401K?"

"A four-oh—"

"Forget it," Colt said. "I'm not worried about getting anything else from him. Just the pay for the work. That's all."

"This whole thing will be yours one day."

"I'm not sure I want it."

"Why the hell not?"

"Just drive."

"You can tell me, Colt."

"I said to just drive, *Caveman*. I'm not talking about it with you."

Sean turned his full attention back to the road. "Fuck you too, Colt."

They didn't talk any more as the van made its way over the roads of West Georgia. The radio played and the windows on both sides of the vehicle went up and down as they smoked to pass the time. With a full tank of gas, the van didn't stop as they cruised through Columbus and LaGrange, then merged onto Interstate 85 to head north toward Atlanta. Colt started to feel the butterflies in his gut as the van entered the city traffic. He hadn't done anything like this before.

Colt decided to break the silence. The talking might help ease the nerves. "What ever happened to the guy that you watched that documentary about?"

"What's that?"

"The guy you told me about earlier. The one out in Montana. You know, the one that didn't have any contacts in his cell phone when the cops interrogated him."

A marked Dodge Durango sped by them on the interstate's shoulder. Its lights engaged. They both watched the deputy's vehicle until it disappeared behind the mass of cars ahead.

"Oh, that guy," Sean finally said, looking over at Colt. "The cops ended up going back and charging him like a week later."

"With hindering the investigation?"

He shook his head. "Nah, they got him on the murder. His DNA was all over this knife they found at the crime scene."

"That'll do it."

"Plus, there were a bunch of witnesses and shit. Can't do anything about witnesses."

Colt nodded his head. "Yeah, witnesses aren't ideal when you're planning to murder somebody."

"Nope."

Even when you do witness a murder, Colt thought, *it's best to just keep your mouth shut.*

"Am I clear over there on the right?" Sean asked as he started to inch the van into the next lane of traffic.

"You're good."

"That's our exit ahead," he said, pointing to an off-ramp. "73A"

A commercial airliner—some Delta flight, of course—crossed above them. With the windows down on the van, Colt could hear the sound of the jet engines over the wind whipping by at sixty miles an hour. *What I'd give to hop on one of those flights headed out of here.*

"Go on and get strapped up," Sean said, breaking his train of thought. "These guys are pretty cool, but you never know."

Colt reached behind him and felt along the back of the seat. He found the handgun tucked inside the seat's cloth pouch. A Sig Sauer P322. As a convicted felon, currently on parole, the firearm and cargo in the van could put Colt away for most of what remained of his life.

"You know these buyers pretty well?" Colt asked, more nervous than before with the extra ten years inside his waistband. He needed some action to even him out.

"Yeah, but it doesn't really matter. In this business, you can't trust anyone."

The van pulled off the exit ramp and they made their way through an intersection, then onto Virginia Avenue. The midday traffic around the airport made Colt feel more comfortable. They edged along with the other drivers until Sean spotted the entrance to a parking garage. A spot that catered to long-term parking for air travelers. He pulled up to the gate and grabbed a ticket from the machine. Colt didn't like it. There were cameras on every corner.

"Looks like there are eyes everywhere," Colt said. "I've counted at least three cameras."

"Relax. If anything goes down, we're not leaving witnesses. Not like that boy up in Montana."

Colt reached into his pocket and readjusted the small recording device. He hoped everything went according to plan.

Sean Caverns backed the van into a space between two newer-model G70s. A younger looking guy, Asian, stepped out of the vehicle parked on Colt's side of the van. He wore a black bucket hat and a graphic T-shirt with symbols on it. He motioned for Colt to roll the window down.

"What's up?" Colt asked as the window lowered.

"Who're you?"

Sean put the van into park, then leaned over to speak. "He's with me."

The man leaned hard on the van's windowsill to talk to its driver. "I didn't ask who he was with, *Sean*. I asked who he was."

"Chill, *Kim*. He's the boss's kid. He's all right."

Colt needed some action, so he reached for the handle on his door and pushed it open. The door shoved the man back and he almost fell into his parked Genesis. Colt stepped out onto the parking garage's deck, pulling the Sig from the back of his jeans. He held it pointed at the ground.

"Yo, Sean!" bucket hat said, his voice an octave higher. "Your guy here needs to cool it."

"He can't help you," Colt growled, taking another step closer. He had at least six inches on the man. "You have a complaint with how we handle things today, you take it up with me."

"I don't know who the fuck you are."

"Sean just told you."

Colt heard the steps of another man coming around from Sean's side of the van.

"Whoa!" Sean called out as he stepped out of the van. He pulled his own pistol out and pointed it at the second man. "You boys better come correct if you're wanting to do business. That's a Hudson boy over there. Wiregrass royalty."

A quiet settled over the parking garage. For a long moment, they all stood there in a standoff, listening to the sounds of the traffic at the street level some thirty feet below. Colt could feel his racing heartbeat in his ears.

Kim tried again. "It appears we got off on the wrong foot."

"I'd say so."

"I'm sorry. I didn't know who you were."

"You ever met my father?"

"I've never had a reason to."

"You want one?"

The man named Kim shook his head.

"I'd keep it that way," Colt said as he shoved the Sig back into his waist-band. "You'll live longer."

"I'm Kim Min-ho," he replied, bowing slightly. "I meant no disrespect. Not to you or your father."

Colt looked over at Sean, then motioned for him to lower the gun. They needed to get to work unloading the van.

"You have the money?" Colt asked when he turned back to Kim.

Kim nodded, then turned to start walking around to the rear of his vehicle. He popped the trunk on the Korean sedan. Leaned inside. Produced a black duffle. "It's all there."

Colt took the bag from the man. He held it for a moment, feeling its weight in his arms. The cut—two hundred twenty-five large—felt lighter than he'd expected. He didn't know what that kind of money felt like, though.

"Tell your guy to start loading."

Colt could feel the small device in his pocket. The Velcro wrapped around his chest, holding the wire in place. He assumed most would feel nervous. Not Colt, though. He rarely panicked once the lights came on.

"Everything in the back of the van?"

Colt nodded. He knew from an early age that his unique ability to maintain calm could be harnessed. Just as he once did as a quarterback on the football field—walking through his progressions in the pocket—Colt went through the wish list of items that Commander Tim Dawson wanted on the recordings. Names of any persons involved. Confirmation that funds were being provided by the buyer. Express understanding that the sale of drugs was taking place. *Nothing to it.*

"There's a lot of weight in our van," Colt said. "You sure these little rice burners can handle it?"

"That's offensive," Kim said. "People don't use that term anymore."

"Yeah?"

He nodded. "You been living under a rock with Caveman over there?"

Colt smiled. "No, I had to go away for a little while."

"Up the road?"

Colt nodded.

"Welcome back, then."

"I appreciate it."

The rear doors to the van slammed and Sean confirmed that everything was out.

"Will I be seeing you around?" Kim asked.

"No doubt, Min-ho. Everyone'll be seeing a lot more of me."

Colt opened the door to his side of the van and hopped back into the passenger seat. Sean cranked the vehicle, and they pulled out of the parking space. As they made their way down to the ground level, Sean turned to his passenger, smiling.

"That shit was nuts, Colt."

"That was fun."

"From now on, I'm making all my runs with you."

"Just drive."

Sean turned his eyes back to the windshield, still smiling. "Yes, sir. You're the boss."

Something like that.

21

Maggie Reynolds opened the front door to Juno, her favorite restaurant in downtown Blakeston. A friend, and one of the restaurant's owners, Kevin June, stood behind the main bar mixing drinks. He noticed Maggie and motioned for her to come sit. As she made her way over to him, she glanced around the front area of the restaurant, searching for Tim.

He's a little late, she thought. *No big deal.*

"Have a seat in my office," Kevin said, pointing to one of the high-back chairs positioned along the front of the bar. "You look—"

"Tired?"

Kevin smiled, folding his arms across his chest. Tattoos peeked out from under the edges of his rolled-up sleeves. "I was going to go with lovely. Maybe even radiant."

"I can't ever trust you," Maggie said as she took a seat at the bar. She looked the small-town restauranteur over with an eyebrow raised. "Look at you in your denim shirt. Wooing your customers with half the buttons undone. You practically give out compliments for tips. It's how you make your living."

"We all work for tips, Maggie. You've never built a client up before handing them the bill?"

Maggie laughed. "It's the other way around in my profession. I usually tell them what a pain in the ass they've been to work with, then spend the rest of the time telling them how great a job I did on their case."

"Then you tell them how your fat bill is only half of what you should've charged them, right?"

"Exactly. You're a quick study."

"No, I've just met my fair share of lawyers."

Maggie nodded but didn't say anything more. She looked down to check her cell phone that sat face-up on the bar. Still no text messages or calls from Tim. She picked the phone up and typed a text: *At Juno. Are you on your way?*

"I take it you've had a long day?" Kevin asked.

Maggie looked back up at her friend. She sighed, a little louder than intended, as she placed the phone back on the bar. "A long week is more like it."

"How about an espresso martini, then?"

"Not tonight, Kev. Let me just start with a glass of your favorite red. Nothing too oaky."

Kevin put his fist to his chiseled chin, obviously thinking hard. "I have a Garnacha you might like. It's my go-to right now. A little fruity on the nose, with fresh black—"

She put a hand up. "Yes."

"Okay, okay," Kevin said, turning to reach for one of the wine bottles at the back of the bar. He found the one he wanted, along with a fat-bowled wine glass, then returned to Maggie. He started pouring. "Where's my second favorite half of the Reynolds-Dawson household tonight?"

"You'll have to ask him. I haven't seen or heard from him since lunch."

"This a date?"

She nodded. "His idea, too."

Like any good buddy would, Kevin tried to cover for his friend. "I'm sure Tim's just running late."

"Right," she laughed, taking her first sip of the wine. She could taste the pleasant notes of some kind of fruit. *Maybe blackberry or cherry?* She knew Kevin would ask her what she thought. "Have you known my husband to be late anywhere?"

"First time for everything."

She smiled. *Yes, there was.*

Another patron seated at the opposite end of the bar called over politely to Kevin. Maggie waved her friend off, encouraging him to continue his work.

"I'll check back with you soon," he said, moving away from her. "I want your thoughts on that vino."

She nodded, then turned in her seat to scan the restaurant once more. Nearly half the tables sat occupied with guests enjoying bits of Juno's ever-changing menu. The restaurant boasted award-winning small plates and handcrafted cheeses, but also offered an assortment of charcuterie boards, hearty salads, and pecan-based desserts that all looked magazine-cover ready when they arrived at your table. On top of the killer food, it was the ambiance of the small restaurant—low lighting, exposed brick walls, trendy artwork—that put the spot over the top, making it a one-of-a-kind establishment in the quaint little town.

For Maggie, the restaurant served as a special place, too. She and Tim met at Juno for their first date. Right on the back patio some seven years earlier. A dinner that preceded it all. Tim being ousted from the GBI. The trial of Lee Acker. Their marriage and move to Florida to start a new law firm. Tim agreeing to work as her private investigator. Their move back to Blake County. The trial of Charlotte Acker. Her first multi-million-dollar settlement. Then—Tim's decision to return to law enforcement.

Full circle.

Maggie's phone buzzed twice on the bar. A text message from Tim. It read: *Got held up at work. Won't be able to make it, babe. Sorry. I'll make it up to you. Love you.*

———

Maggie started to type a reply when she heard a voice over her shoulder. She turned and saw Ben Moss.

"You mind if I saddle up next to you?" the reporter asked.

She paused a second too long.

"Or not..." he started, smiling sheepishly at the awkward moment.

"No," Maggie finally said. "I mean—yes—you can certainly grab a seat."

"It's fine. I was just stopping by to grab—"

"I'm sitting here drinking alone." Maggie pushed the chair beside her back a few inches for him. "It's a bad look. Please, join me."

The young man nodded as he took the chair next to Maggie.

"What're you having, Benny?" Kevin asked from behind the stick. "I've got a wicked little IPA for you to try if you're game."

"Wicked?" Maggie shot toward the bartender.

"Benny Moss went to college up in Boston," Kevin said in a faux New England accent. "I'm just making my man feel comfortable. A little taste of Beantown."

"You know everyone, Kev."

"I did a fluff piece on the June brothers last year," Ben quickly added. "I made the guys get to know me in the process."

"That's right," Kevin said. "Besides, these journalists are always boozing in here. What better place is there than a bar if you're looking for a story?"

"True on both counts," Ben replied. "I'll take that IPA, too."

Once Kevin stepped away, Maggie glanced over at the reporter, waiting for him to start some kind of conversation. He apparently disliked small talk as much as she did, though, because he just sat there humming along to an Alabama Shakes track that played through the speakers in the bar area. She waited until the song ended to break the ice.

"I don't believe we've officially met," she said as their drinks arrived. A fresh beer for the reporter. Another pour of wine for her. "I'm Maggie Reynolds."

"I know who you are," the reporter said as he turned slightly in his chair to better face Maggie. "I don't mean that in a strange way. I'm just familiar with your work is all."

She nodded. It wasn't unusual for local types to know her name.

"I'm Ben Moss."

"Not Benny?"

"Ben is just fine."

Maggie held out a hand. "Nice to meet you, Ben."

They both sipped their drinks for a moment. Another song started. A brassy one from St. Paul and The Broken Bones.

"So, how is the news business today?" Maggie asked.

"Actually, it was a pretty hopping day."

"Yeah?"

He nodded. "A homicide. Right here in the city."

"What happened?"

"You've not heard?" Ben asked. He sounded surprised.

Maggie shook her head. Lawyers often had their ear to the latest news at the local level. Much of what happened in a small-town ecosystem crossed, at some point, someone who inhabited the legal environment. New arrests. Tasty divorces. Surprising bankruptcies. They all had to cross a lawyer or judge at some point in the process.

"Obviously not," Maggie said with a grin. "Do tell."

"You know Trevor Meredith?" he asked. "An investigator with—"

"Yeah, Trevor's with the BCSO. Works drug cases, mostly."

"That's the one," Ben said. "They found him at home this afternoon. Four shots through the chest."

Holy shit, Maggie thought as she absorbed the information. She had a hundred questions already. "How'd it happen?" she asked.

Ben looked down the bar to see what faces he recognized. Maggie knew he had a story on his hands. He probably didn't want to share the details with any of the competition. He turned back to her.

"They are saying someone kicked the back door of his house in. Early this morning, probably. Ransacked the place. Put him down in the process."

Maggie put a hand over her mouth. A home invasion on a member of law enforcement wasn't something that happened every day. Most petty criminals just didn't have the balls for that sort of thing.

"It was a gnarly scene," he continued. "I was able to get close. Not in the house, but close enough to hear the discussions. It sounded awful."

That explains Tim not making it tonight, she thought. *It doesn't explain him not telling me sooner, though.*

"I bet the BCSO has been on high alert."

"Absolutely," he said. "I actually saw your husband out there earlier. Looked like he was helping keep things in line until the GBI showed. I tried to get a comment from him but—"

"He likes to keep things close to the vest."

"That's what I gathered."

The bartender stopped by to ask about food. The reporter ordered a meatloaf of some sort. Maggie didn't feel like eating anymore. She wanted to know why her husband didn't text her earlier about the murder. She would've understood.

"You can tell that the guys respect him, though," Ben added, still talking about Tim. "It's really impressive because—"

"This is your second death investigation in a week, right?" Maggie asked. She didn't want to talk about Tim right now.

Ben paused, probably noticing the pivot in the conversation. "Yeah," he said after he took another sip from his beer. "It's bizarre. Most days I'm struggling to find a story that doesn't put people to sleep. I've had plenty to work with lately, though."

"I bet. How's the sheriff handling all the media attention you're giving his office?"

Ben looked down the bar again to check who was within earshot. This habit gave Maggie the feeling that he believed eavesdroppers were always lurking. When he turned back to her, he spoke in a low voice. "Sheriff Clay doesn't give me anything when it comes to stories like this."

Maggie felt compelled to defend the man. "Well, Charlie is kind of the strong, silent type. You know?"

"I get that," Ben said, still speaking quietly. "His tight-lipped approach kind of pissed me off when the suicide investigation started around John Deese, but I understood. There's the whole liability thing for him to consider."

Maggie agreed. A potential cause of action—one that could be brought under section 1983 of the United States Code—loomed large over any death that took place in the custody of law enforcement. 1983 claims allowed individuals to sue government officials for violations of their constitutional rights. Most saw section 1983 litigation as a way to highlight police and prosecutorial misconduct—excessive use of force, false arrest, malicious prosecution. But section 1983, and its progeny, could be used to address all sorts of issues with local, state, and federal governments. Sheriff Clay knew this, and Maggie was almost certain that the sheriff didn't want the media to take any interest in the premature death of one of his inmates. Especially not one wanted for the murder of a high-ranking politician's wife.

"Makes sense to me," Maggie added. "You make up the Fourth Estate though, right?"

"Damn right," Ben said with a smile. "Now, one of Sheriff Clay's own men is gunned down at home. Does he have time for the media? Of course not."

Maggie listened, trying to get a handle on the young reporter's angle.

"It's small-town bullshit, Maggie. Our sheriff is elected, and he should make himself available to the people and the media for questions about these deaths."

"It's not like they're connected, though."

"Probably not," Ben said as he held up a hand for Kevin to bring him another beer. "But we still don't know enough."

Maggie rolled her eyes. "Come on, Ben. Send a simple open records request and that'll quiet any concern you have about—"

"We already sent one. They won't give us anything."

Maggie paused to think. In Georgia, the Open Records Act was in place to ensure a path for people—like members of the media—to access public records. The broad intent of the Act didn't always sync with its implementation, though. Documents generated by those in public office, in the course of public service, were simply too broad. So, as with any law, there were exceptions. Exceptions that allowed those in power to tell the citizenry that open government is essential to a free and democratic society, but then permitted those same government officials to hold back certain records requested by individuals, companies, and the press.

"They haven't sent you any records around the John Deese suicide?" Maggie asked.

"Nope."

"I assume you've sent a records request already for reports about Trevor Meredith's murder?"

"Of course."

"Well," Maggie said. "If they won't produce them, that's an easy claim right there. Judges who are First Amendment hawks jump all over those sorts of things."

"That's what I hear."

Another beer arrived for the journalist. Maggie asked for her check.

"If they don't give me the records," Ben asked, "can you help me out?"

Maggie leaned her head back a little bit. She didn't want to spar with the BCSO over something like this. She could win the battle, probably, but she'd damage valuable relationships along the way, effectively losing the war.

"I don't know, Ben. The sheriff is a friend. He probably just doesn't want to—"

"This fucking town," the reporter said, shaking his head. "Everyone is friends. So what? It isn't personal."

"It's always personal in this town."

"Well, Maggie, it shouldn't be. It's just the law."

"It's just the law," Maggie said with a laugh. "Mind if I take that slogan for my firm?"

"You can have it if you help me out."

"*If,*" she said, "and only *if* you need help—then I might be willing to move things along."

Ben pumped his fist, then took the check from the space in front of Maggie. "I'll get this. We'll put it on the station's tab."

"That's not necessary."

"No," Ben said, waving her off, "I enjoyed this. Besides, you're my lawyer now."

"There's going to be a much larger retainer than that."

"Just send me the bill."

Maggie shook her head as she stood to leave the bar. Another paying client was never a bad thing. As long as they paid.

"Have a good night, Ben."

"I'll call you later, counselor."

Maggie winked at Kevin, then left through the front door. Once on the sidewalk, she pulled her cell phone from a pocket to check for any new messages from Tim. Nothing.

It sure feels like he's hiding something, she thought. *Maybe the BCSO is, too.*

Maggie climbed into her car and started home. She hoped Tim wasn't there. She didn't want to argue tonight.

22

Tim Dawson pulled his Dodge Charger to the back side of the old Soap-N-Suds, an abandoned car wash on the low side of town. Although Tim wasn't from Blakeston, he knew as much about the low side—a historically Black community—as the other members of local law enforcement. The two communities—those in blue and those that weren't—had been well-acquainted for quite some time now.

Tim cut the lights on the vehicle and rolled the driver-side window down. With the night air pouring in through the open window, he looked out on the old car wash's decaying property. The once-prosperous business sat at the edge of what was now a tough Blakeston neighborhood. In Tim's work with the GBI and his short time with the BCSO's narcotics squad, he'd met a number of the people in that low side community. A community within a community. One that looked like him, mostly.

He knew bits and pieces about the history of the neighborhood. A history that wasn't so different from other small southern towns. Other American towns, really. A strong middle-class neighborhood that flourished after the Second World War, led by men and women rightfully emboldened by their experiences in the efforts to protect America's interests at home and abroad. A community of people who worked to improve their stead in life, even in the harsh environment imposed on them by segregationists. *One imposed on them by the government. By its police.*

In the forties, fifties, and sixties, counties like Blake County, and others throughout southwest Georgia, became notorious for the violent antics of their local police. Tim knew that the local high school teachers tried to inform their students about the region's worst offenders—counties such as *Terrible* Terrell and *Bad* Baker. They did this, though, as a way to minimize their own town's need for change at that time. A way to gloss over the awful years of struggle that forever scarred Blake County and the rest of the South.

Still, progress marched on with the federal civil rights legislation of 1964 and 1965, and those landmark protections ushered in a new phase in Georgia's struggle for racial equality. More Black voters started to make it to the polls, and they started to cast votes for more representative leadership. That leadership then continued the fight through the end of the Twentieth Century. Those leaders, though, as great as they were, still couldn't pull the forgotten communities—like Blakeston's low side—from the edge of the abyss. The vestiges of racism, economic hardship, and income inequality were simply too much to bear. Throw in widespread accessibility to the one thing poor communities couldn't get enough of—drugs—and the hole became almost impossible to climb out of.

Someone had to do something, Tim thought. *White or Black. Crack or Crystal. Legal or illegal. The drug dealers had to go.*

Tim's cell phone buzzed twice on the car's center-console. He glanced down at the screen. A text from Maggie lit the Charger's dark interior. *Turning in. Are you coming home tonight?* Tim picked up the phone and thought before texting her back. He suspected that she was angry with him. An emotion that was well-placed. He'd screwed up. In the day's haste that surrounded the murder of Trevor Meredith, he'd forgotten about their date set for 7:30 at Juno. More than four hours ago.

He texted her back: *I'm sorry about missing dinner. Hope to be home soon. Love you.* Tim watched the screen of the phone as three dots appeared, briefly, then disappeared. No reply.

Tim considered calling her, but then a pair of headlights swept through the parking area behind the Soap-N-Suds. Tim lifted his eyes and saw what looked like an old pickup creeping toward his Dodge. He checked his sidearm, then opened the driver-side door to step out onto the concrete. It was close to midnight.

"You're late," Tim said as the young man stepped out of the pickup. "We agreed on eleven."

"I know that" Colt said as he ambled over. "Some of the guys roped me into a card game. I couldn't get away."

"You win anything?"

"Six-hundred bucks," Colt replied with a glassy-eyed grin. "Why, you want half or something?"

"I'm not shaking you down, Colt. I'm not that kind of badge."

Colt smirked and Tim could tell the young man still seemed unsure about their arrangement.

"What do you have for me?" Tim asked.

"Three or four different recordings. Two with my dad. One from a deal that happened up in Atlanta this morning. Another with the guys during our poker game tonight."

Tim nodded. The boy made quick work of things. "Have you done anything with the recordings?"

"What, like edit them?"

"Anything at all."

Colt shook his head. "I just hit the button on it like you told me, then prayed. It's a miracle these guys haven't asked me to take my shirt off to check for a wire."

"You're all family," Tim replied, like that meant something special. "They trust you."

"Listen to the recordings. You'll see how much they trust me."

Colt handed the recording device over. Tim took it, then passed him back one that was identical. He explained to Colt that it worked in exactly the same manner and gave him the standard admonishments as to editing the recordings and trying to tamper with the device. Colt appeared to understand.

"What was the take on the deal in Atlanta?" Tim asked.

"A little over two hundred."

"That's good. Is your old man planning to keep you on the road?"

"He doesn't tell me anything more than what's happening tomorrow. I'm not sure he even knows."

"He does," Tim replied. He assumed Colt knew that was the case, too. The older Hudson hadn't made it this far in the game without foresight and planning. "He'll let you into the inner circle. Just be patient."

"Can I go?" Colt asked.

Tim held a hand up. "You hear about Trevor Meredith?"

He watched closely for any change in Colt's body language. Nothing.

"Yeah."

"What'd you hear?"

Colt paused a long moment. "That somebody gave him what he deserved. That's all."

"Did Liam call it in?"

"Nope," Colt said as he shook his head. "Why would he?"

The response surprised Tim. He assumed Colt would at least feign some ignorance on the matter. "Because Trevor put you away for half a decade."

"He didn't care about it then and he doesn't care about it now. Besides, my dad's as surprised as you are. Meredith was apparently one of his."

Mindful of his facial expressions, Tim tried to process the information. A cop on the take was nothing new. It'd been around since the advent of policing. Still, Trevor Meredith never gave Tim the impression that he was dirty.

"I don't believe that for a second."

"Okay," Colt said with a laugh. "Believe what you want."

"How long?"

Colt shrugged.

"How long had he been dirty?" Tim yelled. His voice echoed in the stillness around them.

"I don't know," Colt replied in a calm voice. As always, the kid stayed cool. "Listen to the recordings from tonight. It's on there."

"He put you away, though. That doesn't make sense."

"You're preaching to the choir," Colt said, shaking his head. "Look, that's all I know, so can I go?"

Tim nodded. No reason to press the young man on it. Not yet at least. "Be careful getting home."

"Yes, sir."

"And remember, your ass is still on parole. I can smell the beer from here. A BPD officer won't hesitate to take you in."

Colt smiled but didn't say anything as he turned to walk away. A man who goes undercover doesn't usually associate with people who keep their noses clean. To get in, you have to fit in. Tim suspected Colt was being exposed to his fair share of drugging, boozing, and partying. He didn't have much of a choice. The crew that ran the Wiregrass had a reputation for being a wild bunch of alcoholics. Most with a penchant for violence. For Colt to keep up, he'd have to play the game.

Tim watched the truck leave the parking lot. As he stood there under the midnight sky, he considered the veracity of Colt's information. *If Trevor was working both sides of the fence, it meant others could be doing the same.* The idea disgusted him. Tim wanted Colt to help him take down Liam Hudson and his band of peddlers. They'd been distributing the hard stuff to Georgians and the surrounding states for decades. But Tim also wanted the enablers—the lawmen who looked the other way—to go down with them.

As Tim climbed into his vehicle, he looked out on the dark, shabby edges of Blakeston's low side community. People were being arrested every day in their neighborhood for drug possession, and Tim hated the idea that some of those same cops booking the drug users were also taking payments from the crew putting the drugs on the streets.

Someone has to stop it. Why not me?

———————

Tim Dawson pulled into the driveway. No lights shone from the front porch of the ranch-style house.

A bad sign.

He made his way along the brick walkway that led to the house, then did his best to enter quietly through the front door. No dog. No kids. But Tim wanted both.

Someday.

He closed the front door. Locked it. Set the alarm. As he made his way toward the living room, he noticed the blanket and pillow waiting for him on the leather couch. A confirmation that all was not well under his roof.

Such is life.

Before Tim stretched out on the couch, he pulled a pair of earbuds from a drawer in the kitchen. He slipped one into each ear and lay back on his bed for the night. He pressed play on the device handed over at the Soap-N-Suds. The distinct voice of Liam Hudson filled his ears. He listened as the man spoke with his son. The tone sounded serious on the recording, but Tim suspected that it might soften with time. Enough to build some trust with Tim's confidential informant—his *CI*—Colt.

Liam knew more about the BCSO than he did, Tim thought as he listened to the words. *He had to be willing to share that information with someone.*

23

That didn't take long, Maggie thought as she glanced at the screen on her cell phone. It was the morning after her impromptu meeting at Juno with Ben Moss, and the reporter was already calling. *I guess no one gets far as a journalist without a little persistence.*

Maggie answered the phone. "I thought the etiquette was to wait a few days before calling?"

"Not anymore," came a quick, dry reply from the reporter. "Look, I'm sending Trevor Meredith's mom to see you. She should be at your office within the hour."

Maggie glanced at her watch—10:35 a.m. "I'm booked solid for the rest of the day, Ben. I can't see—"

"She won't take long, Maggie. I promise."

"What does she need from a lawyer? And please know that I don't handle any probate work."

"Right now, all she wants is advice. I interviewed her this morning for the story about her son's murder. We talked off the record about the sheriff, his unwillingness to share details about the attack, and one thing just led to another. She asked about lawyers, so I gave her your name."

"Right, but what exactly does she expect me to do about the murder? That's a conversation she needs to have with the DA's office."

"Just listen to her, please," the reporter pressed. "I'm telling you. Something's up. There's a real story here."

For some reason the young journalist's dogged approach didn't bother her. She kind of liked it, actually. "News stories and lawsuits are different things," she said. "They don't always add up to great claims in the courtroom."

"I know that, but—"

The phone on Maggie's desk beeped twice. "Hold on, Ben."

She mashed the mute button on her cell, then picked the receiver up on the office's landline. The receptionist informed Maggie that a woman waited for her in the lobby—a Mrs. Meredith. "Is my eleven o'clock here yet?"

"No, ma'am," the receptionist replied. "I've not seen Mr. Hudson come in the door."

"Okay, let the woman know I'll be right down to meet with her. And please tell her that I only have ten minutes to talk."

"Nicely?"

"Of course. Aren't we always nice?"

The young woman paused on the other end of the line. "I'll take care of it."

Maggie returned the receiver to its cradle, then switched back to her cell. "I'm back with you. Listen, she's here, so I'll try to talk to her. No promises beyond that."

"Excellent. Make sure you ask her about—"

"Bye, Ben."

———

Maggie opened the door to her office building's secondary conference room. A meeting area that she and her small staff called *the pocket*. Tucked in the back corner of the building, the small room offered a perfect setting for Maggie's one-on-one consultations with potential clients. The more intimate setting, with its calming blue walls, abstract art in simple frames, and round meeting table, gave her the perfect space to meet with clients in the midst of crisis.

"Good morning, Mrs. Meredith," Maggie said as she walked toward the small woman seated at the table. The woman started to stand. "Don't get up, please. I'm coming to you."

"My knees like the sound of that," she responded in a raspy smoker's voice. "The girl at the front desk told me that you're very busy today. Thank you for seeing me."

"It's not a problem," Maggie said as she took a seat opposite the woman. "I'm Maggie Reynolds. I'm the sole attorney here at—"

"Yes, I know you well. I've read so much about you over the years. My son—Trevor—even told me several stories about your work on cases here in Blakeston."

Both of Maggie's hands rested on the table in front of her. The woman reached across the small distance between them. She took Maggie's left hand, holding it as she spoke. The woman's palm felt rough, like those of someone who still toiled in their garden on a daily basis.

"I'm Deborah Meredith," the woman continued. "My son was killed yesterday at his home here in Blakeston. I'm sure you've already heard."

"Yes, ma'am, I found out late last night." Maggie said this with her best tone of concern. "I'm so sorry about your son. He was a good man."

A grieving mother was not something foreign to Maggie. In fact, she wanted more grieving mothers in her law office. Most wrongful-death cases, as well as those clients impacted by catastrophic or traumatic events, came with distraught family members. It was part of the deal, and Maggie felt like she was pretty damn good at dealing with those clients. She just needed more than ten minutes to be able to work her magic.

"Yes, he was a good boy."

Maggie plowed forward. "What can I do to help?"

"Well, I spoke with a reporter this morning about Trevor's death. A Mr. Ben Moss, I believe."

Maggie nodded. No need to reveal the fact that she already knew this.

"I wanted to tell him more about the murder, but I felt it was best that I speak with a lawyer first. That way I don't say the wrong thing."

Interesting, Maggie thought. *Not what I was expecting.*

The woman continued. "I felt like he was asking me some questions that required complicated answers. Ones that might affect peoples' memory of Trevor. Do you know what I mean?"

"Sure," Maggie replied, nodding some more. "You should know that you don't have to talk to reporters. You can tell them *no comment* and close the door in their face. In fact, you don't even have to open the door for them when they come by your home."

"Okay," the woman said, shifting in her chair. "Well, now that I've talked to Mr. Moss, do I need to finish the interview like he asked?"

"No, ma'am."

"It's just—" the woman began. She seemed to still be considering what she felt comfortable sharing. "It's just, I think my boy knew somebody was after him. Like he knew this sort of thing might happen."

Maggie considered the mother's words.

Deborah Meredith looked to be somewhere in the neighborhood of seventy. Although a petite woman, her strong arms looked tanned from working under the South Georgia sunshine, and her blue eyes appeared attentive as she waited for Maggie to speak.

"So, you think your son may have known his killer?"

"I'm almost sure he did."

"Have you told the sheriff?" Maggie asked. "I'm sure he'll want to—"

"I don't know Sheriff Clay like that. Besides, he seems to look out more for his people."

Sheriff Charlie Clay was in the midst of his first full term in Blake County. The first Black sheriff in the county's history, Charlie faced mixed reviews from many of Blakeston's long-time residents—mainly the white ones.

Maggie skirted around the woman's comment. "What do you know about this person threatening your son?"

"I didn't say anything about threatening," Mrs. Meredith replied. "All I know is my son mentioned a younger man might be upset with him. One that he sent away to prison years ago but was now back in Blake County on parole."

Maggie knew the GBI would look at those arrested by the drug agent as potential suspects. Those persons at least had motive. "Do you know the man's name?"

"I don't," she said, shaking her head. "I was hoping you might be able to help find that out for me. Then we could talk about whether I should speak to the reporters or investigators about it."

Maggie thought about the request. It wouldn't take long to get the name. "I might be able to find out for you."

The woman smiled. The first of their short meeting. "Thank you, Maggie."

"Do you know about how long he's been back from prison?"

"Can't be more than a week or two."

Maggie nodded. That would be enough to get her started. Besides, her new reporter friend would owe her a favor or two down the line.

"Leave your number with my receptionist," Maggie said as she stood. "I'll call you when I know something more."

———

Maggie stepped into the main conference room. The space—much larger than the pocket room she'd just left—offered a grander, arguably more intimidating setting for meetings with clients. Law books lined the shelves on one wall. Courtroom artwork hung on the other three, each depicting scenes from a jury trial. Ten leather chairs surrounded a large oak table that anchored the space.

"Good morning," Maggie offered, glancing at the watch on her wrist— 11:15 a.m. "I apologize for making you wait. I got behind in my meetings this morning."

Liam Hudson sat alone on the other side of the table. He wore a clean, short-sleeved shirt with a *Hudson Auto* patch on the chest. His forearms flexed as he pushed himself up from his chair. "As long as you're not charging me for those first fifteen minutes, we're good." He said this with a good-natured smile on his face.

"No," she said, smiling herself. "I'm billing you now, though."

He chuckled as he returned to his seat. "Did Harry get you started with a retainer?"

Maggie nodded. They hadn't discussed a retainer the last time she met with Liam and his CPA—Harry Bates. The men paid one, though. A handsome sweetener of fifty thousand to get her locked down for work as a *consultant*, a role she still felt uneasy with.

"Hopefully that'll cover our attorney-client meetings for the foreseeable future."

Maggie took a seat on her side of the table. She wheeled the leather swivel chair back a few inches to cross her legs. "I'm just a consultant, right?"

"Right," Liam said. "Well, hopefully that'll cover quite a few hours of consulting, then."

Maggie smiled again. She knew plenty of lawyers who provided their legal services to clients on an hourly basis. They took in their retainer fees, then billed against them in small increments of time—usually at six minutes a piece. It was the lawyer's responsibility, then, to keep up with those tiny increments of time throughout the workday. They did this over and over and over until they reached enough hours of legal work to carve out a decent living. Some of the most sophisticated clients—the ones that paid the most money, of course—required such meticulous billing practices that their lawyers were forced to drill down on exactly how every bit of the client's money was being spent. All in tiny vignettes at one-tenth the speed. This hourly method of providing legal work could be both maddening and lucrative at the same time. Maggie didn't like to practice that way, though. Even if her way involved taking a few risks every now and then.

"The initial retainer fee is fine," Maggie finally replied. She certainly needed it. "Just so you know, though, I prefer not to do all my work with one eye on the clock."

"How about we just consider that fee as an advance on ten hour-long meetings? That way we don't have to fool with the timeclock."

Maggie lifted an eyebrow. Even if she'd decided to inflate her hourly rate for work as the man's legal consultant, five thousand an hour would have been too rich for the local market.

"That'll work," she said. "Let's get to it then. What do you have for me today?"

"All right," Liam replied. "Same conditions as we discussed before?"

Maggie nodded. "That's right. No recording devices in the room. My cell phone is in my personal office upstairs."

Liam looked pleased.

Maggie gathered from their first meeting that Liam Hudson bent slightly toward paranoia. Not in an irrational manner, though. He just seemed like he wanted to take all available steps to avoid falling victim to an opportunistic eavesdropper. It didn't matter if it was the state, the feds, or his own lawyer—he insisted on being careful.

We all should.

"I've gone back to sending more and more deliveries to the Midwest," Liam began. "See, years ago, I had some connections with a couple of boys out of Detroit. A pair of Greeks that drove their own trucks down. They paid in cash at the point of sale, then handled all the risk of shipping the—"

Maggie jumped in. "They bore all the risk of shipping the auto parts back to Detroit?"

The *consultant* and *consultee* exchanged a glance. Maggie wanted to play this straight. Her job as a lawyer wasn't to assist people in committing new crimes. It was to give them advice—*sometimes on the crimes they'd already committed*—and allow them to make their own decision.

"Right," Liam said after another long moment. "Once they bought the parts, they drove them back home to Detroit. It was always very low risk."

"What prompted you to stop doing business with them?"

"Nothing on my end. They quit doing business with my shop."

While Maggie processed the unsatisfying answer, she pulled a legal pad from the middle of the table. She jotted down a couple of notes. "Keep going."

"Well, I figured they found another supplier, you know? A Mexican shop or something. All my parts are manufactured here in the US of A, and those prices South of the Border are tough to compete with."

Maggie nodded, still writing on the pad. "So, are your customers back or something?"

"Not them, but their names came up again. An investigator with the BCSO came by and dropped them on me the other day."

"Which investigator?"

"Trevor Meredith."

Maggie looked up from her notes. "The one they found murdered at his home."

"That's the one."

"Okay. How'd their names make it back to you?"

"I wondered the same thing," Liam said as he leaned back in his chair. He crossed his arms and peered at her from across the table. "I'm here to get your thoughts on how that might of happened."

"I'm not a police practices expert."

"I know, but you're an expert on why the BCSO seems to do what they do."

Maggie somewhat agreed. Although there was plenty that went on at the BCSO that she wasn't privy to, she still felt comfortable making educated guesses on why they did what they did.

"What did Meredith ask you about?"

"He told me they came across a couple of bodies—an Andrew Karras and a Nick Moralis."

"When?"

"He didn't say."

"They found them in Blake County, of course."

Liam nodded. "The investigator came to me because he seemed to believe I knew the pair of baklavas. Apparently, one of them had my shop's business card in his pocket."

Maggie wrote this on the pad. "Not that it really matters now, but what'd you tell Meredith when he asked about the connection?"

"I said I didn't know them."

"And when he asked about the shop?"

"I told him they probably needed a tire or something. Maybe a tune-up before moving on."

Plausible.

Maggie stood from her chair and started to walk the room. She liked to move when her mind struggled with wrapping itself around the task at hand.

Liam watched her as she paced. "I'm sure the people looking into the murder—the Meredith murder, that is—know he came by the shop to see me."

"It's possible," Maggie replied.

"No, it's more than possible. Another investigator, one from the GBI this time, reached out already. Last name's Abrams. She left a message with my shop. Said she wants to come see me."

"You need a lawyer then," Maggie said. "Not just a consultant."

Liam spread both of his hands out wide, then shrugged.

Maggie started to shake her head. "Call Abe. He'll sit in with you and walk through the motions with the agent handling the homicide investigation."

Liam seemed to grimace at the mention of his personal lawyer—Abe Coleman. It made Maggie wonder again what was going on in his relationship with the old criminal defense lawyer.

"I'll think about it."

She considered asking about Coleman but thought better of it. It wasn't her business to know. In fact, the less she knew about why Liam Hudson decided to shop around for a second lawyer's opinion, the better.

"Anything else?"

Liam started to stand from his chair. The meeting was apparently over.

"What's that over there?" he asked.

"What's what?"

"That," he said, pointing over her shoulder toward the conference room's door. "What's that little nameplate say on the door?"

Maggie turned around and eyed the small copper sign on the door. Written in Japanese script, it read: 道場

"It literally means place of the way."

Liam smirked. "Is that some sort of Buddhist crap or something?"

"Close."

"The place of the way," Liam said, moving his hand in a dramatic fashion, like a bird flying away. "A little hippy dippy, but I can dig it."

Maggie smiled. The sign represented the name of her large conference room—*the dojo.*

"Well, I think that's it," Liam said as he started to make his way around the table. He took his time walking around to her. "I'll just schedule another appointment when something comes up that needs your expertise."

"Looking forward to it."

He stopped just before the conference room's door. "Oh, I almost forgot, I need you to grab something for our next meeting. Something to follow up on today's discussion."

Maggie could tell by the tone in his voice that the *ask* was intended to sound casual. It wasn't. "What's that?" she said.

"The GBI agent mentioned something in her message about photos. She said she came across them in my son's old casefile. I need you to get me a copy of the file."

"This is Colt's casefile?"

He nodded. "That's my only son."

"Didn't Abe handle that case for him?"

"He did, and Abe gave me the discovery from the case. It's all in my office at the shop. Hasn't left its spot for nearly five years now."

"Why get another one?" she asked. "Case has been closed for quite some time. There won't be anything new to look at."

"I want to see for myself."

"I don't know if—"

"Try first before you say it's not possible," Liam said, opening the door now. "If you can't, you can't."

Maggie nodded. Two weeks ago, she wouldn't have thought twice about asking Tim to bring it home one night for her to take a look at. Now, she worried the boy scout would quote her some policy out of the BCSO handbook.

"I'll see what I can do."

"Good."

Liam tapped the nameplate on the back of the door. "I like the room's name, by the way. It's fitting."

"Glad you like it."

"I may have to steal it from you," he said with a wink. "I need my own *dojo* back at the shop."

The comment surprised Maggie. So much so, that she simply watched as Liam walked down the office's quiet hallway. He didn't look back at her. He simply whistled as he walked toward the reception area.

The old country fox wasn't as dumb as he liked people to believe.

24

He pulled the van into the parking lot of a Hardee's off of US 90. A stone's throw away, Colt Hudson saw the sign for the city limits of Chattahoochee, Florida, a town of less than 4,000 that hugged the banks of Lake Seminole. Colt knew the small town. It was one of the last stops on the Blue Memorial Highway before crossing the state line back into Georgia. Aside from the lake, it looked like most of the other inland towns that dotted the highways across the panhandle. A few gas stations. A small grocery. Plenty of churches.

Colt could see from the parking lot that the breakfast rush was still going strong. He stepped out of the van and started to scan the faces of those seated inside. A wholesome group. The kind of weekend morning crowd that might give Colt and his partner a second look. A couple of white, long-haired country boys wasn't unusual for Podunk, Florida, but their tattoos, size, and hardened energy seemed to cause people to cast a wary eye on them. *Even in Florida.*

"Get something quick," Colt said as he leaned against the side of the van. He didn't plan to go inside. Not with three pounds of dope sitting in the Sprinter. "We need to be back on the road in ten."

Sean Caverns slammed his door on the other side of the van. He grumbled something about needing to take a piss inside, but otherwise didn't object to moving on quickly. He and Colt were on their fifth run together and starting to settle in nicely with the natural dynamic. Colt ran point. Sean provided the muscle.

"You want anything?" Sean asked as he started toward the restaurant. "A biscuit or something?"

"Just coffee, Caveman."

"For a guy that just put his feet on the outside, you sure eat like a damn bird."

"I've got a bird for you."

Sean laughed but didn't look back over his shoulder. He just waved a hand over his head and kept walking.

Colt pulled a new cell phone from his pocket—one that Sean insisted he buy—and typed in a number. It rang twice before the voice of Tim Dawson picked up. "You out working today?" he asked.

"I work every day," Colt replied. "Product doesn't move itself."

Tim's voice hovered just above a whisper. "What do you have for me?"

"About to head to another meet. This one's set up outside of Sneads. Everything's changing hands at Three Rivers State Park. You know the place?"

"I know it," Tim replied. "Over on the Florida side of Lake Seminole."

"That's it."

"What time?"

"Here in about forty-five minutes, barring any issues."

"This will be your second run, right?"

"No, it'll be—"

"Hold on," Tim said before half-covering the phone on his end. Colt could hear his muffled voice as he spoke with someone. His wife, he guessed.

Colt started again. "Look, I'm—

"Wait a second. I'm stepping outside."

Colt waited until he had the lawman's full attention.

"I'm back with you," Tim said. "Go ahead."

"I'm ditching the wire from here on out, Tim. I can't keep rolling into these meetings like this. It's too risky."

"I've listened to the first round of recordings you gave me. You sound as cool as Questlove."

"Is he still alive?" Colt asked.

"Of course."

"Right, well, I won't be if I keep running into these—"

"Easy, Colt. Take a breath."

Colt started to, but then noticed a local black-and-white out of the corner of his eye. It rolled slowly into the Hardee's parking lot. Although his heartrate picked up, he continued to lean against the side of the van. A practiced nonchalance, complete with a nod to one of the officers as the car eased by. Colt slowly turned his attention back to the windows of the restaurant. Sean stood in line, waiting to order.

"You still there?" Tim asked.

"Like I said, I'm not wearing it anymore. I'll keep working with you, but I'm not going in wired for sound. Can't do it."

"That's not the deal, Colt."

"The deal has to change, then. I'm the one taking all the risks here. Your ass is just sitting behind a desk waiting to—"

Tim raised his voice. "You're wearing the wire until I say you don't have to. Understood?"

"Fuck that."

"Okay," Tim said with a laugh. "You want me to call your PO? You want me to put you back in the Rut? I don't want to, but I will."

Colt switched the phone to his other ear. He thought about the lawman's words. Tim had promised during their first meeting that he'd send Colt back to prison if there wasn't full cooperation.

"I'm not wearing it, man."

"Yes. You. Are."

"You really going to hold a gun to my head on this?" Colt asked. "I'm telling you they'll kill me. No doubt about it."

Tim paused on his side of the line. Colt knew that the question forced the drug agent to consider his options. If he refused to capitulate, he'd have to send his only CI back to prison, effectively ending his case against Liam Hudson.

"Your safety comes first," Tim finally said. He sounded as if each word was being selected carefully. "Lose the wire for today. We can reevaluate how best to gather evidence."

Colt let the silence sit between them another moment. He wanted his handler to recognize Colt's first step toward asserting some measure of control over their forced partnership. "I'll brief you next time we meet."

"Same time. Same place."

"I'll be there."

Colt mashed the end button just as Sean exited the restaurant. As he did, he held the door open for the two local police officers. A wide grin across his face. Once the door closed, he called over to Colt.

"I went ahead and grabbed you a sausage biscuit."

Maggie Reynolds stood at the kitchen window. She watched her husband as he paced back and forth on their patio with a phone pressed to his ear. She could tell from his facial expressions that the conversation was serious. Although she couldn't hear his words, Tim's body language told her that he aimed to bully whoever was on the other end of the line. She didn't like this side of him.

The door to the patio closed and Tim stepped back into the house. She heard his footsteps on the hardwood floors. Down the hallway. A creak of the door as it opened to the room Tim used as his home office. The sound of the door closing again. Tim's footsteps heading back toward the kitchen.

"I'm running into the office," he said as he came into the room. "Shouldn't be long."

"Do what you need to do," Maggie said. "Should I just plan on dinner alone?"

Tim gave her a face. "Mags, I've apologized for the other night."

He had, emphatically. A sincere apology with kind words and flowers. It didn't matter, though. The tip of the wedge was in place.

"I know you have. I'm just asking the question, Tim."

"Everything in this job is new. I'm working my tail off, and you're giving me grief. Acting like it's a bad thing to—"

"I never said anything about your new job being a bad thing. That's you putting words in my mouth."

"Please don't lawyer me, Maggie. I said *you're acting like—*"

"I don't want to do this, Tim. Go if you need to go. I've plenty to do myself."

Tim crossed his arms. "Here we go. Your job is better. More important."

"Did I say that?"

"You didn't have to."

Maggie rubbed her temples. A version of this argument presented itself from time to time between them. Her first seven-figure settlement earlier that year hadn't helped things, either. Her fee from the Jones case brought them into uncharted waters and they suddenly had more than ever before. Conversations about how best to spend *their money*—an approach she stuck with in all their discussions—turned sideways on several occasions. Finally, after weighing their options, they decided to invest most of the funds into a historic office building in downtown Blakeston, a decision she felt set them up for long-term success in Blake County. The project went over budget—*of course*—so the two decided to go back to their roots for a little while. Tim investigating crimes. Maggie hustling cases.

Maggie turned back to the sink behind her and began to rinse off the mug from her morning coffee. She felt guilty, but she just wanted him to go. "Go onto the office, Tim. I'll just see you tonight."

He didn't say anything, but she heard him leave the room. The front door to the house closed behind him with a forcefulness that cut through the morning silence. Something was wrong between them. That much she knew.

———

Maggie opened the door to the spare bedroom, a room that she rarely entered. Every once in a while, when company came to visit, they opened the space up as a guest room. But mostly, the room doubled as Tim's home office. A place that he needed from time to time. A space with a door.

She flipped on the light.

It's not snooping if I have a reason to be in here, she thought, opening the room's small closet. She pulled a thick comforter that'd been stowed away earlier that year. She planned to throw it on their bed that night. A plausible excuse should anything in the office appear out of place. *The mind of a criminal defense lawyer.*

She walked toward the small desk that sat in the corner. Past the pictures that hung on the wall and the bookshelf filled with paperbacks. Few things sat on the desk's otherwise neat surface. A laptop. A souvenir cup full of pens. A lamp with a little, beaded brass chain.

She leaned down and tried the large desk drawer. *Locked.* She tried the small desk drawer. *Locked as well.*

Her eyes scanned the room as she looked for a spot that her husband might have placed the desk key. He didn't have a reason to hide it, necessarily. At least she hoped not. So, she felt along the shelves of the bookcase. She emptied the cup full of pens. She got down on her knees to look under the desk. *Nothing.*

What am I doing? She thought as she got back to her feet. *This is ridiculous.* The answers to their recent marital problems wouldn't be locked inside the desk. That much she knew.

Maggie did a quick once-over of the desk, making sure everything looked to be in its place. As she went to leave, her eyes rested on a picture that sat on one of the nearby bookshelves. She and Tim smiled back at her from the photo—one taken from a seat they shared at the helm of a Dufour, a 29-footer they sailed from Mobile to Key West. She remembered the trip well—her first on a sailboat of that size. They laughed, enjoyed the trip, and had just enough room below deck. *A long time ago.*

She picked up the frame and held it. As she did, she felt a small key taped behind it. She turned the picture around to examine the metal key. It looked like a match for the desk. *Might as well take a peek.*

Maggie slid the key in the lock for the large desk drawer. Inside it, she found several folders stacked on top of one another. She couldn't believe her luck. She recognized the name on the outside of the folder that sat at the top of the heap. It was a name she'd heard mentioned a few times recently within the walls of her office building. The name of Liam Hudson's only son—*Colt Hudson.*

She crossed her arms, staring down at the folder lying open on the desk. As a trial lawyer with more than a decade of experience handling criminal cases, she'd seen her fair share of casefiles. The pressboard folder was divided into neat sections. She noted the investigator's name on the inside of the front flap—Trevor Meredith—and saw that his initials appeared on several reports found throughout the file.

Maggie paged through the investigator's summary, initial incident report, and results from the crime lab. She vaguely remembered the case. A high school kid who wrecked his car after the homecoming game. His passenger—another high school student—lost her life. A tragic story that took a hard left when first responders came across a large amount—*like, way beyond personal use*—of crystal meth in the star quarterback's trunk.

They arrested Colt Hudson. Charged him with several serious offenses, but the kid wouldn't cop to anything. A younger—apparently more capable —Abe Coleman represented him through the proceedings and negotiated a plea to one count of trafficking in methamphetamine. The kid went to prison for ten years.

Maggie found the final disposition paperwork from *State v. Hudson*. The sentence appeared in bold on the first page. In her early years as a public defender, she'd worked to help all the clients in her heavy caseload avoid prison. Plenty went, though, so she was familiar with the basics around parole eligibility. She knew that most inmates become parole eligible, at the state level, once they served a third of their sentence. A rule that often surprised those unfamiliar with the criminal justice system.

As soon as inmates entered the Georgia Department of Corrections, they quickly became experts as to the rules that governed the parole process. They threw around institutional acronyms in casual conversation and began easily referring to the specifics of the tables that guided the State Board of Pardons and Paroles. Above all, though, they knew that the severity of the crime dictated the time. So, the least serious offenses allowed an inmate to become parole eligible as early as fifteen months into their sentence. The most serious of parole eligible offenses—like trafficking over 400 grams of meth, like Colt Hudson pleaded to—required an inmate to serve at least 65% of their sentence before being parole eligible.

Maggie double checked the date that Colt Hudson was sentenced on.

His recent release didn't line up. He'd made it home right at the half-way point in his sentence. *Unheard of.*

Maggie reached the end of the file. Each piece of paper had been stapled or clipped or fastened in place. All looked to be perfectly organized. Everything except a crisp, new manila envelope at the back of the file. She opened it and discovered a stack of photographs inside. The placement of the envelope seemed odd because the casefile already had a neat section of photos, mostly pictures from the scene and the items taken from the wreckage, at least those held for purposes of investigation. The photos in the envelope, though, looked different.

These must be from the homecoming game back in 2016, Maggie thought, flipping through the photos one by one. She came to a receipt at the back of the folder. One from a local pharmacy that she assumed developed the photos. The date on the receipt read: August 27, 2023. *Nearly seven years after the wreck.*

Maggie placed the photographs back in the file. As she did, she wondered why they'd been added almost seven years after the investigation began. She also wondered how Liam Hudson knew to ask her about getting an updated copy of the casefile.

She planned to get Liam a copy of the file. Not this way, though. Not by snooping through her husband's desk. She could get a copy of the file through the proper channels. Through means that wouldn't cause any additional conflict at home.

Besides, her newest contact with the local media—Ben Moss—owed her that favor.

25

Colt Hudson sat at the wheel of his father's Chevy. Liam rode shotgun, smoking quietly. With the windows cracked, they headed west on US 27. The familiar Bakersfield sound poured from the truck's speakers, and Colt half-listened as Merle Haggard went on about being a branded man. *He would know.*

"I got a complaint from one of our customers," Liam said as the station switched to commercial. His tone sounded relaxed, almost fatherly. "Guy told me you pulled a gun on him for no reason."

"You have a complaints department?" Colt asked. He couldn't help but grin.

"Always something smart to say. Just answer the question, please."

Colt looked over at the passenger seat. "Caveman and I drew on a couple of guys up in Atlanta. It's no big deal."

"Any reason?"

"One of them got smug with me. I figured I'd better give him something to remember me by."

Liam took one more drag on his Marlboro, then flipped it out onto 27. He pointed to a clay road that shot off the highway. "Turn up here."

Colt did so, slowing the truck as its tires rolled onto the two-track that sliced between the hog farms owned by Mel Darden, and the deep woods surrounding Kelley Hill Plantation. To the left, a well-defined tree line and a four-foot fence protected the boundary of the hunting preserve. To the right, rows of sugarcane fields provided a natural barrier, somewhat obstructing the view of the roofs of the swine houses. The divide ran as far as the eye could see.

Liam started in again on his inquiry. "I can't have any of that cowboy shit, Colt. It's bad for business. You understand?"

"I'm sure you had to throw some muscle around back in your day."

"My day was different. I was working retail. This is wholesale, now. The clientele expects a certain level of professionalism."

"And discretion, right?"

Liam ignored the question. "I need your word that you'll quit with the act. We're not leg-breakers. We're deal-makers."

Colt kept his eyes on the road. The man seated next to him was arguably the most successful drug dealer that the South had seen in almost three decades. He'd facilitated the growth of an unfathomable tonnage of marijuana in the fields of local farmers, put enough cocaine on the streets to dam the Mississippi, and now had enough cooks to start a Crystal-fil-A franchise. His longevity in the business was unheard of, and Colt suspected he knew why.

"Dad, the only way I know to protect myself is to stay aggressive. That's how I played ball. That's how I survived in prison. That's how I'll survive now."

Liam didn't respond.

"I mean look at me. I have no protection. I either do what you want, or—"

"You have protection, son."

"Not protection from what the DA will do to me if—"

"You're going to have to trust me."

Colt laughed. He didn't love the concept.

"In the meantime, Colt, can you not put yourself in a position where you might end up killing someone?"

Colt thought about Natalie as soon as the words spread through the cab of the truck. He'd already killed once. That was enough for a lifetime.

"I'll be more patient out there. I just can't guarantee Sean will."

"He works for us. You've got my blessing to handle it if he steps out of line."

Colt nodded. There wasn't anything else to say on the matter.

"Tell me about the investigation," Liam said, switching subjects. "Where are we now?"

The truck's low ground clearance forced Colt to be careful as he navigated the bumpy farm road. He considered his response as he eased around a deep rut on the right.

"I whet his appetite with the recordings we agreed to," Colt finally said. "A sampling of the operation, if you will."

"Good."

"He's got two of you and I discussing logistics. One from the deal up in Atlanta. One from the boys and I playing poker the other night."

"Do you know if he listened to them yet?"

"He has," Colt said. "That's why I was able to convince him to let me lose the wire. Old Timmy Tim seemed resistant at first, but he wants this case so bad he can taste it. He wasn't willing to risk sending me back at this stage."

Liam lit another. He rolled the window all the way down on his side of the truck, inviting the smell of the pig farm into the cab. He didn't even flinch.

"Keep bringing him in slowly," Liam said. "That's the only way to deal with a bull like Dawson." Liam waved his free hand in front of him like a matador's cape. "You keep them transfixed on the prize. Chasing it, until they can almost touch it. Then, you pull it all away, right as the lights go out."

"Is that what happened to Trevor Meredith?"

"Trevor was my bull, but he wasn't even in the same class as this one we're dealing with now."

Colt didn't like the answer. He tried again. "Right, but who took care of Trevor?"

Liam paused a moment. "Don't ask questions like that."

"I deserve to know, Dad. People already think that it was me and I—"

Liam's voice rose. "Let them think, Colt. That's all I'm going to tell you, so drop it."

Colt gripped the wheel. He was about to say something more when his father pointed ahead.

"There's a gate up on the left," Liam said. "Turn there. It should already be open."

Sundown looked to be almost upon them, but Colt spotted the break in the clearing with ease. He turned onto the path. A metal gate sat propped open with a sign across the front that read: *Kelley Hill Plantation.*

"Why are we—" Colt started to ask.

"Listen to me, boy. I need you to understand something right now. This here business is family business. When I say family, that's just you and me. You understand?"

Colt kept driving slowly through the open entrance. The darkened road ahead looked to be a single lane that led up a steady slope of wiregrass and tall pine trees.

"I didn't choose this life, and you know that," Colt said.

"I didn't ask if you chose it. I asked if you understood it."

Colt nodded.

"Then you need to know that these people I'm about to meet with, they're not family. They don't give a shit about me, you, or even their own."

Colt tried not to think about the fact that he'd spent almost five years doing time for *the family*—a.k.a. Liam Hudson.

"I understand."

"And no one is to know about this."

"Who would I tell?"

"Say it, dammit."

Colt looked over at his father. A serious gaze met his eyes. "No one will know about this."

"Okay, good."

Colt followed the narrow lane up the hill and around a turn. Ahead, he saw the lights of a large house. A house that most people probably referred to as *grand.*

"Park up there," Liam said. "I'm leaving you in the truck."

Colt didn't protest. He simply pulled up to where his father told him, right alongside a row of black SUVs. The closest Tahoe didn't have a license plate on it, but Colt recognized the look of the vehicle. Dark tinted windows. Next-generation frame. Brush guard on the grill.

Government types, Colt thought. *What's he up to?*

Liam opened the glove box and placed his cell phone inside it. It fit neatly beside his trusty S&W.

"Are you meeting with Senator Collins?" Colt asked.

Colt watched his father's face for any sort of reaction. He knew that Kelley Hill Plantation—a large private estate owned by a wealthy, embattled United States Senator from Georgia—welcomed only select visitors.

"Don't ask questions like that," Liam said after a short pause. He said it in almost the same tone as before. "You'll know when you need to know."

Liam slammed the passenger door and started up toward the house. He hollered back over his shoulder in Colt's direction.

"Stay in the truck!"

26

As Maggie Reynolds drove to the office on Monday morning, she called Ben Moss's cell phone. It rang four times before going to the reporter's voicemail. She left a message that urged him to call her back. She needed him to get started on a request to the BCSO. As she ended the call, her phone started ringing through the car's speakers. Assuming it was the reporter calling back, she picked up without glancing at the name on the screen.

"Hey," Maggie said, starting in, "thanks for calling back. Look, I need you to help with something. It's not going to—"

"Uh, Maggie?" replied a familiar voice. "Can you hear me?"

Maggie took her eyes off the road to glance at the screen on her dash. Charlotte Acker's name glowed on it beside a green phone icon.

"Hey there," Maggie said, trying her best to recover. "Sorry about that. I thought it was someone else at first. How are—"

"I'm hearing something different."

"Yeah?" Maggie asked. "Different how?"

"Like, maybe you wouldn't have picked up this call if you'd known it was me." Charlotte let the silence hang between them a moment. "Am I pretty close?"

"No, Charlotte, that's not it at all."

"It's okay, really. I understand you don't want to deliver the bad news to me. I get that the case is probably over."

Maggie paused a moment to appreciate her client's head-on approach. Although Charlotte Acker was only in her second year of law school, she spoke of courtroom matters like a seasoned associate. Which made sense, because she'd seen the courtroom from some ugly angles already. Once as the daughter of a man accused of murder, then later as a defendant herself. Maggie sat at counsel's table for both trials and she knew the Acker family well. They trusted her and expected her to come through for them. *She always had, until now.*

"I was going to call. I'm just still trying to work it all out in my head. I didn't want to get you on the line to discuss some half-baked theory that—"

"No, I'm game for that. Let's do it."

Maggie pulled up to a red light at the center of downtown Blakeston. Her favorite coffee shop—Beans on Broad—sat at one corner of the intersection. A few familiar faces eased out of its front doors, coffee cups in hand. She'd planned to pick up a smoothie that morning, but her conversation with Charlotte didn't appear to be ending anytime soon.

"Are you sure?" Maggie asked.

"Walk me through it."

"Okay, well, the original plan was to go at John Deese with everything we had. Hit him with our lawsuit while the BCSO had him in custody at the county jail. Get us some standing in a Blake County courtroom."

"Wouldn't we have already had that in the criminal case against him?"

"Not the kind you needed, though."

Victims to a crime are crucial when it comes to a prosecutor proving their case, but the victim is only a witness in the case against a criminal defendant. Victims don't control the prosecution of the case. The State does.

Charlotte sighed. "I guess it doesn't really matter. There won't be any kind of case to go after him with now."

Maggie paused a moment before responding. Her client was probably right, but she wanted her to know that they'd at least tried to make something happen. "You remember Michael Hart, right?"

"How could I forget our friend at the DA's office?"

"Well, he already had an indictment when they picked Deese up in Peru. Hart planned to apply as much pressure as he could to get information out of him. Our civil suit would've gone at the problem from the other side. Hart seemed comfortable with the idea of us working the problem from different angles. The worst we expected Deese to do, though, was take the Fifth in the discovery process, not—"

Charlotte interrupted. "Do you think he did it?"

The light turned green, and Maggie started through the intersection. It wasn't that long ago that Charlotte stood trial for a murder charge in Blake County. She'd been accused in the high-profile killing of Lucy Kelley Collins—the late wife to Senator Bill Collins. The ordeal pushed Charlotte to the edge, only to be saved in the late stages of the trial by one of the men who helped frame her—a law professor, her lawyer, and brief lover— Lawton Crane. The disgraced lawyer, now disbarred, took a sweetheart deal as penance for his trespasses. In exchange for crucial testimony that implicated John Deese as the principal in the murder of the senator's wife, Crane pleaded guilty to one count of conspiracy to commit murder. His cooperation sealed the deal for the case against Deese and pointed to the senator's involvement as well.

"There's no reason to believe he didn't commit suicide," Maggie replied. "They found him dead in his cell at the county jail. A bedsheet wrapped around his neck."

"How can you say that?"

"That he's dead?" Maggie said with a laugh. "I didn't expect you to have any sympathy for John—"

Charlotte shot back a quick response. "I don't have any sympathy for him."

"Then, what?"

"How can you say that there's no reason to believe this might not have been a suicide?"

Maggie Reynolds sat in her office, trying to review a stack of medical records. They'd been provided in one of her cases involving an injured worker at the local railyard. The case checked all the boxes. It involved a client that she could truly help, one with serious injuries that equated to real value for her firm. And it fit squarely within the kinds of cases she needed to put her time and energy into. Yet, she couldn't seem to get locked in. Other matters gnawed at her. *Unresolved matters.*

The phone on Maggie's desk beeped twice. She picked it up, grateful for a distraction.

"There's a reporter in the lobby who says he needs to see you. Should I send him away?"

Maggie picked up her cell phone to check her missed calls. Nothing.

"What's his name?"

"Ben Moss. He's with—"

"Send him up."

Maggie's second-floor office sat at the front of her large, elongated office building. Its high, floor-to-ceiling windows allowed plenty of light to enter during the daytime and offered a perfect view onto the brick streets below.

Ben Moss sat on the office's small sofa. Maggie in a high-back leather chair. The soft, mid-morning light eased through the tall windows and onto the office's sitting area.

Maggie took a sip of her coffee. "You could've just called."

"I know, but I was already in the area."

"This is a small town, Ben. We're all in the area."

"True," he said with a smile. "I figured we might as well talk about what you needed in person. I'm new to all this, so it helps me understand the process."

"Want to try that again?"

Ben crossed one leg over the other. "Fine. I don't like to talk on phones, okay?"

Maggie shook her head. All these men—Liam, Ben, Tim—they all seemed to think that their work was so important that someone had to be monitoring their every move. The only difference in the three was Liam Hudson and Ben Moss seemed to believe they could confide in her.

"You've been reading a little too much about big brother and—"

"I'm not some kind of tin-hat person. I just feel like it's good to be careful."

"Careful is good, Ben, but I'm not here to share top-secret information. I just need you to put in a request or two for me."

The conversation with Charlotte earlier that morning prompted Maggie to consider expanding their inquiry into the BCSO's unwillingness to share information.

"What do you need?" Ben asked as he pulled a tablet from his bag.

"Have you had any luck getting records from the BCSO's investigation into Trevor Meredith's death?"

"They finally sent me the bare minimum last Friday. Basically, a copy of the initial incident report and a redacted version of the 9-1-1 call. The GBI has the case now, though."

"Did they give you any reason for not providing anything more?"

"Of course," he said. "Told me it was an ongoing investigation. Same as always."

Maggie nodded. Those additional records were mostly exempt from disclosure under the Open Records Act. Mainly to protect the investigation.

"Okay, how about the investigation into John Deese's death at the county jail?"

"Even less," he said, typing away on the tablet. "My parents go to church with the coroner, so he's a family friend. Most of what I know about Deese is off-the-record information. The GBI has that one, too."

Maggie respected the privilege journalists were entitled to, so she didn't want to ask for the information unless it was offered. "Did the BCSO cite a reason for not providing you anything more on Deese?"

"Same reason. Active investigation. Blah, blah, blah."

"Okay," she said, thinking. She felt like she could set the play up with the reporter. "I need you to request another file for me."

"What's the name on it?"

"It's an older case."

"So, it should be closed, right?"

Maggie nodded. The exceptions in the Open Records Act that allowed law enforcement to hold back information about their active investigations didn't usually apply once the case ended. The casefile Maggie wanted had been closed for five years now.

"The name on the file is *Colt Hudson*."

Ben typed the name into his tablet. "You know how old the file is?"

"Closed for close to five years now."

"It might be in archives. I'll ask them to check."

"Okay," she said, knowing damn well it wasn't in the BCSO's archives. It sat tucked away in Tim's desk drawer at their house. "That would be great."

"Is that all?" Ben asked.

Maggie looked over at the young reporter seated on her couch. Educated in Boston, but working the crime beat, among other things, in small-town Blakeston, Georgia. She figured he must be hungry for more.

"How much do you know about Senator Bill Collins?"

27

Colt Hudson pulled into a parking space that fronted the Department of Community Supervision. DCS handled the supervision and reentry services for felony probationers and parolees across the state. Its office in Blakeston took up two units at the corner of an aging strip mall. One on the wrong side of town. A laundromat, vape shop, and fast-tax service occupied the strip's only other remaining storefronts that were suitable for commercial tenants. A few other cars, all early-two-thousand models, sat parked in the otherwise empty lot.

He cut the engine on the Chevy and stepped out into the afternoon sun. It was the second week of November and temperatures still hovered in the low seventies. He needed a break from the heat. He needed a break from everything, really.

Colt pushed through the front door of DCS and nodded to a skinny white woman who sat at a counter behind double-pane glass. He could see the yellowing on her teeth when she smiled at him, a reminder that he needed to quit the budding habit stuffed in the back pocket of his jeans.

"Afternoon," Colt said as he stepped to the window. "I'm Colt Hudson. Here to check in with the boss."

The woman offered him another yellowed smile as she pushed a clipboard through a slat at the bottom of the window. "Fill this out, sweetie. He'll be with you soon."

Colt took the clipboard, then turned to select one of the metal folding chairs that lined the walls of the empty lobby. He guessed the space used to be a restaurant of some kind. He could still see the markings on the walls from where the booths rubbed at the paint and the stains from odors on the drop ceiling tiles.

Might've been the old Panda Garden, Colt thought, before turning his attention to the questionnaire in his lap.

The form asked all the standard questions: *Have you changed employment since your last visit? Have you been charged with a new offense since your last visit? Have you used drugs or alcohol without doctors' approval since your last visit? Have you been outside the state since your last visit?* Colt checked the box for *No* after each. He knew, as did the brilliant people at DCS, that no ex-con would affirmatively answer one of the questions on the form. Not if it meant potentially going back to prison.

A man's voice drew his attention away from the questionnaire. "Colt Hudson?"

Colt stood from the flimsy chair. "Officer Rope, good to see you, sir."

The parole officer offered Colt a quick smile, then pointed with a thick forearm toward the open doorway. "Come on back, Colt."

"Yes, sir."

Officer Ronald Rope took the clipboard from Colt as they started down the office's main hallway. He asked about housing, and how the work at Hudson Auto was going as he reviewed the questionnaire. Colt provided him with satisfactory responses and the PO initialed the bottom right-hand corner of the form.

"I'll have you piss first," he said, "and then we'll sit down to talk after that."

Colt nodded. He'd slammed a Gatorade and a bottle of water on his way over to the meeting. The word on *Ronald the Rope* was that he was fair with his parolees, and a decent guy if you stayed on his good side. He didn't hesitate to send someone back up the road on a violation, though. True to his name, he gave his guys just enough rope to hang themselves.

"Works for me, sir. I've got the phony ding-dong ready to go."

Rope laughed. "I've seen a few of them come through here, Colt. I'm sorry to break it to you, but they don't make a model that's small enough for you."

"You would know," Colt replied, laughing as well. "You're the one who spends all day talking to ex-cons and looking at wieners."

"More than most working girls in the area." Rope said this with a smile, then pointed to an open door at the end of the hallway. "Last door on the left. I'll go grab the cup and follow you in there."

"Yes, sir."

Rope fired back one last jab. "That'll give you a head start on finding that thing."

After Colt passed the standard five-panel drug screen—one that tested for marijuana, cocaine, PCP, amphetamines, and opiates, none of which Colt used—he followed Rope back down the hallway to a small meeting room. His previous two check-ins had taken less than ten minutes, so Colt already had his mind on getting out the door. As soon as he sat, though, he was reminded why guys back in prison told him to never trust his parole officer.

A familiar face entered the room. That of a serious looking Cam Abrams.

"I'm Special Agent Cam Abrams," she said, taking the chair across from his. She slid what looked like a recording device to the center of the table. "I'm with the GBI's Region Fifteen Investigative Office and I need to ask you—"

"I know who you are, Cam. Hell, I just saw you a few weeks ago at—"

"It's Agent Abrams, Ms. Abrams, or Special Agent Abrams. Not Cam. Not ever. Is that understood?"

Colt turned to look at Rope. "You could've warned me about this, you know?"

He folded his arms across his barrel chest. No longer playing the friendly PO. "Answer her question."

Colt turned back to her. "Okay, *Agent Abrams*, I know who you are."

"Good."

"Can we take a beat and just talk for a minute?" Colt asked this in an almost pleading manner. "You've never given me a chance to apologize for—"

Cam ignored him. "Are you aware that an investigator with the Blake County Sheriff's Office was murdered recently in his own home?"

"Yes, Agent Abrams. I'm aware of the fact that someone killed Trevor Meredith. That's what this is about?"

"Our reports suggest that the break-in occurred at his home sometime around 11:20 a.m., on the morning of October twenty-fourth."

"Was that a Tuesday?"

She narrowed her eyes. "This isn't a game, Colt. I'm getting the feeling that you're being a little uncooperative, maybe even trying to obstruct my investigation."

"That's not at all what I'm—"

"So much so, that Officer Rope here might need to consider violating your parole on this interaction alone."

Colt showed her both of his palms. "I'm not sure what's going on here, but I didn't kill him."

Cam turned and spoke in the direction of the parole officer. "Your guy here says he didn't kill him, Ron. I guess we just believe him?"

"I guess so," Rope replied, matching her condescending tone. "At least we tried, right?"

"Are you sure?" Cam asked. "Maybe we should be a little more thorough. I feel like some ex-cons aren't always all that honest."

"Come to think of it, you're right. I say you ask him one more time."

Cam turned back to face Colt. "Where were you the morning of October twenty-fourth?"

"Isn't someone supposed to read me my rights?"

She asked the question slower this time. "Where were you the morning of October twenty-fourth?"

"Not at Meredith's place," Colt said, mindful of the tone in his voice. "I was working that day."

"Where?"

"Up in Atlanta."

"The entire day?"

Colt nodded. "We left sometime around five that morning and probably didn't make it back until sometime after dinner. I can't remember the exact time that—"

"We?" she asked. Every word that left her mouth sounded harsh, accusatory. "Who is it that can vouch for your whereabouts that day?"

Colt hesitated a moment. Sean Caverns wasn't the ideal candidate for someone to serve as an alibi witness. He was a wildcard, but Colt didn't have any other options. Also, it was the truth. *Whatever that was worth.*

"His name is Sean Caverns. I'll get you a number if you need one."

Cam leaned back in her chair for a moment. A welcome break in the onslaught. Still, she glared across the table at him with an unmistakable look of disdain. "Give it to me."

"I don't know the number by heart," Colt said, easing a hand toward the front pocket of his pants, "but I have it in my phone. Should I get it?"

Rope slid a piece of paper over. Then a pen. "Write it down."

Colt scratched the number on the paper, then his interrogators stepped out into the hallway. Neither said another word to him as they closed the door. *Click.*

Tim Dawson sat in the administrative offices of the BCSO, waiting for an afternoon meeting with his boss—Sheriff Charlie Clay. A nearby radio squawked occasionally as deputies and other personnel called in requests to dispatch. Most started their messages to the dispatcher by identifying their command and assignment, then providing a short update or request.

Tim heard an unfamiliar voice call in over the radio. The voice sounded clear as he notified dispatch that he had one Colt Hudson in custody at the offices of DCS. A potential violation of parole. The male voice proceeded to request a criminal history and address check on another person of interest —Sean Caverns.

The dispatcher notified the individual that he must call in by telephone for the information, then provided the number.

"Who's that calling in?" Tim asked, walking over to the deputy that sat on desk duty.

The young deputy picked up his radio and requested the information. They waited a moment for the man to respond.

"It's an Officer Ronald Rope," the deputy said. "A parole officer with DCS."

"Tell him not to do a thing with Hudson until I get there."

"Sir, I believe he—"

Tim turned to look over at the door to Sheriff Clay's office. Still closed.

"Let the sheriff know that I had to deal with an emergency. And you tell Ronald Rope he'd better not do a damn thing with Colt Hudson until I get there."

The startled deputy pulled the radio to his mouth and relayed the information to Rope. As Tim ran out the door, he realized that the message would go out over a frequency shared by all deputies with the BCSO. Probably a few eavesdroppers, too.

Colt Hudson checked the time again on his cell phone. It'd been more than twenty minutes since Cam stepped into the hallway to make the call to Sean Caverns. He could only imagine the kind of story Caveman cooked up in an attempt to provide cover. The guy could throw a right-hook better than most and knew how to take care of himself in a tight spot. He didn't know a thing about concocting an alibi on the fly, though. Especially not one that was carefully crafted to avoid putting Colt in hot water with his PO, or the GBI for that matter.

He had his head in his hands when the door to the room opened. He looked up and saw Tim Dawson coming through the doorway. In a smooth motion, the lawman picked up the recording device at the center of the table and slid it into his back pocket. "Get up," he said. "Let's get you out of here."

Behind him, a fired-up Cam Abrams came through the door. "This is my investigation, Commander Dawson. I've not confirmed this suspect's whereabouts on the date of the Meredith murder. He's not leaving until I do."

A homicide investigator carried a supremely difficult task. They chased killers of all kinds. Those that killed maliciously, accidentally, justifiably, or with reckless disregard. A good investigator had to make sure their cases received the requisite amount of attention. Those that murdered another member of law enforcement, though, they received a special interest from all involved in the investigation. It wasn't just the attack on one victim—as if that wasn't enough. No, it was an assault on the entire profession. One that they'd dedicated their lives to.

"It wasn't him," Tim growled. "Now, get out of the way so I can get him out of here. He's my responsibility."

"With all due respect, this might be a cop killer. I'm going to need more of a reason to let this—"

"You need to watch what you're about to say," Tim shot back. He appeared to be making no effort to deescalate the situation. "I'm not going to lecture you about the importance of investigating suspects based on the facts, but someone needs to. Your emotions are in your head. Get a handle on them."

Cam bristled. "He wanted Meredith dead, Commander. That's plenty of motive for me. It should be for you, too."

"That's not what this is about, Abrams."

Tim's decision to drop titles seemed to embolden Cam. It put them on the same level.

"That con over there hasn't been out of prison but a month. I bet he thought about killing Meredith every night he sat in prison."

"Are you going to tell me you haven't had those same thoughts?"

Cam took a step closer, staring her opponent down.

Tim continued. "I know your history, Abrams. I know your sister was in the car with Colt the night of the accident. I bet you've wished him dead, too."

"That's ridiculous!"

"Is it?" Tim exclaimed. "Now, I don't believe you plan to murder Mr. Hudson here, nor do I believe that he went about the business of killing one of our own."

"I'm a member of law enforcement. Colt is a convicted felon. You're going to give the same benefit of the doubt to that piece of—"

"Watch it, Abrams."

"Give me something solid and I'll back off."

Tim glanced over at Colt, then back at the blonde agent. He seemed to be weighing his options.

"You don't have anything to back your gut on this, do you?" Cam chided.

"I can place him in Atlanta on the day of Meredith's death. I have Colt on a recording, making a delivery to a couple of Korean buyers. That's definitive proof that he was more than two-hundred miles away when someone kicked in Meredith's back door."

Cam stood there, silent. She'd obviously not expected that kind of response.

"Is that proof enough for you, rookie?"

She still stood in the doorway. "I want to hear it."

Tim laughed. "No."

"I need more—"

"Is wrecking my ongoing investigation just to satisfy your personal vendetta against this young man something you want to do?"

"I need to hear it to believe it."

"Not a chance," Tim said as he shook his head. "Now, I need you to move."

"No," Cam said again. She stood taller now. "I want to know what kind of work you have him doing for you."

Tim started to push past her, but she shoved him back.

"Try that again," Tim said, starting toward her.

She kept her stance strong in the doorway, then shoved him once more as he tried to pass her.

"I'm warning you, rook—"

Colt watched—from a front-row seat—as Natalie Abrams' little sister pulled a fist back and drove it into the narcotics squad commander's jaw. The blow connected squarely, knocking the 6-foot-3 lawman to the carpet. As he hit the ground, Cam's eyes flashed to Colt. He held her gaze for what felt like a long moment.

"Oh shit," she said, smiling.

There it is, Colt thought, looking back at her. *Been waiting a long time to see that.*

28

Tim Dawson sat up on the carpet, stunned. The shot to his jaw had been unexpected, with enough force behind it to spin his head quickly to one side. He felt like a humiliated prizefighter. One dropped to the mat by a smaller opponent and his own hubris. He looked up at the faces of Colt Hudson and Cam Abrams. Both stood a safe distance away with expressions that were a mixture of fear and amusement.

Cam spoke first. The titles were back. "I'm so sorry, Commander Dawson. That was incredibly out of line and—"

"Just help me up," Tim said, extending a hand. "That'll be enough for now."

She tried to finish her apology as she helped him off the floor, but Tim waved her off. He knew he deserved the right cross from the young agent. Although somewhat embarrassed, he felt his senses beginning to clear.

"For the record," Colt said, "I didn't hit anyone."

Tim smiled. The jaw already felt stiff. "Shut up, Colt."

"Yeah," Cam added, "shut up."

Tim found a chair at the table and sat. He rubbed the left side of his face with one hand, shaking his head. *What a trainwreck*, he thought. He was a little over one month into his tenure as commander of the BCSO's narcotics squad, a position he didn't expect to hold much longer if things didn't start heading in a better direction. Between one of his investigators being murdered in his own home, his prized confidential informant refusing to wear a wire, and his wife no longer speaking to him, he had his hands full.

He needed some help.

"Special Agent Abrams," Tim said, looking over at the young GBI agent, "you said you wanted to know what kind of work Colt here is doing for us."

Cam bent down to the carpet and tipped one of the chairs back up onto its legs. "I'd certainly like to know," she said, taking a seat. "That is, if you're able to share that information with me."

"It's my investigation," he replied with another smile. "I'd say I'm allowed to do whatever the hell I want."

Colt was still on his feet, leaning against the wall. "I'm not sure I like where this is going."

"Can we put him in jail for a little while?" Cam asked. Her voice sounded lighter. "A little solitary confinement for him might do us all some good."

"No," Tim said. "His old man already put him in prison once. Seems cruel for us to do it to him again."

"That's not true, Tim. I deserved the time I did up at the Rut."

"Not all of it, though, and certainly not for trafficking meth."

Tim watched the young agent as she looked over at her contemporary. The anger that'd clouded her judgment earlier seemed to be dissipating as she considered him for another moment. She directed her question to Colt. "What does he mean by your dad put you in prison?"

Colt looked away from her.

"You've been asking to talk to me about my sister for years," she pressed. "I read every single one of your pathetic letters that you sent me. Now you're not going to talk to me?"

Tim tried to help them along. "I came across some evidence recently—a set of photos—that led me to believe that Colt didn't know those drugs were in his Mustang the night of your sister's death. That he probably didn't commit that—"

"I still caused the wreck," Colt said in a low voice. "I was guilty of that, which was enough."

"Maybe so, Colt." Tim kept his voice calm. "You didn't plead guilty to vehicular homicide, though. You pleaded guilty to trafficking."

Colt shrugged. "It doesn't matter. That's just what the lawyers put together. I took Natalie away from her family and that kind of thing couldn't go unpunished."

"You know that's not the same thing."

"Maybe not," Colt said as he turned to look at Cam, "but that wreck was my fault, and not a day goes by that I don't think about Natalie. I'm not asking you to forgive me. I just need you to know that I'm sorry."

Tim thought he saw the GBI agent's eyes start to water at the mention of her sister's name. She sniffled, then wiped her eyes with the sleeve of her shirt.

Colt continued. "I should've gone to the hospital during that game. I should've told Coach Weeks I couldn't play. That my head was jacked up—"

"Colt—" she started.

"And I sure as hell shouldn't have been driving that night, Cam. I don't know what I was thinking…"

The reports that surrounded the tragic death of Natalie Abrams painted Colt Hudson as the villain. A piece of trailer trash that was nothing more than the product of the misplaced importance that rural towns gifted to their star athletes. Colt became the symbol of what crystal meth was doing to small, southern communities. Ruining good families. Poisoning good people. Killing good children.

"We can talk all about the things that *shouldn't* or *should've* happened," Tim said. "Your coaches should've taken care of you. The whole town shouldn't have given them a pass, while they pushed you away. The people that—"

"What good does it do for me to blame them, Tim? The school, the doctors, my coaches, they all turned their backs on me."

You're right about that, Tim thought, as silence entered the room. It hung there as they processed it all. The disproportionality of punishment. The lack of accountability. The loss of someone so young. *It all seemed unfair.*

Cam finally spoke up. "It was an accident, Colt. You need to stop blaming yourself and try to let it go."

She stood from her chair and opened her arms to him.

"I need to let it go," she said. "Me hating you for a mistake isn't going to bring my sister back."

Colt hesitated, then stepped in for the embrace. The moment continued for a short while, and Tim watched as a few tears rolled down Colt's cheeks. Unresolved guilt only festered with time, and he knew that Colt never had a chance to reconcile with the Abrams family after the wreck. Seven years since the accident. Five years in prison. It all started to wash away with one act of kindness.

"So," Cam said, clearing the emotions from her throat as she stepped back, "you're turning over a new leaf or something?"

Colt pulled the collar of his T-shirt up and dried his eyes. He laughed. "Something like that."

"Grab a seat," Tim said as he directed Colt to the open chair in the room. "I think it's time we tell Agent Abrams here about our arrangement."

"Call me Cam," she quickly added. "I figure we should be on a first name basis if you're going to cut me some slack for decking you."

Tim laughed. "Sucker punch is more like it."

Cam smiled as she glanced over at Colt for a ruling. The young CI looked like he'd do anything for her in that moment.

Tim Dawson walked Cam Abrams through the last month and a half of work. He explained to her that when Sheriff Charlie Clay offered him the job as the commander of the narcotics squad, it came with one condition.

"The sheriff told me that he wanted to put a plan together to take down a drug ring being operated right in his backyard. One headed up by a man who owned a local garage on the outskirts of Blakeston."

Cam nodded. "That would be Colt's daddy—Liam Hudson."

"That's the one," Tim said. "And at first, I assumed this was just going to be some group of local meth heads. A bunch of jackoffs cooking up dope out in the woods. One bad batch away from blowing themselves up."

"I know the kind."

"That's not this group, though. They're different than any other operation within at least five-hundred miles. Everything's organized, efficient, and handled by a nearly impenetrable group of loyalists at the top."

"No one has been able to get in?" Cam asked.

Tim shook his head. "Not that I'm aware of. There's never been anyone to go after at the local level. No one that they could flip on a small-time drug bust, then trade up with to climb the ladder."

"No one except Colt," she said, starting to put the pieces together. She paused a moment as she appeared to consider the information. "I bet someone went after him pretty hard after the wreck with my sister."

Tim looked over at Colt. His young CI wasn't contributing to their little briefing. "Colt?"

"Trevor Meredith tried to get me to come in," he said. "I couldn't do it."

"So, you chose to go to prison to protect your dad?"

Colt shrugged. "I didn't choose my family, Cam."

Tim dismissed the evasive response and turned back to the agent. He explained that from the beginning, it was the sheriff who turned him onto Colt Hudson's case. They worked it out so that Tim could approach Colt at Rutledge State Prison and offer him a deal. One that came with the opportunity to return home to Blakeston immediately.

"Okay," she said, eyes on Colt. "That's probably about what Trevor offered you seven years ago. What changed?"

"Look," Colt began, "I don't want to rehash the decision not to take the deal with Meredith. I just didn't know then what I know now."

Another evasive answer, Tim thought. *Interesting.*

"You didn't know about the photos?" Cam asked.

"Tim brought me the photos when he came to see me. Pictures from that homecoming game seven years ago. The images showed a couple of boys my dad worked with—two Greeks from Detroit—hanging around my Mustang with another guy. From what you can see in the photos, it looks like they were setting me up."

She nodded to Tim. "Let's bring those two in for questioning, then."

"We can't."

"Why not?"

"They're dead," he said. "Both of them."

She offered a heavy sigh. "Where'd that happen?"

"The bodies were found here in Blake County. That much we know. The case is frigid, though."

"So, we may be looking at Liam Hudson for those two bodies, along with a laundry list of drug offenses. What's the interest looking like over at the district attorney's office?"

Tim leaned back in his chair. "I've not spoken with them on this yet. My plan was to meet with the sheriff today to get approval, then set up a sit-down with Michael Hart at the DA's office."

Colt jumped in. "I think you should look at him for another homicide, too."

"Which one?" Cam asked.

"Trevor Meredith's."

Tim raised an eyebrow at his CI's decision to volunteer this information. It was the first he'd heard of it.

"Why?" Tim asked. He carefully watched the body language on the young con.

"I think Liam may've done it—or had it carried out—to get some additional leverage on me. The morning of Meredith's murder, he sent me to Atlanta on my first run. He knew my alibi would be a shit one that wouldn't hold up in court. He just didn't anticipate me having insurance strapped around my chest in the form of a wire."

Cam raised an eyebrow. "It's plausible."

Tim agreed. "It's not the worst theory I've heard."

Like most cops, though, Tim prided himself on his intuition. Something about Colt's idea felt wrong, and Tim knew it in his gut.

"Let me get in on the meeting with the DA," Cam quickly added. "I'll pitch Hart the Meredith angle. It's my case."

"And what am I supposed to do once the word gets out?" Colt asked. "They'll kill me if they find out I'm involved with—"

Tim interrupted him. "If Hart is on board, he'll want you to testify before the grand jury. Then, he'll place you in protective custody after that. Somewhere safe."

"How long?"

"Until the trial. Maybe longer."

"Let's not get ahead of ourselves," Cam said, sounding like a seasoned vet. "First, we need to present a solid case to Hart."

"She's right," Tim said. He already liked having Cam Abrams in their camp. "That's step one."

"Tim, I'll need access to Colt's old file to get up to speed."

Tim nodded. He'd have to grab it from the house.

"I'll need the case on the two boys from Detroit, too, and anything you have on Liam Hudson's history, known associates, holdings—"

"And the photos," Colt said. "She'll need to see the photos you showed me up at Rutledge."

Tim considered his young CI's words. Another well-placed recommendation, but the energy felt off. The tone sounded wrong.

"Right," she said. "I'll need to see those photos."

"Of course. They're in the file."

"By the way, where did they come from?" Cam asked.

Tim leaned forward with his elbows on the table. This question had been expected. It was one he'd already answered a couple of times with a harmless lie. Once when Sheriff Clay asked about them. Another time during his and Colt's first meeting in prison. *What's one or two more?*

"Someone sent them into the office," he said, calmly. "They were in the file when I took the job."

That was the official story. The photos found their way into the file before Tim took over as commander of the narcotics squad. Probably added by an administrative assistant at the BCSO.

"Who on your team supplemented the file?" she asked. "We need to figure out who they received them from. It might help us out."

Tim nodded. The unofficial story was one that no one else knew. *Nor would they.* The mysterious photos weren't sent to the BCSO's office to be added to the casefile. They'd arrived in Tim's mailbox at home—in an envelope addressed to him.

"The BCSO casefile doesn't say who added them," Tim said. "We can look into it, though."

"Let's try to get with Hart as soon as possible," Cam said. "We need the DA's office in on this early."

"What should I be doing?" Colt asked.

"Just keep your head down and keep doing what you've been doing."

"Easy enough."

Tim caught himself smiling as he looked at the two seated with him at the table. A sort of innocent man, and a soon-to-be-hotshot investigator. An unusual duo.

"Let's try to move fast," Tim said as he stood from the table. "The grand jury convenes next week, and I want to have our star witness in front of them."

29

Colt Hudson dropped by the shop later that evening. As he pulled the Chevy to the rear of the building, he found several vehicles parked out back. He only recognized one of them, though. A black-on-black Challenger that Sean Caverns kept showroom ready—and rarely out of sight. Colt eased around the tail-end of the Dodge and spotted its owner. He stood just outside one of the garage's open bay doors, smoking a cigarette with Harry Bates. Both wore serious expressions until they noticed the Chevy pulling into a nearby parking space. The two exchanged a comment of some sort, then acknowledged Colt with a nod.

As he cut the engine on the truck, it crossed his mind that this small after-hours meeting might have been specially called. Colt considered this as he sat for a moment behind the wheel. He never asked Cam Abrams if she spoke with Sean earlier that afternoon. If she did, though, that meant she asked him plenty of questions about Colt's whereabouts over the last couple of weeks. Questions that would've made someone like Sean, along with the rest of the crew, nervous about Colt being back in the fold.

Harry called over once Colt stepped out of the truck. "It's been a long time, young man. Get your ass over here!"

The wily accountant looked like he could barely suppress. a smile as Colt walked his way. Colt knew that Harry had partnered up with Liam

back in the early days, before baby Colt came into the picture, and the partnership was one that'd held strong over nearly three decades, mostly
because Harry provided the *yang* to Liam's hard-ass approach at life. He
offered sound counsel when it was requested, and ensured the legitimate
businesses stayed that way. He'd been around Colt's entire life. Never
serving as a stand-in father figure, but always nearby to provide a different
perspective when Colt needed it.

"You didn't think you needed to come around and see me?" Colt chided
as he went in for a bearhug with the big man. "Not hide nor hair since I've
been back. I figured you must've died or something."

Harry started to put Colt in a chokehold. "See, that's just a shitty thing
to say, Colt. I damn near almost did last year."

"Oh, I'm sorry," Colt replied, easily breaking free from the aging money
man. "I didn't know you'd gotten so sensitive while I was away."

"I'm telling you it was close. A heart attack almost got me in the middle
of the night. Can you believe that?"

Colt could, actually. "Get out of here!"

"It was as serious as it gets. Thank God I had a friend in bed with me.
She called 9-1-1, and they sent the paramedics over to my hotel room just in
time."

"Was this friend a hooker?" Colt asked.

"Young Hudson, that term's no longer popular in the industry."

"Well, I'm just glad your ex-wife wasn't with you that night. She
might've rolled over and gone back to sleep."

"Which ex?"

"Both of them."

"Probably so," he said with another laugh. "It's good to see you back.
You planning to come inside?"

Colt looked over at Sean for a moment. With both hands tucked in his
pockets, he seemed to be keeping his distance from the quasi-family
reunion.

"What's good, Caveman?"

"Just chilling." Sean offered nothing more.

"All right," Colt said after a moment. He motioned over his shoulder to
the Dodge. "Challenger looks clean tonight."

"Always," he replied. "We're taking her out."

"Where to?"

Harry put an arm around Colt's shoulders and started to lead him through the open bay door. Colt turned back toward Sean to get a response to his question, but realized his partner was already headed toward the parking lot. Harry started in again on how long it'd been since they'd seen each other, and how good it was to have Colt back in Blake County. Not a word was mentioned about Harry's unwillingness to visit the Rut over the last five years.

"Is my dad around tonight?" Colt asked.

"He's in the office finishing up some work." Harry walked with his arm slumped over Colt's shoulder. "I'll go find him for you."

"No, it's fine, Harry. I'll go see if—"

"I don't mind," he said, then pointed over to a vintage Nine-Eleven parked on the opposite side of the garage. "Go check out my new project over there. I owned one of those babies back in 1981. Should've never sold it."

Colt glanced over at the door that led to his father's office. "No, I need to—"

Harry interrupted, again. "There's beer in that fridge on the back wall, too."

"All right," Colt said with a nod. Message received. "I'll check the Porsche out. Let my dad know I'm here, though."

"Of course."

"Anyone else around?"

Harry made a showing of glancing about the large, empty garage. "Looks like pretty much everyone took off for the day."

Colt thought about the other vehicles parked out back. A Cadillac, Sean's Challenger, a newer-model Ford truck, and a Range Rover.

"Who else is back in the office?" Colt asked.

Harry ignored the question. "I'll let your old man know that you're here."

Colt watched him as he disappeared into a hallway that led to the office, all the while wondering if he should hit the door.

Maggie Reynolds sat on a tattered leather chair in Liam Hudson's office, waiting for him to answer her question. He stared back at her from the seat behind his desk. She'd been there for almost thirty minutes. A house-call of sorts because the client now insisted on meeting in the only place that he considered absolutely secure—his personal office inside the walls of Hudson Auto.

"I need to know," Maggie pressed. "I can't help advise you on any of this if—"

"Look," Liam said, "I like you, Maggie, but I don't think we—"

"You didn't come to me because you liked me, Liam. You came to me because you needed my help with something specific. Something that you don't trust your own lawyer to handle for you."

A knock started on the door to the office, and Maggie heard the voice of Harry Bates coming through from the other side.

"Do you mind getting that?" Liam asked.

"I do, actually. If I get up to go open that door, I'm leaving through it."

Liam slowly shook his head as he stood from the desk. He walked to the door and unlocked it for his business partner.

"Are you two about done?" Harry asked as he entered the room.

Maggie called over her shoulder. "Pretty much, Harry. Come on in and sit."

"No," Liam corrected. "We're still working through some details right now. Trying to come to an understanding."

The smell of smoke and strong cologne wafted by as Harry took a seat in the chair next to Maggie. He crossed one leg over the other and leaned back in his seat. Although his appearance in the room gave Maggie's consultee slash client a reason to continue to sidestep her inquiry, the large man did ease the tension for a moment.

Harry looked over at Liam. "Your son is here. I asked him to hang out in the garage."

"That would be Colt?" Maggie asked, before anything else could be said.

Liam nodded. "That's right. Like I told you during our first meeting, he's my only son."

Maggie remembered their first meeting well. In it, Liam explained to her that his son had been released early from prison at the request of local law enforcement. A claim she somewhat doubted at the time because Liam couldn't—*or chose not to,* she now believed—tell her the name of the individuals at the BCSO that brokered the early-release. Now, she felt certain she knew who was behind it.

"I'd like to talk to him," she said. "I can't offer you much more in the way of advice until I speak with him about—"

"Is this about the GBI agent's call today?" Harry asked. "I was just talking with Sean about it."

Maggie noticed as Liam shot a glance toward the accountant. She decided to play off of it, quickly.

"What do you think about the call?" Maggie asked, turning to look at Harry.

"Well, we know Colt didn't murder Trevor Meredith because of—"

"Harry," Liam interjected. "Let's hold off on all that right now."

The two men stared at one another for a moment. Harry appeared to understand.

"How about you go back out into the garage and check on Colt?"

"You're serious?" Harry asked.

"Does it look like I'm not?"

Harry seemed frustrated by the curt dismissal, but he did as was expected. Maggie and Liam both waited for the CPA to close the door to the office. A part of her wanted to leave, too.

"I'm going to give you sixty seconds to tell me why I'm here," Maggie said. "If you can't break it down for me in that time, I'll walk out that door and won't work with you anymore. Understood?"

Liam didn't respond, at first. His eyes stayed glued to a wall covered in picture frames. Most looked like photos from dirt-track races. They showed him holding cheap trophies or standing beside brightly numbered race cars. He looked a lot younger in the photos, happier even.

"Forty-five seconds."

Liam turned to look at her. "I need you to start working on a deal for me."

"Okay," she replied. "What kind of deal?"

Maggie liked that they were finally getting to it. Although they both knew what he was talking about, she wanted him to come out and say it.

"The kind that'll allow me to step away from all of this. Retire to somewhere quiet."

"That isn't in prison," she added.

"Right."

"Have you been charged with anything?"

"Not that I know of," he replied. "I expect I will be soon, though."

"Did your son tell you that?"

"He didn't have to. He wore a wire a few weeks ago on a deal I brokered up in Atlanta. He also recorded some conversations he and I had about moving some product. Another between him and some of the guys that work for me."

"Are the recordings solid?"

"Very."

Maggie considered the man's options. In her experience, the prosecution of large-scale drug cases depended heavily on witness cooperation from those on the inside of the conspiracy. Most of those witnesses, if not all of them, tended to be characters with colorful pasts, and records an inch thick. Their testimony didn't come voluntarily before the jury, either. It usually came as a condition to some deal with the State. Some *quid pro quo* that required full cooperation from the witness, in exchange for a sweetheart plea deal. Recordings always changed things, though. They made the prosecution's job ten times easier.

"That's not good," she said. "Not good at all."

Liam shrugged. "I guess we'll have to see, won't we?"

There it was again—that Taoist approach.

"How'd you find out about the recordings?" she asked.

"He and I discussed them before he handed them over." Liam's tone sounded even, almost business-like as he said this. "That was probably two weeks ago."

Throughout Maggie's career as a lawyer, she'd been able to spread her talents over several disciplines. It was in the area of criminal defense work, though, that she'd amassed the most experience. Never had she encountered someone who knowingly handed over recordings such as these. Not ones that would provide the foundation for a case of this magnitude. Never.

"You obviously know my next question, right?"

He nodded. "You want to know why?"

"Of course."

Liam stood from his chair and walked around to the other side of his desk. He took the seat beside her, the one occupied earlier by his CPA, and turned to face her.

"If I'm going to tell you, Maggie, I need to know that you're willing to help me."

"Who's leading the investigation?" Maggie asked.

Liam didn't even pause before responding. "Your husband."

"How long have you known this?"

Again, no delay. "Since the first time I met with you at your office."

"Dammit, Liam. You've been lying to me."

"I had to."

"Well, that makes this easy because I'm not going to be your lawyer on this," she replied. "It's that simple. I won't defend you on charges brought by my husband."

"What if you can convince him not to charge me?"

Maggie laughed as she started to stand from her chair. *Unbelievable,* she thought. The man faced the tip of an investigation that would most likely stretch across much of the Southeast. A process that might last decades if Liam chose to fight the cases brought by each individual state, not to mention the various agencies in the federal government's alphabet soup.

"What could you possibly give me to negotiate with, Liam?"

"It's not *what,*" Liam said. "It's *who.*"

"They'll get everyone else, Liam. They'll use them all to get to you because you're at the top. There's no one else to give when you sit in your seat. Don't you understand that?"

He looked up at her. His expression was one of patience, calm.

"Sit back down and give me sixty more seconds, Maggie. I'll give you the best name I have."

"I'm telling you, Liam, it doesn't matter."

"Sixty seconds."

Maggie considered him for a moment. No matter how hard she tried to leave behind the work of a criminal defense lawyer, it always seemed to show back up at her door, pawing at it to be fed one more time. Maggie took a seat.

"You're on the clock."

While Colt waited in the garage area of Hudson Auto, he thought about the unexpected meeting from that afternoon at DCS. He didn't mind leading Tim Dawson along with empty promises. He owed the lawman nothing and had no reservations when it came to the game that he and his father had in place. The addition of Cam Abrams to the equation changed things, though. She made Colt weigh his next steps and seriously consider whether he wanted to be part of Liam's plan.

Maybe she'll understand, he thought. *Maybe.*

Colt had his eyes on the eighties-something 911 when he heard the office door open on the other side of the garage. He turned and saw the vehicle's owner exiting quickly. Colt couldn't remember the last time he'd seen Harry frustrated, but the old CPA seemed to be bordering on angry as he took long strides across the shop's floor.

"I like the new project," Colt hollered over to Harry. "It's going to be a fun one to work on."

Harry didn't look back over his shoulder. "I'm heading out."

The throaty growl of an engine started somewhere outside of the garage. Colt took a few steps toward one of the shop's open bay doors and saw the black Dodge pull around to meet Harry. From where he stood, Colt could see the passenger-side window roll down. Harry leaned low enough to see through the open window and then began to speak with the driver. The sound of the radio playing inside the large garage, along with the *pat, pat, pat* of the Challenger, masked any bits of the conversation between Harry and Sean.

Colt called over as he walked right to the edge of the asphalt parking lot. "Where are you heading, Harry?"

The big man leaned against the Challenger's windowsill, still in discussion with the driver. The two looked to be arguing about something. Colt called out to the accountant again, but he couldn't tell if the old man heard him or not. He was about to call to him a third time when another truck pulled up alongside the Dodge. The same truck that Colt had encountered a few weeks ago at the river—right before being handed his welcome-home beating.

Harry looked over at the truck, then turned back to the shop. "Your daddy should be done with his meeting soon," he said, once he spotted Colt. "He'll come find you."

Colt stood there, watching as two men hopped from the bed of the truck. The pair seemed to recognize Colt as they walked around to the passenger side of the Challenger. As one of them climbed into the rear of the muscle car, the butt from a pistol poked out from the top of the man's jeans. Harry climbed into the passenger seat and slammed the door.

He looked back at the garage and seemed to realize that Colt still stood in the same place.

"What is it?" he asked.

"Tell Sean to give me a call tomorrow. I need to go over a few things with him."

Harry turned inside to say something to the driver, then leaned back out the window. "He says he doesn't have your number memorized."

"I'll give it—"

"Don't worry about it."

Colt started to step closer to the Dodge, but it pulled away and the pickup truck followed. Colt watched as the two vehicles disappeared around the corner of the building, the sounds from their engines fading into the night.

"Where are they all off to?" asked a familiar voice from over Colt's shoulder.

"Harry wouldn't tell me," Colt said as he turned to face his father. "I figured you had them out working a job tonight."

Liam stepped to the edge of the large bay door and looked out onto the dark parking lot. A waning crescent moon hung in the sky beside stars that shone brightly above them. Colt could see his father's breath as it spread into the crisp November night. They stood there, silent.

"Where'd you send them out to?" Colt asked.

Liam pulled a pack from his chest pocket, then cupped his hands around the stick as he lit it. He hacked a few times after the first drag, then went back to the silence.

Colt watched him carefully. "Dad?"

"I didn't send them anywhere tonight, son. I'm about done with that kind of work."

30

Tim Dawson sat on the front porch with a thick sweatshirt on. As he sipped from a warm coffee mug, he looked out onto the quiet neighborhood street. It was almost ten o'clock and Maggie still hadn't pulled into the drive. No text that she was working late. No call that she planned to meet friends for dinner. Nothing.

I don't want it to be like this, he thought, waiting there on the porch like an outside dog. *There must be a way to make it all work.*

A pair of headlights came around the corner at the end of the street, and Tim recognized Maggie's SUV as it passed under a distant streetlight. The Rover slowed once it neared the house, then turned into the driveway. From the porch, Tim could hear the muffled sound of a narrator's voice coming through the speakers inside the vehicle. An audiobook of some variety. He waited a long moment for the door to open, prepared for the worst.

She walked quietly toward the porch. A black laptop bag looped over one shoulder. A small load of groceries in the opposite hand. "What're you doing out here?" she asked.

Tim stood to meet her at the top of the porch's brick steps. "I was waiting on you," he said, reaching for the reusable grocery bag. "I—"

She clutched the bag. "I've got it."

He turned and reached out for the front door, opening it as she walked right by without another word. Tim followed her inside.

"I thought we might be able to talk, Mags."

She kept on through the living room. Toward the kitchen.

"I'm tired, Tim. Can't we just talk another night?"

"We haven't really talked the last couple of weeks. I don't want to keep doing this."

"Then don't."

She disappeared through the door that led to the kitchen. He heard the fridge open as she tucked away whatever cold items she carried in the bag. He waited in the living room, reminding himself not to get excited. *That wouldn't help.*

"You were out of yogurt," she said, once she started back through the room. "I'm going up for bed."

Tim noted the small act—*a good sign*—then held out a hand to her. "Can you wait a minute?"

"Everybody just wants a minute," she muttered as she brushed by him. "What can you possibly tell me in sixty seconds that'll—"

A loud ringtone started from the cell phone in Tim's pocket. He'd turned the volume up to the loudest setting earlier in the night, not wanting to miss a text or call from Maggie.

"Hold on," he said, glancing at the device's screen as he pulled it from his pocket. It was the sheriff, *of course.* "I actually need to take this call from—"

"Go ahead," she said. "I'll just see you in the morning."

"Come on, Mags, it'll take just a minute. I have to—"

"I really don't care," she said. "Take the call, Tim."

The phone continued to vibrate in Tim's hand as he watched his wife walk toward the stairs. He didn't plan to give up that easily.

"This is Tim," he said as he pressed the phone to his ear. "What's going on?"

Charlie Clay's voice filled the other end of the line. He sounded strained as he tried to talk over the sounds of sirens and other emergency activity in the background. Whatever was happening, the sheriff was already on-scene.

"We have a situation out on county line road, Tim. I need you to get out here."

Tim started to walk toward the kitchen as he listened. His shoes, keys, and wallet sat by the back door.

"I'm at home, Charlie, but I can probably be there in fifteen minutes. What's happening out—"

Another voice started in the background. Someone asking for the sheriff's attention. Clay asked Tim to hold.

"Of course, Sheriff."

As Tim started out of the kitchen, he turned the corner and bumped into the edge of Maggie's laptop bag, knocking it out of the chair. A stack of paperwork spilled out onto the ground, along with pens and a legal pad. Tim could still hear the muffled conversation between the sheriff and someone else on scene, so he knelt down to scoop up the mess. Phone still pressed to his ear, he glanced at the name on one of the documents in the pile.

"You there, Tim?" Charlie asked.

Tim held up one of the sheets of paper that'd poured out of Maggie's bag. He stared at it a moment longer, confused.

"Tim?"

"I'm here, Sheriff."

"Look, we need you out here—"

"You never told me what the situation was."

"It's a fire, Tim. I need everyone out here that I can get."

Tim tossed the paperwork onto the chair and left Maggie's bag on the floor. He didn't even bother with trying to put everything back in order. She could figure out how to reorganize Colt Hudson's casefile. Her new client—Liam Hudson—had to be paying her enough to at least do that.

"I'll be right out there, Sheriff."

Tim started for the door.

Cam Abrams stepped out of the shower. As she dried off, she noticed the faint sounds of sirens wailing in the distance. Unusual, because she and her roommate, Ashley, rented a modest home on the northwestern edge of Blake County. *Way out in the sticks.*

The couple that owned the home, a pair of empty nesters from Central Florida, had built the house five years earlier with plans to retire to South Georgia. The twenty-three-hundred-square-foot gem—a three-bedroom, three-bath farmhouse—sat on an acre and a half of land that backed up to a small pond mostly surrounded by tall pine trees and wiregrass.

When the owners built the house, they chose stylish fixtures, top-of-the-line appliances for the kitchen and laundry areas, and energy-efficient systems to make it all more cost effective. The home had it all, and the couple from Florida loved everything about the property. They just didn't love their neighbors—the Darden Family.

"The smell isn't always bad," the landlords had told her, when they first walked Cam and her best friend through the house. "If the wind kicks up, though, that's when the stench becomes unbearable. We just can't live here."

The owners hadn't been wrong about the pig smell down the road, but Cam and Ashley told the couple that they thought they could handle it—especially for the price.

Cam stepped to the bathroom mirror and started to apply her face cream. As she rubbed it over her face and neck, she could still hear sirens in the distance. *Maybe I left the television on*, she thought, wrapping the towel around her body. She knew no one else was in the house. Ashley worked late most weeknights as a PA in the hospital's emergency room and had started staying over more and more with her new boyfriend in town.

Cam knew she'd already locked up.

As she started toward the bedroom, the lights in the house flickered twice before going out for good. Cam stopped where she stood and listened for a moment, waiting for the automatic generator to kick on outside. Darkness filled the room around her, so she started feeling her way toward the bedside table. *Where did I leave it?* she thought, feeling around for her cell phone to use as a flashlight.

"Are you looking for your phone?" a voice asked from somewhere in the darkness. "I may know where you can find it."

Cam felt her body stiffen as the sound of the intruder's voice registered in her ears. The words seemed to slither toward her from some unknown place in the darkness. Still, she willed herself not to scream as she tried to visualize the layout of her dark bedroom. The voice came from the corner closest to the door to the hallway. Almost on the other side of the room. If he hadn't yet moved, that meant she had about twenty-five feet of separation from the man.

"Who's there?" she asked, trying to keep her voice from shaking. She eased toward the bedside table and reached down to feel for the top drawer. Inside it, she kept a Taurus revolver with five rounds chambered. Her hands shook as she slid the drawer open and felt inside it. *It's gone.*

"The Judge is over here," the voice said, sounding amused as he said it. "I don't see any reason we should be getting the court involved, right?"

Cam always kept her GBI-issued service weapon in a gun safe downstairs. The Judge—a small revolver that almost functioned as a short-barrel shotgun—stayed in her nightstand for home-defense purposes. Her intruder obviously knew this, or at least did a good job of searching her room while she showered.

"Yes—I was looking for the gun," she replied, trying again to keep her voice from shaking. "You should know that I'm an agent with the Georgia Bureau of Investigation. You don't want to do this."

A small light illuminated the opposite corner of the room. The young agent's eyes tried to start making an identification. All she could see was a tall man in a dark ski-mask, shaking his head back and forth. It terrified her.

"What do you want?" she asked.

"I want to know if you're planning to get the court involved."

Cam readjusted the towel around her as she felt it begin to slip. Beads of water dripped from her wet hair to the back of her neck. She stood there, confused, considering the question. She thought he'd only been talking about the revolver earlier. A firearm branded as *The Judge* because of its use as a self-defense tool for those that sat on the bench. She didn't realize he was actually asking about the judicial process itself.

"Are you?" the voice asked again.

The sirens continued from somewhere relatively close by. Cam turned for a moment to sneak a glance out the bedroom window. She almost did a doubletake as she noticed an orange glow hovering above the trees in the distance. A fire.

"I'm not an attorney," she said. "I don't argue things in front of a judge. I just give the prosecutors what they need and they—"

"Stop helping them, then," the man said. "Stop investigating the death of Trevor Meredith. Stop looking into the deaths of Karras and Moralis. Stop looking into—"

A loud sound rushed into the room—*Smash!*

The window to Cam's back exploded as an object of some sort came through it. She felt shards of glass pepper her bare shoulders. The sounds from outside intensified as they rushed through the now open window. She moved to the side just as a second object—another brick, maybe—flew through the window. This one hadn't been slowed by the glass barrier, so it soared through the opening and nailed the faceless intruder.

The man groaned. "Arrggh, my face! What the—"

Without thinking, Cam raced toward the window. Glass lay scattered all over the hardwood floor, and she felt it under her bare feet as she leapt high enough to dive through the hole in the window. She heard the intruder yelling profanities at her as she hit the grass on the ground outside of the first-floor bedroom. The towel fell from her body as she rolled over to push up from the ground. She grabbed it with one hand and scooped it up, then started sprinting toward the orange glow that illuminated the tree line.

She looked back toward the house, hoping the brick thrower wasn't already in pursuit. She saw no one, though. Only the headlights of two vehicles. A black car of some sort, shiny even in the darkness, and a pickup truck. She heard their deep exhaust systems grumble—*vroom, vroom*—as the vehicles seemed to be turning around to leave.

She didn't plan to wait and see, though. She turned back to face the woods. No one shouted behind her. No gunshots cracked through the night. Still, Cam strode it out with every bit of speed she could muster— eyes on the fire ahead.

Tim cut off from the county two-lane and followed a clay road that ran along the fence line of Kelley Hill Plantation. Ahead, he saw the lights from the vehicles of all those First Responders already on-scene. Firefighters. EMTs. Deputies from the BCSO. They all seemed to be huddled together for a briefing. Tim pulled his SUV as close as he could and hopped out.

A forester, along with a member from one of the volunteer fire departments, stood at the front of the group. They explained that the fire looked to be spreading quickly through the woods, and they expected it to jump the clay two-track, onto the farms owned by Mel Darden and his family.

"The river should contain the western edge of the fire," the forester said, almost yelling as he spoke, "but we expect it'll run east into the spray fields owned by Mr. Darden. I'm looking for spotters to line the road with radios to help us monitor the fire's progress while we work on the firebreaks."

Men and women in the group began raising their hands to volunteer for assignments. Tim did the same. A ranger with the DNR walked around and confirmed that everyone had radios, flashlights, and understood where to position themselves along the roadway.

"I see you made it," Charlie Clay said as he walked over to Tim. "I appreciate you coming out."

Tim nodded. He looked around at the faces of those dispersing toward their vehicles. The BCSO looked to be represented, but mostly by road deputies and others considered lower on the totem pole. "Of course, Sheriff."

He leaned in close to Tim. "Where are they having you set up?"

"A couple more miles up the road, almost at the intersection with Five Forks."

The sheriff unfolded a laminated map. He pulled a penlight from his chest pocket and shined it down on the geography of Blake County. The roads, rivers, and woods all looked to be depicted in detail. "Right up here?" the sheriff asked, pointing to a spot on the map.

"That's right."

"You see that clearing in the woods right there, Tim?"

Tim looked at where the sheriff pointed. "I see it."

"There's a nice little house back there in the woods. Probably the only piece of property along this stretch of road that isn't owned by Mel Darden or Senator Collins. Do you mind doing a quick welfare check on them?"

Tim started to tell the sheriff to go have one of his young guys check on the house, but he thought better of it. It wasn't too far from where he planned to set up and monitor the fire.

"I'll drop in on them," Tim said, "and make sure they know about the fire."

The sheriff smiled. "Good man."

31

Tim Dawson drove slowly along the clay road. He passed orange-vested spotters at half-mile increments, each standing with flashlights along the edges of Kelley Hill Plantation. As he peered out into the dark woods, he couldn't help but think of the people who would be pleased by the news of the fire raging across the private estate. And he couldn't help but think back to that night when the senator and his family scorched their legacy—along with that of the Ackers.

He rolled the windows down and smelled the scent of charred earth. He welcomed it, along with the chilly night air that poured into the vehicle. *It was cold on that night, too.* That night that he waited in the woods at the edge of the family cemetery. Their resting place that sat atop a hill that bore the name Parker's Knoll. Tim remembered that night well, but he and Maggie rarely ever spoke of it. He shared every detail with her the morning after it all went down, but that conversation stayed between them. Like a secret kept only for her. Like the one she still kept for her late client—Lee Acker.

It's the secrets, Tim thought as he followed the dark road ahead. He beat his fist on the steering wheel as he recognized the error in his ways. It wasn't her passion for defending the accused that held them back. No, for the two of them to work, they had to know each other's secrets. *All of them.*

A pair of vehicles approached from a side road and interrupted his thoughts. The lead vehicle, a black Dodge, came to the intersection with the clay road and turned north, heading away from Tim. A second vehicle, an older-model pickup, slowed little as it tore around the corner, following the same path. Tim eyed the plate on the second vehicle as it sped away. An Alabama tag: *HGK 685.*

"For just being out riding dirt roads," Tim murmured to himself, "you boys sure seem to be in a hurry."

He slowed to a stop at the rural intersection. He watched the lights of the vehicles until they disappeared into the night. That cop intuition tickled his belly, so he called the descriptions in on the two vehicles. He guessed the drivers would soon be in Clay County or somewhere over the state line. A fact that would've troubled him in his early days as a lawman, but one he'd come to accept in his return to the work of county policing.

Tim turned right at the intersection and started down the side road. The one that the sheriff told him crossed in front of the secluded country house in need of a welfare check. As he took his time along the graded road, an almost putrid smell began to fill the interior of the vehicle. *Pigs,* he thought, looking down for a moment to find the button for the power windows.

When he looked back up, his headlights centered on a woman standing in the middle of the narrow roadway. He jerked the wheel to the right, barely missing her as she leapt in the opposite direction. He bottomed out hard in the ditch, then ran up onto one of the pig farmer's wire fences. His heart pounded as he peered through the cracked windshield toward the front of his vehicle. No airbag obstructed his movement, so he unbuckled his seatbelt and turned around to look for the woman in the road.

I didn't hit her, did I?

Tim grabbed the flashlight from the passenger seat and quickly hopped out. As he trapsed through the ditch, he saw the woman struggling to get to her feet on the opposite edge of the roadway. She worked to wrap a bath towel around her otherwise naked body. With the back of her head still to him, he called out to the blonde-haired woman.

"Holy hell!" he shouted. "Are you okay?"

He tapped the button on the flashlight and turned it on her. He could see blood running down her upper back and her feet looked to be caked in mud. The towel around her had briars and stickers across it and showed tears at its edges.

"You're safe!" he yelled, realizing then that he needed to announce himself to the wild woman. "I'm Commander Tim Dawson. I'm with the Blake County Sheriff's Office and I won't hurt you—"

The woman looked back at him. With her face illuminated, he immediately recognized the young GBI agent. He couldn't believe his eyes.

"You almost ran me over," she said, breathing hard. "That would've sucked."

Tim stared at her. In the beam of the flashlight, he saw her smile.

"Are you okay?" he asked.

She nodded her head, still trying to catch her breath. "I think so."

"What the hell happened?"

She evaded the question with a laugh, then pointed over at his vehicle in the ditch. "Is that thing drivable?"

"I don't know," Tim said as he turned to look at the wreckage. "We can call in a ride, though. Preferably an ambulance for you."

She waved him off. "There's no time for that. We have work to do."

"First, you take care of you."

"Fine," she said, her voice clear and in control, "but we need to get a message to Colt tonight."

"I can make that happen."

"Tell him they already know we're working to expedite the investigation. That they tried to take me out, and that he may be next."

Tim thought of the truck and the Dodge that he'd seen pull out of the side road ten minutes earlier.

"Who came for you?" Tim asked.

"I don't know," she said, shaking her head. "I didn't get a good look at him."

"But you think it was Liam's crew?"

She nodded. "Call us in a ride. I'll tell you all about it."

While Tim waited for the EMTs to finish their evaluation of the young GBI agent, he admired the orange and red glow put off by the fires in the distance. Reports that'd been passed along from the foresters and fire-fighters suggested that the fire might continue to burn well into the next day or two. That although they felt they'd contained the worst of it, the unruly flames still burned hot throughout swaths of the private estate—a part of nature that no one could control.

Cam eased up beside him. She leaned over and bumped his shoulder with hers. "Quite the bonfire, isn't it?"

Tim looked over at her. She now wore a set of borrowed clothes. An oversized pair of sweatpants and a baggy T-shirt from The Sandbar. With her hair pulled up in a ponytail, Tim could see the dried blood that'd begun to crust around the cuts on her face and forehead. He stared at her a moment, finding it hard to believe that they'd resorted to fisticuffs less than twenty-four hours ago. He respected the mettle in the young agent and was pleased to see her in one piece.

He smiled. "It's fair to say that someone got a little carried away down by the river."

"People are saying it's the biggest fire in the history of Blake County. It's certainly the biggest one I've ever seen."

The consensus among those watching the fire burn from a distance was that the flames would have to eventually destroy most of the buildings on the property. They simply looked to be burning too bright and too long to not make it to the steps of the main house.

"I hate it for those trees more than anything," Tim finally said. "You don't find many places full of trees like that anymore. Not down here in the South."

"Old trees," Cam mused. "That's what came in number one on the list."

"I'm not worried about that mansion tucked back in there. The senator can build himself another one with the insurance proceeds."

Cam smiled. "We'll never get those trees back, though. Not in our lifetime."

"You can joke," Tim said, "but that senator has destroyed about every-thing around him. There'll be nothing left of that place when he's finished."

"Maybe so," she replied. "This sure is an eerie, somewhat beautiful way to go about it, though. It's like it doesn't matter how much you have, it all goes back to the earth, you know?"

Tim nodded. "Hopefully sooner rather than later for Collins."

Cam turned to him and looked as if she was about to say something, when a familiar SUV pulled up alongside the ambulance. The driver-side window lowered, and the sheriff waved them both over.

He spoke first to Cam. "It's good to see you on your feet, Agent Abrams."

"Thank you, Sheriff. I consider myself very lucky. It could've been much worse."

"Nonsense," he said. "That's good training and better instincts. I'm sure the folks at your office will feel the same way."

Tim could barely see past Charlie's stout frame, but he noticed that another man sat in the passenger seat of the vehicle.

"I hope so, Sheriff."

"Now that this fire is under better control," Charlie said, "I have a few extra deputies that I can send over to your house to secure the crime scene. Would you like to ride over with me?"

"Sure," she said, "give me one moment. I want to make sure the paramedics don't need anything else from me."

Cam stepped away to find one of the EMTs. Tim moved closer to the window on the sheriff's Yukon. He recognized the passenger seated in the vehicle. It was one of the new guys on the narcotics squad—Deacon Campbell.

"Commander," Deacon said as he turned toward Tim, "looks like we've got a little excitement tonight."

Tim noted the wide smile on the young drug agent's face. The swelling and bruising around his right eye, too. "Plenty of it to go around, Campbell."

He nodded. "That's the way I like it."

Tim shifted his eyes back to the sheriff. "Who's handling the investigation at Cam Abrams's place?"

"Right now, I'm going to have Deacon here handle it."

Tim considered his boss's face for a moment. They both knew that

Deacon Campbell recently came off the road, and only had about a month of work under his belt as an investigator. A narcotics investigator at that.

"Are you sure? There might be some heat on this one, Charlie."

Deacon leaned forward in his seat. He didn't say anything, but he seemed like he wanted Tim to know he was listening.

"Come on, Tim," Charlie scoffed. "This is probably just some sick puppy that singled this house out. Smashed his way inside and thought he might be able to recreate his prom night. Deacon here can handle that for us."

Deacon nodded. "I'll do everything by the book, Commander."

Tim started to say something, but Cam returned from the ambulance.

"Bad news," she said. "They're taking me over to Blake County General. Something about me possibly needing a CT."

Charlie smiled. "Health comes first."

"I'm sorry about this, Sheriff. I'll walk the scene with your investigator as soon as they release me."

Tim waited for Deacon to offer something from the passenger seat, but he stayed quiet. A sorry start to his work as the investigator on the case.

"You take care of you," Charlie said, sounding much like a politician. "We'll be able to catch these guys when you're ready."

She turned to Tim. "Let's get together tomorrow on—"

He interrupted her before she said a name. "Call me in the morning. We'll set up a time."

She nodded back to him. "Okay."

As Tim watched her walk back toward the rear of the ambulance, he heard the sheriff's Yukon shift into gear.

"We'll catch up later," Charlie said in Tim's direction. "You still owe me that update on your investigation."

"How about I just ride over to the house with you?" Tim said, turning to reach for the rear door on the Yukon. "We can talk while Campbell is taking a first look at everything."

Tim pulled at the handle. *Locked.*

"Not tonight, Tim. It's already late and I'm sure you're wanting to get home to that pretty wife of yours."

"I don't mind, Charlie."

"We'll talk later, Tim."

Sheriff Clay rolled the window up and started back down the dark little side road. Headed in the direction of that secluded country house that'd been in need of a welfare check. As Tim watched him drive away, he tried to ignore that tickle in his belly.

32

Tim Dawson woke up later than usual the next morning. He lay in the spare bedroom, still smelling of smoke and sweat from his work the night before. The mattress and sheets on the guest bed felt uncomfortable under his back. He missed his bed in the primary bedroom. He missed Maggie sleeping next to him.

As he sat up, he reached over to the bedside table to check the time on his cell phone—*8:48 a.m.* A string of notifications filled the screen. Unanswered calls. Texts. An update from ESPN. He opened the call log and saw a few missed calls from Cam Abrams. Two from Colt Hudson. Another from Charlie Clay. *No one leaves voicemails anymore.*

He checked the text messages. True to their generation, Colt and Cam communicated most effectively via text. He checked the young agent's messages first. Hers thanked him again for being there the night before, then informed him that they already had a meeting scheduled with Michael Hart at the district attorney's office. *Good news,* a message read, *ADA Hart says he already knows the basics. See you at ten.*

He smiled at the prosecutor's arrogant response to their meeting request. *Then why hasn't he gotten off his ass to do something?* Tim thought, recognizing that it was the kind of thing he and Maggie laughed about back when they worked together. When they spoke to one another.

Tim opened the message from Colt. It fit his young CI's typical style. Cryptic and free of any context. Tim stared at it for a long moment. *Bingo* was all it said. Tim swung his feet off the bed and got to his feet. He didn't need any other information from Colt. He knew what it meant for the young man. What it meant for the investigation.

It was now or never. The young CI had been made.

Tim and Cam sat on the same side of the conference table. Across from them, Michael Hart paged through a stack of documents that'd been requested from the BCSO and the GBI. From what Tim could see, he appeared to be holding Colt Hudson's original casefile. Portions of other files that'd been compiled in connection with the unsolved murders of Trevor Meredith, Andrew Karras, and Nick Moralis, sat nearby.

Hart positioned a well-used legal pad in front of him and stared across the table at Tim. "Commander, thank you for coming in."

"Of course, Mike. We appreciate you making time for this meeting."

"Especially on short notice," Cam added.

Hart seemed to force a smile as they first touched on the latest updates that surrounded the massive fire at Kelley Hill Plantation. They'd all heard that the fire was now under control, but most reports suggested that it'd left a path of destruction that encompassed much of the historic property. Now, in the wake of the destruction, theories as to the cause of the fire itself started to spread throughout town, almost as quickly as the flames themselves.

"It's such a shame," Hart said. "All that history gone in a matter of hours."

Tim didn't agree, but he offered no such comment on the matter. He just nodded along until they reached the end of the obligatory five minutes' worth of idle chit-chat.

"Now, Agent Abrams," Hart said, clearly switching gears, "I've been looking through these files that you mentioned to me this morning."

"Good," she said. "I appreciate you taking a look. I know there's a lot there to process on short notice."

"There certainly is."

"What do you think, Mr. Hart?"

"I was about to ask you the same thing," he replied, offering her a grin. "I'm interested to know where you see a connection between all of these cases."

Tim noticed that the prosecutor's legal pad appeared to be filled with notes, which made him wonder how early the man had begun his day in order to prepare for their meeting.

"It's simple," Cam said. "It all comes back to Liam Hudson."

Hart leaned back in his chair and appeared to consider the agent's succinct theory. He placed his hands together, steepling his fingers in a manner that Tim found to be somewhat pretentious. *Maybe that's what he's going for.*

"Are you familiar with Liam Hudson?" Cam asked.

"I'm familiar with the name. I know the man apparently has a history of coloring outside the lines when it comes to his businesses."

Tim snorted. "Liam Hudson's a drug dealer, Mike. A high-level one at that. You know this."

He smiled back at Tim. "I know this office tried to nail him down on something years ago. I've never had enough to take a serious run at the man."

"Well, now you will, Mike."

He arched an eyebrow, then tapped the large casefile in his lap. "I assume you're talking about some information that you've received from Mr. Hudson's sole heir—Colt."

"That's right. I've had him working an operation inside his father's crew."

"Really?"

"I have him willing to cooperate with you as a witness to drug trafficking, money laundering, murder—"

"Did you say murder?" Hart asked.

"That's right," Cam added, seeming eager to jump in with the boys. "I spoke with Colt yesterday after his meeting with parole, and he indicated to me that he's willing to assist on the theory that his father called in the hit on Meredith."

"Why would Liam Hudson do that?" Hart asked.

"It's a working theory," she said, "but there's certainly motive, opportunity, and—"

The prosecutor picked up a piece of paper from one of the stacks in front of him. "I have here a confidential memo—one sent over to me by Sheriff Clay—that says Investigator Meredith was under investigation himself, apparently for violation of his oath of office. They apparently have some evidence that he was receiving bribes in exchange for his willingness to obstruct certain investigations within the BCSO. His death is still a shame, of course."

Tim absorbed this. The same piece of information had been offered to him by Colt during a late-night meeting at the Soap-N-Suds. Tim hadn't been sure what to do with it, though. Sheriff Clay apparently already had the crooked lawman on his radar.

"Obstructing for who?" Tim asked.

"For *whom*, you mean?"

"Right," Tim said, mindful of his tone, while also wanting to call the man a prick. "Does the report say?"

"It does, but I'm considering our options before doing anything more with that information. Trevor Meredith served the people of this county for a long time, and I'm not sure any justice comes from us revisiting some of the poor decisions he made during his lifetime."

Tim understood the message behind the prosecutor's words. The people that Trevor Meredith may have wronged during his work as an investigator weren't important enough to his office. Not deserving of a full-on investigation into the practices of the BCSO.

Cam started in again. "Regardless, every angle is worth looking at when it comes to Liam Hudson, and I think we have to move fast."

"I'm a man of patience when it comes to my work, so I doubt this is something that can be rushed by—"

"I was attacked last night in my own home, Mr. Hart. Someone came to my house, broke in, and threatened my life because of this investigation. There is no time to be patient because they'll do it again, and again, and—"

"I understand," Hart replied, "so let's get your man in here. I'll talk to him as soon as possible."

"When does the next grand jury convene?" she asked. "He says he'll testify in exchange for protection."

Hart paused a long moment as he seemed to consider his response. The prosecutor sat across from members of law enforcement. A group he worked closely with on a weekly, if not daily basis. Still, Tim had been around lawyers long enough to know that when it came to certain legal matters, they considered *laypeople*—persons without the specialized training that Hart and his colleagues possessed—to be undeserving of certain information.

"Let's take this one step at a time."

Tim pressed him. "When do you have your grand jury coming in again, Mike?"

A grand jury is different than what most consider to be a jury. The jury that one is typically exposed to—the kind shown on television and depicted in movies—is a *petit* jury, or trial jury. It is a jury that is typically comprised of twelve individuals. In a felony case, those twelve strangers listen to the evidence offered by the prosecution—as well as the defense on occasion—and are then charged with the duty to return a verdict. If the State meets their burden at trial—proof beyond reasonable doubt—then the jury is authorized to return a verdict of *guilty*. If the State fails to meet that burden, the jurors must then return a verdict of *not guilty*.

The grand jury, however, is tasked with a wholly different responsibility within the process. It's larger—as the name would lead one to believe—and is comprised of sixteen to twenty-three individuals. Those individuals—all citizens with their civil liberties intact—are required to serve longer, and usually hear evidence on more than just one criminal case. They are impaneled for one term of court and meet regularly to hear evidence presented by the district attorney's office, members of law enforcement, and select witnesses. The grand jurors don't determine guilt or innocence like a trial jury might. They only determine whether there is probable cause to believe that a crime was committed, and that the accused committed it. If the grand jurors believe probable cause does in fact exist, then they return a written indictment outlining charges brought against the accused.

One key difference in the *petit* jury and grand jury is how those jurors receive the information they must consider. The twelve jurors at a trial receive all evidence in a setting that is open to the public. They deliberate in private, but the evidence they are charged with weighing is out in the open. It is the opposite for those that serve on a grand jury. They receive the evidence in secret. Away from the eyes of the public.

Hart smiled. "You know that information is kept private, Commander?"

"When did the DA's office decide to stop sharing that kind of information with their local agencies?"

"I didn't mean to insinuate that I wouldn't tell you," Hart said, again with his fingers steepled. He paused another moment before giving up the goods. "My grand jury will be here in a couple of days, Commander."

"That's enough time for us."

"So, you're asking me to consider presenting this Hudson matter to them?"

Tim nodded. "At least the drug trafficking side of things. I can't speak for—"

"I'll consider it," he said. "Get your boy in here this afternoon and I'll talk to him."

Tim thought about this offer as he stared back at Hart. *I'll have to make sure I can find him.*

"That'll work," Cam said. "We'll run him down and have him here by three o'clock."

Hart nodded over at Tim. "Does that work for you, Commander?"

"Of course, Mike. We'll see you then."

33

Maggie Reynolds and Ben Moss sat together in the law office's large conference room. Over a working lunch, they discussed the latest on the reporter's story. A two-part series was in the works. One being directed at the BCSO's handling of certain higher-profile investigations. Through a series of records requests sent by the local journalist, along with Maggie's snooping in her husband's home office, they'd been able to put together a few pieces of the puzzle—at least the pieces she needed.

Ben kicked it off. "Let's talk first about Colt Hudson."

"Okay," she said, "he's a good place to start. I'd say he's the lynchpin in all this."

"I have him on early release from Rutledge State Prison up in Columbus," Ben said as he worked through his angle out loud, "but the State Board of Pardons and Paroles doesn't have anything on him. They don't even have any record of him being granted clemency. It's as if someone deleted him out of the system."

Maggie chewed a bite of her salad, nodding along as she listened. The state's department of corrections didn't have a stellar record when it came to management of their prisons, but losing an inmate in the system just didn't happen anymore.

"I also stopped by our local DCS office, and they refused to give me any information about him. The lady at the desk told me point blank that she couldn't release any information about Colt Hudson. Then she threatened to have me arrested as I was kicked out of there."

"Did they at least confirm that he was being supervised by DCS?" Maggie asked.

"They didn't have to," he said with a smile. "Their reaction to the request told me everything I needed to know."

"True."

"Anyways, so we have this ex-con back in town. A guy that we know went away to prison after Trevor Meredith put him away."

Maggie kept her expression even. She needed to tread carefully when discussing anything that touched on an area of privileged information. She knew from conversations with her client that Colt had a reputation for being a stellar athlete and a capable fighter. Liam never dissuaded her from the idea that his son possessed a propensity for violence. She was banking on the reporter arriving at the same conclusion.

"Right," she said, "Colt comes back to town, and, within the week, everything goes down at Trevor's place."

Ben nodded back. "That's the coincidence that's worth looking into. One we know probably didn't happen."

Maggie wavered some on this point. She needed to push the reporter in the right direction, while also playing devil's advocate with him. "You have to admit, that's a pretty big leap. For all we know, the GBI could still be looking into arresting Colt for the murder."

"Of course," Ben replied, "and I'll make that point in my story, but the big question is *why* haven't they already done it, right?"

"Cop killers are typically some of the highest-priority cases," Maggie mused. "People won't like that this guy is out there, potentially getting a pass."

Ben smiled. "Which takes me to the next point in my article, and I plan to just come out and say it. Colt Hudson is receiving special treatment from the BCSO, so that they can draw his father into an investigation. So much special treatment, that they're willing to overlook the murder of one of their own to take down a man that doesn't have anything more than speeding tickets on his record."

"I want my husband's name kept out of this as long as you can. Is that clear?"

"Based on what we know, Maggie, I'm not sure that's possible—"

"Our deal was that you wouldn't name him in your story."

"And I'm not going to," he said. "I just think him getting wrapped up in all this is a foregone conclusion."

Maggie ignored the reporter's sentiment. "Again," she said, "I'd be careful with making that leap that the BCSO is just blindly protecting Colt. I know you want clicks on the news story and all but—"

"I'll be careful."

"Okay," she said, satisfied. "Next piece of the puzzle, then."

Ben nodded. "My parents finally convinced our family friend, the coroner, to go on record. He understands it's probably the right thing to do."

"And you're sure he's good with putting his name out there on this?"

"He's not planning to run for reelection next year, so he doesn't have any real concerns around losing the sheriff's support."

"Okay, he just has to know that his small-town political career will be over."

"He does, Maggie. He'll say what he needs to say."

Maggie considered the implications of it all. An hour after the body of John Deese was discovered in his cell at the county jail, the coroner arrived on-scene. From what Ben gathered in his discussions with the man, everything in the small cell pointed to a painfully obvious cause and manner of death. Suicides in jails and prisons—particularly by hanging—occurred more often than the average person realized. With increasingly harsh conditions, coupled with widespread mental health issues, self-harm prevention continued to be a difficult hurdle for those who managed correctional facilities, so it'd been logical for the coroner to initially conclude that the event was just another in-custody suicide.

Ben glanced at a set of notes before him to hit the details. "He says he'll go on the record and admit that he initially performed an external exam of the body, and that he could see ligature marks on the neck, which pretty much ruled out another cause of death as far as he was concerned."

"Okay."

"Well, as you probably remember, it was a Saturday morning when they called him out there to the county jail. He had a family event that day, so he didn't finish up all of his paperwork before he left."

"But his findings were made public that day, right?" Maggie asked.

Ben nodded. "That's right, he gave Sheriff Clay an unofficial report before he left, and Clay released it to the public."

"So, how many hours passed before he went back to finish up his report?"

"He told me it was at least eight hours later. He stopped in at the funeral home where arrangements had been made and spoke with the director as he was locking up. They chit-chatted about this and that as the coroner took one last look at the body. I guess it was then that he noticed all the swelling on Deese's face. He knew then that it all probably came from some form of blunt-force trauma."

"Pretty much somebody whooped his ass before he hung himself, right?"

"Right."

"Does the jail have any record of that?"

"Of course not, Maggie. What they do have a record of, though, is who else had been placed on that hallway the night of the death."

Maggie smiled. "Colt Hudson."

"That's right," Ben replied. "Colt had the cell right next to Deese, and no one else was on the hallway that night."

Maggie leaned back in her chair, trying to predict how this information would be received by the public. She knew Liam's son didn't murder John Deese, but that's what the young reporter needed to imply.

"Another coincidence," Maggie added, pushing the reporter along. "You know what they say about coincidences, right?"

The reporter shook his head as he took a bite of his sandwich.

"That it takes quite a bit of planning for God to make them fit just right."

"Well," Ben said as he wiped a napkin across his mouth, "it's a miracle I've even gotten this far in my research. I still don't know who attacked this guy, but our system isn't supposed to allow murder suspects to be killed in jail before their trial."

Maggie usually agreed. She didn't feel any sadness around how Deese met his demise, though, nor did she feel invested in locating the person who stepped into his cell that night to murder him. What mattered to her was that there *was* a killer, and that only meant one thing. *That somebody ordered it.*

"Be careful with this story, Ben."

"Why do you say that?" he asked with a chuckle.

"Take it from me. Powerful people can be difficult to deal with when you get on their bad side."

"You mean the sheriff?"

"Maybe."

Ben paused a moment as he seemed to weigh her ambiguous response. "Do you think the sheriff is involved, Maggie?"

Maggie didn't want the reporter to go down that rabbit hole. She felt that in her interactions with Charlie Clay, she'd been able to get a feel for what motivated him. She guessed that maybe the politics of being *Sheriff Clay* warped his judgment on certain policy matters. That at some point, he'd just decided poorly when presented with opportunity. The public wouldn't buy that, though, so it needed to stay out of the article.

"I don't think so," Maggie finally said, trying not to let her face give anything away. "I feel like that'd be a bit of a stretch."

"Agreed," Ben said. "Wouldn't that be something, though."

"It would."

The reporter glanced at his watch and announced that he needed to get back to work on finishing the story.

"When do you plan to release the article?" Maggie asked.

"I'll have it to my editor tonight," he said, bagging up the trash from his lunch. "If she gives me the green light, it could go live as soon as tomorrow."

Ben started for the door.

"Remember our agreement," she said. "Tim's name doesn't go in the story."

"I've got you, Maggie."

As Maggie watched the young journalist leave, she couldn't help but think about how Tim would react to the article, one that would attack the BCSO in the court of public opinion—a court that once ran Tim out of the GBI because of their relationship leading up to the trial of Lee Acker.

It's going to happen again, she thought, *and it'll be because of me—again.*

Maggie knew that her husband was a good man. That he was a good cop. But she knew that every lawman like Tim encountered decisions in a career that forced him to balance his own desire for power with that of the responsibility to do what was right.

Tim had arrived at that point in his own career. Although she didn't like what he was up to, she at least understood why he was doing it. He wanted to do something right for the people of Blake County. He wanted it so bad that he could almost taste it. So bad that he couldn't help but take the bait.

34

Tim Dawson pulled around back of the Blake County Courthouse and found a parking spot on the curb designated for law enforcement. As he walked toward the historic building's rear door, he spotted Colt Hudson leaning against one of the porticoed entryways. As Tim had suggested, his young CI wore a button-down and a pair of dress pants. The long hair had been chopped down and he now wore it brushed back into a style that made him look like a poor man's James Dean. He no longer looked like the wayward son, but instead appeared presentable for the *good people* of Blake County.

Tim smiled. "Looking good, Hollywood."

Colt ran a hand through his shortened mane. "I'm already feeling lighter."

The back door of the courthouse opened as two lawyers in suits exited the building. They seemed to be rehashing a hearing that'd just taken place inside. Tim recognized one of them, a local ham-and-egger who ran Blakeston's quickie-divorce mill.

"I saw your wife inside," the divorce lawyer said as he passed by Tim. "Always good to see her around a courtroom. It's been too long."

"You handle something against her today?"

"Nah," he said, shaking his head as he kept on walking. "I talked to her for a minute, but she was in a hurry. Had to run into Mike Hart's office for a meeting on something."

Tim considered the information as he watched the lawyer continue toward the street. Maggie wasn't actively taking criminal defense work—as far as he knew—so he wondered what brought her into the DA's office for a formal meeting.

"Your wife is a lawyer?" Colt asked.

The question pulled Tim from his thoughts. "Yeah, she has her own practice here in Blakeston. Her office is only another two blocks over. Right next to Stack's."

"I didn't realize that."

The revelation seemed like it surprised Colt—something that struck Tim as odd because most in the area knew him as Maggie Reynolds's husband. He'd been almost certain that Colt knew that, too.

"You ready to go inside?" Tim asked.

"As ready as I'll ever be."

Tim and Colt walked through the metal detectors at security, then started down the main hallway that ran the length of the first floor. Aside from providing the main stage for most of the county's court proceedings, the Blake County Courthouse also housed a number of government offices that were tied to the work of the county and its local court system.

As Tim passed the open doorways to each office, he casually glanced inside. He knew from the countless hours he'd spent waiting around courthouses, that most any information worth spreading passed through the people who worked in the offices like these. He also knew that it wasn't unusual to find local lawyers milling around those same clerks, mining information that they could leverage in their practices. Part of him hoped Maggie was doing just that today, but he couldn't find her anywhere.

They climbed the front stairs to the second floor of the courthouse, passing a few more of the local lawyers who were on their way down. The building's second floor was comprised of essentially four areas. The largest of the four was the main courtroom, followed by the district attorney's office, the judge's chambers, and a secure room used for jury deliberations. As Tim reached the top of the stairs, he noticed that the doors to the handsome wood-paneled courtroom sat propped open. Court looked to no longer be in session.

Tim stopped in front of the open doorway and stuck his head inside the courtroom. Two lawyers remained in the otherwise empty space. They talked quietly with one another on the opposite side of the room. From where Tim stood, he admired the profile of one of the lawyers—a serious-looking brunette who'd been his wife now for five years. She looked to be engaged in an intense discussion with the local prosecutor, Michael Hart. Neither seemed to notice him standing in the doorway to the courtroom— and at that moment, Tim wasn't sure he wanted them to—so he backed away to continue down the hallway. As he did, he almost bumped into his shadow.

"Is this where we're meeting?" Colt asked.

Tim shook his head. "No, the DA's office is just down this hall. Come on."

Colt lingered by the door for another moment, then did as he was told.

———

Tim pushed through the main door to the district attorney's office and offered a smile to the woman seated at the desk in reception. She seemed to recognize him, so Tim dispensed with the introductions.

"We're here for a three o'clock with Mr. Hart."

"Of course," she said as she reached for the phone on her desk. "I'll see if I can find him. I'm not sure I've seen him come back into the office from court yet."

"Did he have anything on the docket this afternoon?" Tim watched the woman's face closely after he asked this. "I glanced at the calendar, and it looked to be all civil matters today."

She paused only a moment, then pressed the phone to her ear to attempt to reach her boss, or at least cover for him. "I believe he had some-thing on the calendar, Commander Dawson. It's hard to keep up with everywhere he has to be on a daily basis."

"Well, when we passed the doorway to the courtroom earlier, it looked like they'd already adjourned for the day."

"Then, I'm sure he won't be too much longer," the receptionist replied as she returned the phone to its cradle. "How about I go ahead and set you gentlemen up in a conference room?"

"That'll be fine."

The receptionist stood and led the men to a hallway. On one side of the narrow corridor, Bankers Boxes had been stacked to about waist height. The receptionist took the lead, while Tim and Colt fell into a line to follow her toward their destination. As they passed the open doors to the other rooms in the DA's office suite, Tim found them to be equally overwhelmed with boxes and stacks of paper.

"Are you all getting ready to move or something?" Tim asked.

"We're bursting at the seams," the receptionist said as she opened the door to a small conference room. "I think the county approved another storage building for us, but we can't get in there until next week. What we really need in this office is another prosecutor or two to help shuttle these cases out of here."

"Another lawyer isn't usually the answer," Tim said with a smile. "I'd be careful what you ask for."

The receptionist offered them both a polite smile and assured them that Mr. Hart would soon be in, then she closed the door to the cramped little room. Tim took a seat in one of the four chairs that surrounded the room's circular table. He looked around the space. One small window. A fern that looked to be on life-support. More Bankers Boxes.

Colt stayed on his feet. "Is this guy going to record my statement today?"

"I doubt it," Tim replied. "I understand this is a meeting for the prose-cutor just to feel you out."

"What's that supposed to mean?"

"What's what supposed to mean?" Tim asked.

"You said you *understand this is a meeting* for—"

"It's a meeting for Hart to hear what you have to say," Tim said, trying to calm his young CI's nerves. He didn't want him to get spooked for some reason and lawyer up. "There's nothing to worry about, Colt. These kinds of things are routine."

The door to the room opened. It was the receptionist again, with Cam Abrams right behind her. She informed them all that Mr. Hart was running late, but that he would soon be with them. Cam took one of the three remaining seats at the table as the receptionist exited the room.

"Sorry I'm late."

"You didn't miss anything," Colt replied. "Our man is apparently running late, too."

Tim noticed that Cam smiled at Colt as she looked him over. The cleaner-cut Colt Hudson seemed to meet her approval. She looked like she was about to say something more when the room's door opened yet again. Michael Hart strode in with his jacket off, tie loose at the collar, and a legal pad in hand.

"I see everyone is here," he said. No apology for his tardiness. "So, I say we get started with this little interview."

"Mr. Hart," Colt said, before Tim could start in with the introductions. Colt walked a step in the prosecutor's direction and offered him a firm handshake. "I'm Colt Hudson. I appreciate you letting me come in to talk with you today."

Colt's polite, yet strong approach impressed Tim. He expected Hart's ego would like it as well.

Hart released Colt's hand, and they both took a seat. "And I appreciate you being here, Colt. I understand you've been doing some good work for Sheriff Clay and his team over at the Blake County Sheriff's Office."

"I've not met the sheriff yet, but I've spent plenty of time with Commander Dawson here. He has been shepherding me along and showing me the ropes."

Hart smiled over at Tim. "That's good."

"What do you want to know, Mr. Hart?"

Tim couldn't help but be a bit surprised with Colt's preparedness for the meeting. He seemed to be in better control than anyone else at the table.

"Let's start with what you can tell me about how your dad makes a living."

"How much time do we have?" Colt asked, grinning.

Hart chuckled and Tim could tell that the prosecutor liked the young CI.

"Start with what you yourself have personally witnessed and heard," Tim said, wanting to have some involvement. "You can walk it out from there to all of the things you're aware of based on second-hand knowledge."

"I like that idea," Hart said as he pulled a cell phone from his pocket. He placed it at the center of the small table. "Mind if I record this?"

Colt shot Tim a glance.

"You sure you need that?" Tim asked.

"I'm a slow note taker, Tim. I'd rather have it for—"

"It's fine," Colt said. "No big deal, Mr. Hart."

"Good," Hart said as he tapped once on the phone's screen. "Now, I have a group of grand jurors coming in tomorrow."

"Okay."

"Do you know what a grand jury is, Colt?"

Colt nodded. "The commander here explained it to me."

"He would know," Hart said with a smile. "He's testified in front of a number of them."

Tim considered telling the prosecutor that he'd never spoken with Colt about the grand jury process, but then figured it wasn't a problem. Maybe the young man misremembered a conversation they'd had about the next steps in the investigation.

"Now," Hart said, continuing with his preliminaries, "I need you to make sure you're telling me only the things you'd be comfortable telling a group of sixteen to twenty-three strangers. Do you understand?"

Colt nodded.

"All right," Hart said as he leaned a little over the cell phone, "this is Chief Assistant District Attorney Michael Hart, and I have sitting with me Mr. Colt Hudson, along with Commander Tim Dawson from the Blake County Sheriff's Office, and Cam Abrams from the Georgia Bureau of Investigation. My understanding is that Mr. Hudson is here pursuant to an agreement with Sheriff Clay's office. One that requires his serving as a confidential informant, in exchange for early release from a correctional facility managed by Georgia's Department of Corrections."

The prosecutor looked over at Colt for a long moment.

"Is everything I just said true?" Hart asked.

"It is."

"Then tell me what you know, Colt."

35

The next morning, Maggie Reynolds woke early to start her day. With the forced distance still between her and Tim, they'd not slept together in the same bed for almost two weeks. Maggie missed going to bed together. She missed that time at the end of the day when they read together or talked about the little things in their lives. When they snuggled up together to watch a movie she'd never finish. When they snuggled up together to not talk at all. She missed all of it, and all of her husband. *There was still work to be done, though.*

Maggie showered, did her make-up and hair, then chose one of her favorite outfits from the closet. She pulled on her pants—*one leg at a time, just like the next man,* her father always said—then slipped into a blouse, a Veronica Beard single-breasted jacket, and a pair of conservative black pumps. As she checked her reflection in the mirror, she looked over one more time at the empty side of the bed. *He'll come back.*

As she headed downstairs, she found Tim waiting for her in the living room. Over the last week or so, Maggie had made efforts to vary her morning routine. She'd leave the house earlier than usual on some days, then intentionally wait until after Tim left the house on others. All of this was in an effort to avoid an awkward confrontation. An effort to avoid a series of questions that she knew her husband might have for her about her work as of late. A series of answers she didn't want to hear if she asked him the same. This morning, however, it appeared she wouldn't get away without a few words between them.

"Good morning, Mags," he said from his seat on their leather couch. He had a mug in front of him, along with a boiled egg and a half-eaten piece of toast on the coffee table. "There's a fresh pot in the kitchen if you want some coffee."

"I'll grab a cup on my way into the office," she said, trying to sound rushed. "I need to get—"

"Give me just a moment, please."

He stood slowly from the couch and turned around to get a good angle on her. He looked to be dressed accordingly for the day. A starched white shirt and a red tie. His good suit jacket hanging over a nearby chair.

"Come on, Tim," she said with a sigh, "we don't have time to get into everything today. I have a—"

"You look great," he said, ignoring her response. "I've always liked that trial jacket on you. Are you arguing something in court today?"

She fiddled with a button on her cuff for a moment. He knew her so well.

"I need to go."

"I just haven't seen much of you lately, Mags, and I wanted you to know that—well, I miss you."

She tried to tamp down the corners of her mouth as they edged toward a smile. Knowing how good her handsome investigator was, she figured he'd noticed. *Only another day.*

"I know," she finally replied. "I miss you, too."

"Then, stay for just a few minutes."

"Not today, Tim. I told you I need to get going."

Tim nodded slowly as he looked down at the floor for a moment. He seemed to be considering a response as his cell phone dinged from somewhere nearby. Maggie used the brief break in their interaction to collect her laptop bag from a chair in the living room. She started toward the door. As Maggie turned back to look at him, she saw him staring down at something on his phone. His eyes moved back and forth. Reading.

"I'll see you later," she said. "Have a good—"

"It looks like there's some article in the local paper today about the BCSO," he murmured. "Something about Sheriff Clay's handling of high-profile investigations at his office."

Maggie's heart pounded in her chest. She'd hoped to make it out the door before the article started spreading around town.

"I'll have to read it," she said as she opened the door. "Have a good day today."

He looked up at her from his phone. She could see hurt in his eyes. A message to her that he'd seen the documents the other night in her laptop bag. The ones that had to do with *his* investigation. *His* confidential informant.

"Sure," he said, looking away from her. "I'll just see you later then."

She could see it in him at that moment. She knew that he knew.

"I love you, Tim."

He didn't say anything as she walked out the door. Maggie didn't look back, either. She didn't want to.

36

The legal advisor to the grand jury is the district attorney. Lawmakers recognized long ago that for criminal indictments to be put together fairly, the entire citizenry needed to be involved in the process. The average citizen, however, was unfamiliar with the countless technicalities that existed in the law. For that reason, grand jurors must rely on the prosecutors for answers to any questions they have about the law. They are not permitted to, as a whole, employ their own attorney to advise them on certain points of the law. That privilege is reserved for the DA's office.

Michael Hart stood at the front of the large courtroom on the second floor of the Blake County Courthouse. In the gallery before him sat twenty-three people. All citizens of the United States of America. All residents of Blake County for at least the last six months. All over the age of eighteen and considered to be intelligent, experienced, and upright citizens. The men and women of the grand jury knew the prosecutor, as they'd met with him before to hear the presentation of a variety of criminal cases. Most of those cases, however, were run-of-the-mill felony offenses. Aggravated assault, theft by taking, possession or distribution of varying kinds of controlled substances, family violence, felons in possession of firearms, and the occasional felony murder case. The list went on, and they knew the drill.

"Good morning, Mr. Hart," said a gentleman by the name of Vernon Kilgore. Mr. Kilgore sat in the front row. A man with seventy-three years on earth, he could have asked to be excused from his civic duty to serve as a grand juror. However, as was the case with many retired individuals that found themselves with a summons for jury service, Mr. Kilgore wanted to serve, as did his wife who wanted him out of the house. "I saw we had ourselves a little crowd out there in the hallway."

Hart smiled at the man. "We have a rather large list of witnesses for you today."

"That's good to hear," Kilgore replied. "I look forward to it."

Hart glanced around at the faces of the other grand jurors. In the group, he had about an even split as far as individuals who straddled the age of forty-five. More women sat on the jury, but the racial diversity suffered as there were no Black residents on the panel, and only two Latinos, both of whom were men. He had several professionals with demanding schedules, one farmer, a stay-at-home parent, several office workers, and a few skilled laborers who grumbled each time the grand jury convened because they were losing valuable time. Still, as a whole, Hart felt comfortable with this group and expected they would weigh the day's information with interest.

No judge sat on the bench at the front of the courtroom. No members of the media or the public sat elsewhere in the gallery. Only a court reporter and an assistant from the DA's staff sat at one of the tables typically assigned to counsel. It was Michael Hart—and Michael Hart alone—who stood at the center of attention. *For now.*

A woman named Angela raised her hand from the second row. Her married name was Dalton, but she and her husband had been separated for almost two years now. She'd asked the prosecutor to use her maiden name, Carter, when he referred to her.

"Ms. Carter?"

"Have you read that article from the *Blake County News* this morning?" she asked.

Hart nodded at the mention of *that article*. He'd expected some discussion on this issue today, so he was happy to see someone get it out of the way.

"Yes, ma'am, I read it while I ate breakfast this morning."

"Is that something that we should be looking into?"

Hart smiled at the question. Angela Carter worked at the local Toyota dealership as a bookkeeper. She graduated high school at five months pregnant and had another two kids not long after that. Raising babies with a dead-beat husband made it hard for her to jump into a technical program or junior college to pursue additional education. The woman was sharp, though. Probably the smartest in the group, even though several college graduates sat among them.

"We can certainly talk about that," he said, "but like I told you on the first day we all met, I can't make you to do anything."

Grand juries can consider more than just the cases and evidence that the prosecutors ask them to. They play a unique role in the administration of justice. They can investigate matters themselves. Subpoena witnesses and documents. Seek approval to take on special investigations of departments and offices that make up county government. They can do all of this, and more, because they have the responsibility to protect the public from those who commit crimes, while also safeguarding their fellow citizens from those who make up the branches of their local government.

"I don't know if we necessarily need to today," Angela said as she looked around at her fellow grand jurors, "but I might be interested in hearing more about Sheriff Clay's office in the future."

Words of approval could be heard as several heads nodded in the gallery.

"I'll see what I can do," Hart said. "Now, any other questions before we get started this morning?"

Colt Hudson waited in the hallway outside of the courtroom. Several deputies from the BCSO, investigators from the BPD and GBI, and a few other suits huddled in small groups along the hallway. He'd noticed a few hard eyes on him as members of local law enforcement began to put two and two together. The article that morning targeted some of their own, something Colt imagined they didn't take too kindly to.

Colt kept his eyes down until he heard the door open to the courtroom. The prosecutor stepped out and looked up and down the hallway.

"Has anyone seen Special Agent Abrams?" Hart asked.

"I'm right here!" a voice called from somewhere in the stairwell.

Colt couldn't see around the corner at the top of the stairs, but he soon saw Cam Abrams's face appear. She held a large binder under one arm and had a bag slung over the other. She nodded to a few of the other cops she knew as she looked up and down the hallway. She didn't so much as smile at Colt.

"You're up," Hart said. "You ready to go?"

"Let's do it."

Colt watched her and Hart reenter the courtroom. Neither acknowledged him as they did.

Cam Abrams looked out onto the group of grand jurors from the courtroom's witness stand. She pulled the microphone to her mouth as she introduced herself. In her short time with the GBI, she'd testified in front of several grand juries, mostly in Blake County. She knew from experience that only the prosecutor and grand jurors would be allowed to ask her questions about her testimony.

It was an easy task, though, when compared with testifying in a full-on court proceeding. The grand jurors didn't need to be shielded from hearsay, rumors, and other kinds of testimony that wasn't usually allowed in front of a jury at trial. It was all fair game. And best of all—there wasn't a criminal defense attorney in the room that she had to worry about cross-examining her. In fact, the accused, along with their defense lawyer, didn't get to appear in front of the grand jury at all. That's just how it worked, *usually*.

"Agent Abrams, tell us what you know about Colt Hudson."

Cam paused a moment before beginning her response. Although her testimony that morning was being offered under oath, as well as being transcribed, it didn't come with the pressure—nor require the preparation—that came with testifying in open court. She collected her thoughts, then pressed forward.

"Colt Hudson is a recently released convicted felon, still serving a portion of his sentence for trafficking in methamphetamine," she said. "He went away to prison in 2018 after being involved in a fatal car wreck some two years earlier. A wreck that led to the discovery of a large quantity of crystal meth in his vehicle."

"Were you involved in that investigation that resulted in him going to prison?"

She grimaced as she shook her head. "Not as an official member of law enforcement. My older sister lost her life in that wreck, though, so I kept up closely with the progress in his case. I was there at every stage of his prosecution and testified at his sentencing after he pleaded guilty."

"From the standpoint of the victim, right?"

"Of course, Mr. Hart."

"Now, when did you become reacquainted with Colt?"

"I first saw him in the county jail about a month and a half ago. I was called in on a Saturday morning to handle an investigation into the death of an inmate."

"Was he involved in that incident?" Hart asked, seemingly trying to let the question hang in the air a moment.

"No," she said as she scanned a few faces on the front row. An older white man seated closest to the aisle looked to be hanging on her every word. "The incident was ruled a suicide. The decedent—a man by the name of John Deese—had been placed in a holding cell, alone."

"What about—"

"Colt Hudson had been placed in the holding cell next to his. Alone as well."

"Did you lead the investigation into the incident?"

Cam nodded as she described the entire scene at the county jail. The hallway and points of entry. The size of the individual holding cells and keys required to access them from the outside. Her opinion that there was no reason to suspect Colt's involvement.

"Did he provide you with any information about suspicious activity that night at the jail?"

Cam shook her head. "He told me he couldn't recall anything suspicious. After a discussion with the coroner and Sheriff Clay, I didn't see any reason to look any deeper into the matter."

A woman seated in the second row of the gallery raised her hand.

"Mr. Hart?" she asked. "Can I ask the agent a question?"

"Sure," the prosecutor said. He appeared somewhat perturbed by the interruption, though. "Do you want to wait until the end?"

"I think it's best we ask it now."

"Okay," he said, turning back to Cam. "Can you hear her just fine?"

Cam nodded as she looked over at the woman. "Yes, ma'am?"

"Have you read the recent article that Ben Moss wrote for the *Blake County News*?" she asked. "The one about Sheriff Clay and some problems with his office?"

Cam smiled at the woman. She'd read the article that morning and wasn't surprised that it was quickly causing a stir in the small community.

"I read it."

"Did you see that the coroner suspected foul play to be involved in Mr. Deese's death?"

Cam paused again to consider her words. "While I think that's what the reporter meant to imply, I don't believe that's exactly what the article said. I did read that the coroner apparently observed bruising on Mr. Deese, though, so I took the article to mean that this led the coroner to have some concerns about the matter. Specifically, whether Mr. Deese had been beaten prior to taking his own life."

"I'm sure you got a good look at the man," the woman said. "Didn't you see any of that same bruising?"

Cam remembered more so being enraged by the unexpected presence of Colt that morning. To a point that it seemed to cloud her memory regarding the details of the scene.

"No, ma'am. I don't recall seeing that kind of bruising on the man."

"Was there any video footage from the hallway that night?"

"Again, we felt confident at the time that it was a suicide and nothing suspicious."

"Does that mean you didn't look for any video?"

Cam looked over at the court reporter who sat typing away. She reminded herself that a skilled criminal defense attorney might do worse to her in a cross-examination, but the agent guessed it wouldn't be much worse.

"No, ma'am."

The woman shrugged to her fellow grand jurors and returned to her seat.

Hart resumed his position of control in the questioning.

"Let's talk now about your investigation into the murder of Trevor Meredith."

Colt sat in his same spot in the hallway outside the courtroom when Cam exited from inside it. She looked frustrated as she stepped into the now quiet corridor. Several of the officers and deputies who'd shown up earlier had been excused by one of the personnel from the DA's office. He'd over-heard the woman as she informed the lawmen that the office's presentation of evidence was only going to be focused on one case that day. *His father's case.*

Colt called over to Cam. "How'd it go?"

She let out a sigh. "It went."

"You were in there a long time," Colt said, trying to get a little more information. "They must've really drilled you about my father."

She shook her head. "Not really."

"Well, what happened in there?"

"Look, Colt, I'm not really supposed to get into all of that with you. It's kind of how they like these things to be done around here."

"Sure, I understand."

She kept her eyes on him for a long moment. It was a look he'd not seen in a long time.

"Have you seen Tim?" she asked.

"He was here earlier, but I've not seen him in about thirty minutes. He asked me to wait here."

"Did he say when he'd be back?"

Colt figured she didn't want to share her testimony with him, but it sure seemed like she wanted to share something with Tim.

"He didn't say. You need me to tell him something?"

She glanced up and down the empty hallway. No one looked to be within earshot. Still, she took a step closer to him before she said anything.

"Tell him he might want to talk to someone about that article in the paper before he goes in front of the grand jury."

37

Sheriff Charlie Clay chose not to sit in the witness stand at the front of the courtroom. Instead, he pulled a chair to the center aisle that cut down the middle of the large room. The move struck Michael Hart as odd, because the sheriff had always stepped up to the witness stand during their past presentations. Still, regardless as to where the man positioned himself in the room, he always made for an impressive witness—a strong, good-looking lawman one would expect to be tasked with protecting the good people of Blake County.

The prosecutor walked to a seat in the gallery—one on the aisle—so that he could clearly see the witness. Hart understood the sheriff's strategy was to make his own testimony feel more intimate, and the questions from the assistant district attorney seem misplaced.

"Thank you for being here, Sheriff."

Clay smiled at a few of the faces around him, before turning his attention to the prosecutor. "It's part of the job, Mr. Hart."

Hart cleared his throat as he looked back down at the notes on his legal pad. The night before—a little after nine o'clock—Hart called the sheriff to ask that he be in court for the presentation before the grand jury. The big man initially seemed frustrated by the idea, but soon came around once he understood that the prosecutor intended to use Colt Hudson as an unsuspecting witness. A plan that the sheriff seemed more than willing to help execute.

"If you will, Sheriff Clay, tell us what you know about Colt Hudson."

"Well, Mr. Hart, I didn't know a whole lot about the young man until rather recently. A new investigator of mine, Tim Dawson, took over my narcotics squad a couple of months ago, and turned me onto the idea of working with him. Tim planned to use young Hudson as a CI, mainly to eavesdrop on the kid's father, Liam Hudson, and determine whether there was anything illegal going on in the family's auto repair business."

"Is Tim Dawson still working for you?"

Clay nodded slowly. "He is for now, but I've come to learn quite a bit about the way my man has been handling our informants. I'll need to reevaluate his performance next week and determine whether a change in leadership is needed."

Hart felt strange just sitting in one of the seats in the gallery, so he stood to be able to pace back and forth in the center aisle. The sheriff looked comfortable in his chair. One leg crossed over the other.

"We spoke with Special Agent Cam Abrams earlier this morning about a death that occurred in your jail on—"

"Yes," the sheriff said, "I don't have many deaths under my watch, so I know you must be talking about Mr. Deese's suicide."

"That's correct, Sheriff. Now, have you looked at—"

"The man's death was originally ruled a clear-cut case of suicide, but it was recently brought to my attention that this opinion was a bit, let's say, premature. I understand our local coroner found some suspicious bruising that appeared to have happened before the man's death. For some reason, our good coroner neglected to inform me of this situation. He thought it best to instead provide that pertinent information to a local reporter."

Hart smiled along with a few of the other grand jurors in the gallery. The prosecutor hoped that they were all getting the impression that their sheriff wasn't one to take responsibility for the mistakes in his office.

"You're talking about the article written by Mr. Moss?"

"That'd be the one," the sheriff said as he nodded. "A story that one of our local hacks decided to write about my office. I hope to meet with the editor over at the paper soon."

"Right, but—"

"I'll also add that this story was done without asking me first whether any of the *reporting* was in fact true. I mean, what's journalism coming to in this country, am I right?"

Hart could see a few grand jurors nodding along. He recognized the play as one out of the modern politician's handbook.

"Let's stick with what you know, Sheriff. I'm not sure—"

"I'll just make this easy for you, Mr. Hart. I've read that article and I can tell you what the connection is between all of Mr. Ben Moss's conspiracy theories."

"Okay, what would that connection be?" Hart asked, trying not to appear frustrated by his witness's frequent interruptions.

"Colt Hudson, of course."

Hart offered a strategic pause as he looked down at his notes. He hoped the sheriff might continue with his theory. Which he did.

"This young man came into my jail the day John Deese was killed and—"

"Sheriff," Hart said as he looked back up from his pad, "I'm sorry to interrupt you, but did you just mean to share your opinion that John Deese was murdered?"

Clay leaned forward and placed his elbows on his knees. He had the attention of all in the room.

"You folks know everything that's said in here is supposed to remain secret, right?"

Most nodded their heads.

"Good," he said, nodding back at them. "See, I've started an investigation of my own into this suspicious suicide, and I'm not convinced it's all what it appears to be."

"What do you mean, Sheriff?" Vernon Kilgore asked from his seat in the front row.

"Well, I come to find out that my cameras in that part of the jail somehow quit working the night Mr. Deese lost his life. A bit of information that somehow didn't make it into that GBI agent's casefile."

The older juror crossed his arms as he took in the new information.

Hart considered the body language of the other men and women in the gallery as they seemed to weigh the information as well.

"What else has your investigation revealed?" Kilgore asked.

The sheriff smiled. "My team hasn't had a lot of time to work this up yet, but I've found some other interesting issues that've caused me some concern."

"Like what?"

"Well, for one, the doors in my jail are all wired with sensors on them to help keep the facility secure. When a door opens, we know about it. When they quit working, we know about it."

Kilgore and the other jurors nodded along, listening. Eager for more.

"I've asked my team to go back and look at the logs from the night of this tragic incident. It looks like Mr. Deese's cell door was opened while our cameras were down. Someone had to of opened it from the outside."

"You're certain of that, Sheriff?" Hart asked.

"My cells don't open from the inside," the sheriff said as he winked back at the prosecutor, "it's sort of a security measure of mine."

The jurors chuckled at the lawman's humor. Hart didn't mind, though. He wanted to continue to narrow the witness's testimony, especially about his team's *investigation.*

"So, your suspect in this killing is Colt Hudson?"

"Who else would it be, Mr. Hart?" the sheriff asked this without leaving any room for an answer. "I mean, this guy comes back to town, and I've got two bodies within a matter of days. The first is an inmate a door over from Hudson's cell, and the next is one of my investigators. The same one that sent the young man off to prison."

Hart let the statements hang around for a moment.

"Wasn't your key suspect locked away?"

The sheriff took in a deep breath. "Look, Mr. Hart, I'm not happy about the direction in which my investigation is headed. There are more problems my team is going to need to grapple with."

Hart raised an eyebrow. "As in?"

"My logs show that another cell door opened while the cameras were down. The door right beside Mr. Deese's cell—the one occupied by Hudson."

Hart scratched a note on his legal pad. He noticed a few of the jurors had eyes on him as they waited for the prosecutor to help further unpack the issues.

"That sounds like an internal investigation that—"

"And on top of that, Mr. Hart, the GBI agent that investigated this incident at the jail, she was assaulted in her own home a couple of nights ago. It's a miracle the girl made it out alive."

"This is Agent Abrams you're talking about?"

Clay nodded. "If we hadn't been out in that part of the county working the fire at Kelley Hill Plantation, she might not have been here to testify this morning."

A voice spoke up from the end of one of the pews. It was one that hadn't ever engaged with a witness in their past presentations. It was the deep voice of a local hog farmer, Mel Darden.

"I can't thank you enough, Sheriff, for having your people out there that night."

"Of course, Mr. Darden," the sheriff replied. "I understand we kept that fire off your property."

"That you did, and I couldn't believe you and your man were already out there when we called it in."

Hart noticed the expression change on the sheriff's face. It quickly went away as he smiled back at the hog farmer.

"You fine people elected me, so I figure I need to always be working."

"Well, I do appreciate you."

Hart wanted to get back on track. He waited a moment for the exchange between the wealthy hog farmer and the sheriff to conclude, then pivoted back to the task at hand.

"We know you're a busy man, Sheriff Clay, but can you tell us what else you know about Agent Abrams's assault?"

"Sure," Clay said as he leaned forward again onto his knees. "Now, mind you, I'm still piecing together my investigation."

"Of course."

"My gut tells me that I can help you prove who assaulted that young agent, though. Maybe even who started the fire out at Kelley Hill Plantation."

"Do you believe it was Colt Hudson?"

"Maybe," the sheriff said as he scanned the faces before him, "but you all have to know that I rely on my investigators to help prevent crime in this county. If they don't tell me what I need to know, I can't help with catching the bad guys."

Kilgore offered his understanding. "We know, Sheriff."

Hart pressed on. "Then what is it you do know about Agent Abrams's assault?"

The sheriff paused another long moment. All eyes in the room were on him. Hart knew that the sheriff had to decide what direction he needed to go with his narrative. If the information from Hudson was solid, the sheriff knew he needed to be playing defense.

"Well, first off, you'll all need to know who it was that found her in the woods that night."

38

Michael Hart arranged for lunch to be delivered for his grand jury. He'd expected the move to receive pushback from the group, as they all had jobs, families, and other obligations that required their attention throughout the rest of the afternoon. He didn't hear a single complaint, though. *Another good sign.* One that meant they were at least intrigued by what they'd heard that morning.

"I'm stepping into the hallway," Hart announced from his post at the front of the room. "I'm trying to be mindful of the time that we have today, so I'll bring our next witness in to offer testimony in about twenty minutes."

Sandwich wrappers could be heard rustling as the jurors unpacked their lunches from a local deli. Hart wanted them fed, caffeinated, and back to work by twelve thirty. Angela Carter, the group's foreperson, confirmed the schedule and Hart made his way toward the door. As he stepped out of the room, Hart heard the beginnings of a discussion about the morning's witnesses.

"Mike, what's the deal in there?" a voice asked as Hart stepped into the hallway. "We need to talk strategy for this afternoon."

The prosecutor recognized the frustration in Tim Dawson's tone. He needed to tread lightly.

"I'm out here in the dark," the commander continued. "I need an update on how things are going with the case against Hudson."

"Have you eaten, Tim?"

Dawson shook his head. "I'm good, Mike. I've been out here for over three and a half hours now. I need to know—"

"It's going to be a long afternoon, so go grab something to eat. The food will help calm your nerves."

The two men were the only ones standing in the hallway that fronted the courtroom. Hart turned his back to the investigator and started toward the district attorney's office that sat just down the hall.

"My nerves?"

Hart kept on walking. He didn't want a confrontation. "I'm not planning to bring you into the room until late this afternoon. Get something in your stomach."

Tim called out once more. This time loud enough for his voice to carry down the long second-floor hallway. "Mike, when the hell is Colt going to testify?"

Hart didn't break stride as he turned the corner at the end of the hallway. He heard a few choice curse words directed at his back. All warranted, given the tactics being employed. Hart didn't have a choice, though. Hunting big game required patience.

As Hart stepped inside the door to the DA's office, he smiled at his receptionist and reminded her that no one should be allowed in to see him. He warned her that a rather agitated investigator might be walking through the door within the minute. She promised to handle it and Hart continued on toward his personal office.

"They're already waiting for you in your office," the receptionist said. "Do you all need anything?"

"I just need you to help me keep this quiet. At least for another few hours."

Hart reached the door to his office and stopped to listen. He heard two muffled voices in conversation with one another. Hart took a deep breath, then stepped inside.

"Good afternoon to you both," he said as he came through the door. "I hope you've been comfortable waiting here in my office."

Maggie Reynolds spoke first as she stood from her chair. She looked sharp in her blazer and sculpted pants.

"I've never been all that comfortable in these offices, Mike."

"This work isn't about the comfort," Hart said as they shook hands. "Not for me, and certainly not for lowly criminal defense lawyers slinking through our doors in search of deals for their clients."

Maggie smiled. "You need to work on your sales pitch for future recruits."

Hart shifted his eyes from Maggie to the man still seated in the chair next to hers. Liam Hudson appeared indifferent as he stared back at the prosecutor.

"Mr. Hudson," Hart said as he extended a hand, "I appreciate you agreeing to be here."

He looked over at his lawyer before making a move to stand. Before making a move of any kind. Maggie nodded her approval and Liam rose to shake the prosecutor's hand.

"It sounds like we'll be seeing a lot more of each other."

Liam didn't respond. He simply returned to his seat and recrossed his legs. One ankle resting on top of his opposite knee. The smug expression on the man's face told the prosecutor everything he needed to know about the level of trust that existed between them.

"Have you heard from the AG?" Maggie asked.

Hart turned his attention back to his soon-to-be comrade. "I heard from him this morning."

"And?"

Hart took another deep breath in before he responded. As a career prosecutor, he didn't focus so much on the names of the people that worked on his side of the aisle. He just wanted to work with lawyers and investigators that sought justice in all that they did.

"He told me that if you two can deliver, Maggie, you can prosecute the case. It's yours if you want it. I've consulted with the Prosecuting Attorneys Council as well. They're also in agreement with the decision."

It pained Hart to admit it—and he only ever would to himself—but Maggie Reynolds proved to be better suited for the big stage than he was.

They'd squared off twice against one another, and Maggie walked away both times without a guilty client.

"We can deliver, Mike."

The prosecutor took a seat on his side of the desk. He certainly hoped so.

"It can all be official today if you're ready to take the reins."

"I'm ready."

Hart nodded as he leaned back in his chair. This was all new to him and he expected most prosecutors across the state would feel the same. A special prosecutor wasn't something unheard of in legal circles across the state, but the appointment of a veteran criminal defense attorney to that position certainly was.

Liam directed his first words at Hart. "What happens next?"

"The AG will appoint Maggie as a special prosecutor," Hart said, slowly. "She'll be allowed to act on behalf of the State for the time being. I'll serve as her co-counsel if she'll have—"

"Which means I'll then be granted immunity from prosecution?" Liam interrupted.

Hart looked over at Maggie for a moment, then rested his eyes back on the long-time drug dealer.

"Are you ready to go this afternoon?" Hart asked. "Your cooperation —*full cooperation*—is at the center of the decision not to prosecute you. The AG made it clear to me that he wants us to go after your ass if you renege on our agreement."

"What about the feds?"

Hart shrugged. "You're not talking with a federal prosecutor right now."

Liam looked over at Maggie. Hart could only assume that the two had already discussed the intricacies of concurrent prosecution by state and federal agencies. He didn't have any control over what the US Attorney's Office might do with the case, much less what other states might decide to do with the innumerable sins committed by Liam Hudson over the years.

"Murder is typically a state matter," Maggie said. "That's what we're focused on right now."

"What about my son?" Liam asked, turning back to the prosecutor. "What happens to Colt?"

"I almost have my grand jury primed and ready to go," Hart said, pressing because he didn't want to blow their deal. "They've heard from Sheriff Clay already and he did a nice job of starting to dig his own grave."

"Clay wasn't always dirty," Liam replied. "When he started at the office back in 2019, he refused to play ball. I think both of you need to understand that."

"What changed?"

"The money," Liam said, seeming more at ease now. "That's how it always is in my business. These cops have families. Kids that need braces, and cars, and tuition for college. Clay wasn't any different than any other man we've bribed. It just took him a while to come around."

Hart leaned forward and placed his elbows on his desk. He wanted to take the sheriff down for any misdeeds that they could prove. He was willing to work with any prosecutor who felt the same. A recently corrupt sheriff deserved prosecution as much as those long since corrupted by greed. They had their sights set on higher office, though.

"I think it's probably true that most people would have a hard time turning the money down," Maggie said. "You know that's not how those grand jurors will feel once they hear from you."

Liam stood from his chair and slowly walked over to the small window in the office. He stood there for a moment before speaking again.

"I'll bet you're right," he said. "It's easy for those people to judge others from where they sit."

"They'd be deciding what to do with you if it weren't for what you can give this office," Hart said. "I'd focus more on that if I were you."

Liam turned from the window. "I'd focus on being—"

Maggie interrupted her client as she turned to the prosecutor. "Mike, I want to go over the terms of our deal one more time. Then, I want everything reduced to writing."

Hart kept his eyes on the witness in the room. The man obviously took the cue from his lawyer to stop speaking—and he listened. Hart wondered how this unique relationship might interfere with Maggie's role as a special prosecutor. That conversation was for another day.

"I wouldn't expect anything less from you," Hart said as he turned back to Maggie. "I assume you already have a draft agreement for me to review?"

Maggie offered her own smile back at him. She didn't need to say anything more.

"Hand it over," Hart said with a sigh. "I'm already giving you everything you want."

39

Colt Hudson stepped into the large courtroom. As the tall wooden doors closed behind him, the twenty or so seated in the gallery seemed to all turn at once in their seats. Colt felt their eyes on him as he started the long walk down the room's center aisle. The six-foot-wide walkway that divided the long rows of wooden pews felt like a plank under his second-hand oxfords. Although he kept his eyes up, he couldn't keep his thoughts from drifting back to those first days in prison. Days that he walked along unfamiliar hallways. Terrified of what might be just around the next corner. Terrified of what might become of him.

The prosecutor—Michael Hart—held a low gate open at the end of the hardwood aisle. It, along with a short wall that ran along the front of the gallery, served as a divider of sorts. The front area of the courtroom, the space where the lawyers typically worked, seemed to be one that was meant to be accessible by invitation only.

"Take a seat up there on the witness stand, Colt."

Colt shook the prosecutor's hand as he passed by. "Good to see you, Mr. Hart."

Hart returned the firm handshake. "We appreciate you being here."

Colt wore the same dress shirt and pants from their meeting the day before. He figured the prosecutor might notice, but Colt didn't care. He felt confident in his appearance and didn't have much need for multiple sets of slacks, polos, and button-down shirts. He hoped to avoid courtrooms and professional meetings for the rest of his days, if possible.

Hart got right down to business. "Madam court reporter, can you please swear the witness?"

Colt stopped just short of the witness stand and turned to a middle-aged woman seated nearby. She asked him to raise his right hand. "Do you solemnly swear, or affirm, that your testimony today will be the truth, the whole truth, and nothing but the truth, so help you God?"

Colt lowered his hand. "I do."

He turned back to the elevated platform and stepped up to take a seat at the small desk. The five-by-five space, with its short walls, felt like a tight enclosure in the large, high-ceilinged room. He settled into the chair and pulled the microphone close. As he did, Colt felt that old, claustrophobic sensation begin to tickle his senses. The same one that'd crept into his cell during those first nights in prison. That feeling of being trapped in an open cage. Protected by guards, yet always in danger.

"Mr. Hart, before we get started, can I ask young Colt here a question?"

The query came from an older man seated on the front row of the gallery.

"Let's just get into his testimony," Hart said with a twinge of frustration in his voice, "then you all can start asking him questions. Will that work for you, Mr. Kilgore?"

"It won't take long," the man said, already starting to stand from his seat. "I've been wanting to ask him something about this for years."

"Well, I guess go ahead," Hart said, taking a few steps back to lean on the low wall at the front of the gallery. He motioned for the man to continue. "Let's try to be quick, though."

"I'm seventy-three," the man called Mr. Kilgore replied. "I'm quick about everything."

The grand jurors chuckled as the man plowed forward. He placed one hand on the barrier, and another on his cane as he spoke.

"Son, I know you probably don't know me, but I know you. I watched you play ball for many years."

Colt didn't recognize the man, but the comment was one he'd heard often in his prior life. As a young star, one that many in Blakeston once believed might make it to the big stage one day, local people often proclaimed their fandom. He usually chose to be grateful for the attention.

"It's good to see you, then. I wish we were on a ballfield right now. I'd be a heck of a lot more comfortable."

Kilgore smiled. "I worked as an official with the GHSA for many years. On the rare Friday night that I didn't handle a game in another county, I always chose to come see you play. It was always worth the price of admission."

"That's very kind of you to say, Mr. Kilgore."

"And I remember your last game. I remember it like it was yesterday. I was working the game here in Blakeston as a back judge that night. You boys looked tough all game."

Colt nodded, listening.

"I saw the hit you took to the head. A nasty one that I don't think I've seen a player take since, and I've watched some big games over the years."

"I watched the game film once," Colt said, shifting in his seat. "That was enough for me."

"I bet it was," Kilgore said, "but I'll tell you this, Colt, it was much worse in person. My stomach hurts thinking about it now. I still blame myself, along with every other adult at that stadium that night, for not making you sit down for the rest of that homecoming game. It wasn't right."

"I don't know what—"

"Do you remember the game that night, Colt?"

From his seat on the witness stand, he could see the faces of all the grand jurors seated in the gallery. They, along with Kilgore, wanted to know the answer.

"I'll be honest, Mr. Kilgore, I've tried to forget a lot about that night."

"I'm sure you have, but do you remember the game?"

Colt looked up at the ceiling as he considered his response. He remembered parts of the game. Parts of the night. Not the ones that mattered, though.

"I don't remember the hit, if that's what you're asking about. I don't remember the long touchdown pass from late in the second half. I don't remember Deacon Campbell's fumble recovery in the final minutes of the game. I don't—"

"How about your girlfriend talking to you before you went back into the game?"

Colt didn't remember anything like that from the night. Maybe it was because of the hit to his head. Maybe it was just a mental block he kept in place to shield himself from the pain.

"I don't believe so, Mr. Kilgore. A long time has gone by since—"

"She tried to convince them to not put you back in the game. I remember her yelling from the other side of the fence. Telling the coaches. Fans. Anyone that would listen. She tried to get them—"

Colt cut the man off. "I chose to go back out there, Mr. Kilgore. It wasn't the right decision, but it was mine."

The old man appeared pleased with the response. He started to say something more, but instead eased back down into his seat.

"Anything else?" Hart asked.

Kilgore motioned for the prosecutor to carry on.

"Okay, then let's get down to it."

Colt nodded.

"Let's talk about your father, Colt."

40

Maggie Reynolds started down the hallway toward the courtroom. She'd received a text from Hart, letting her know that it was almost time. As she turned the corner, she found Tim waiting on the bench outside the doors to the courtroom. His tie hung loose around his collar, and his jacket lay stretched out on the space beside him. His eyes were down, reading something on the screen of his cell phone.

"Do you have a minute to talk?" she asked.

He sat back up straight in his seat, then looked over at her. He didn't look frustrated. He just seemed tired.

"What're you doing up here?"

"I was going to talk to—"

"Are you coming from the judge's chambers down the hall?"

Maggie could hear the tension in his voice. She paused a moment, considering her response. Choosing to lie wouldn't defuse anything.

"I'm coming from the DA's offices because—"

"Because you're working the Hudson case," he said with a laugh as he stood from the bench. He picked his jacket up and started to put it on. "You must think I'm some kind of a moron."

"No, I never—"

"You could've picked any other client's case to work on in this entire county. This entire state, really. Instead, you decide to pick up the one I'm running an investigation on. How can you even begin to explain yourself, Mags?"

"If you'll let me talk, I'll tell you what's going on."

"Let me guess," Tim said, "you need me to step away from the investigation into Liam Hudson, right?"

Maggie realized that the message she planned to deliver to her husband was one that required him to do just that. It wasn't because of a conflict of interest between them, though. It was because she needed Liam to help prosecute a bigger fish.

"The conflict is going to cause *you* too much trouble." Tim said this in a condescending tone. "Did I get that about right?"

As Maggie started to respond, the door to the courtroom swung open. Out stepped Michael Hart, and Colt Hudson followed close behind. They both looked surprised when they encountered the couple standing almost nose-to-nose.

"Are we ready to go?" Hart asked.

"I'm ready," Tim said as he turned to look at the prosecutor. "Let's get me in there."

Hart looked at Maggie, then back at her husband. He obviously wasn't sure how to broach the topic of Maggie's involvement in the case.

"Look, Tim, there's been a change in plans."

"What kind of change?"

"The kind that involves us deciding not to target Liam Hudson."

Tim took a step back from the prosecutor. A decision she wanted to applaud her husband for at that moment. She could tell he was beyond pissed, and she didn't feel much like watching him go to jail on a simple battery charge.

"Since when did *we* decide to let pieces of garbage like Liam Hudson walk?"

Hart shook his head. "That's not it at all. I just don't want to get into it—"

"The man spent almost thirty years of his life stuffing drugs up peoples' noses. People in the poor communities here in Blakeston, and all across the South. Now, he puts more crystal on the street than all the other cooks in the state—combined. Grow some balls, Mike, and let's take this asshole down."

The sound of footsteps could be heard coming up the stairway. Boots on tile.

"We have a bigger fish now, Tim. You know that's how it goes sometimes."

"Who is it?" Tim asked.

Maggie saw the faces of two men appear at the top of the stairs. Both in BCSO uniform.

"Mike," Tim said, almost yelling now, "I asked you a question, dammit."

Maggie placed a hand on Tim's arm to try and calm him. He shook it off as he turned toward the men walking their way. Sheriff Charlie Clay, along with another large investigator, offered a nod as they turned to open one of the doors to the courtroom.

Hart put a hand up. "The grand jurors are having a discussion, Sheriff. You can't go in there right now."

"They need to be made aware of some of my recent findings, ADA Hart."

The sheriff pulled the door open wider and started inside. Maggie watched as the late-forty-something prosecutor reached out and pulled back on the shoulder of the well-built lawman. The action spun the sheriff around, probably more out of surprise than from Hart's strength.

"What do you think you're doing?" the other man with the sheriff growled. He looked younger, somewhat wilder. "You'd better—"

Hart's voice rose. "Stay out of there, both of you!"

Before Maggie could move out of the way, Hart came flying back in her direction. She saw Tim stepping in front of her from the corner of her eye. He stood tall, blocking her with his elbows out as several voices started shouting at once.

"Settle it down, Deacon!" Colt said as he went to grab the young investigator's shoulder. "This isn't how this needs to be handled."

Maggie stepped around her husband's frame. As she did, she got a good look at the man called Deacon. Bruising ran down one side of his face, from his temple to his jaw. It looked as if he'd been on the wrong side of a fight recently. He looked ready to jump into another one as he lunged at Colt.

The younger Hudson seemed ready, though, as he took a smooth step to the side once the hulking man came within inches.

"Stop it!" Maggie yelled. "All of you."

"She's right," Tim added, "this is way out of line."

Before Maggie could say anything to the sheriff, she watched him disappear behind one of the courtroom's tall wooden doors. The prosecutor started toward the entryway, but Deacon raised a hand in warning.

"He's just reporting some of our findings."

"Findings as to what?" Hart asked.

Deacon motioned in Tim's direction. "We've got a dirty commander in our ranks. The sheriff is going to make sure they know about it."

"That's bullshit and you know it."

The big man stood firm in the doorway, shaking his head. "Those people in there are going to hear the truth."

Tim started toward the door just as the latching sound on the courtroom's door filled the hallway—*click.*

41

When the door to the courtroom opened again, it wasn't the sheriff that exited. Instead, the grand jury's foreperson—Angela Carter—stood holding the door open. Maggie waited at the edge of the small mis-matched group. She, along with Tim Dawson, Michael Hart, Cam Abrams, Colt Hudson, and Deacon Campbell, stared at the woman for a moment. Maggie assumed they were all thinking the same thing—*where did the sheriff go?*

"Sheriff Clay asked us to invite you back into the courtroom, Mr. Hart."

"I apologize for the commotion," the prosecutor said as he stood from the bench. He looked down as he straightened his suit jacket and ran a hand through his hair. "I know that was rather unusual."

"That's okay," she replied, "I grew up in a house with four brothers. A *small* house."

"I'm guessing you held your own, Ms. Carter."

"I certainly tried."

Hart smiled as he started toward the open door. He glanced over in Maggie's direction and waved her toward the courtroom.

"Let's go, Maggie, you'll be in on this last presentation."

Maggie felt those familiar butterflies flutter in her stomach. She'd made countless appearances in front of jurors just like the one standing in the hallway. Still, she always felt nervous before stepping back into the well of the courtroom. A good indication that the work still mattered. That it still excited her.

"That must mean I'm the last witness," Tim said as he started to stand from the bench. "I feel like I've been hiding out here all day in plain sight."

The juror looked warily over at Tim, then to Maggie. "Is Commander Dawson your last witness?"

"No, I have someone else that I need you to hear from."

The woman scanned the faces of the others standing in the hallway. She didn't look like she wanted to hear from any of them.

"Which one of you is it?"

42

Liam Hudson stepped onto the witness stand. At a few minutes after four o'clock, the court reporter swore him in. He added his first few words to the record—a transcript that would be rehashed for years to come—then looked out onto the faces of the people who'd been summoned for service on the grand jury. He recognized at least half, nodding to the few he knew well enough to call by their first name. Liam felt light, sitting there on display for the group to see. All ready to judge him, along with his decisions, from the perspectives of their quiet lives. *Let them judge.*

"Tell this group of jurors about yourself," Maggie prodded from her place at a nearby lectern. "Some in this room may know you, while others may not."

Liam glanced down at his hands. Strong hands that'd served him well throughout life. Best for driving, working, and screwing. Now he held them folded in his lap, though, wondering if they could've done anything more in this world. He would never know.

"Well, I grew up right here in Blake County," Liam said as he lifted his eyes to Maggie. "My mom liked to say that I grew up in God's country."

"So, you're a South Georgia boy?"

Liam nodded. "The wiregrass region is my home. The only one I've ever known."

"Is your family still alive?"

"My parents passed in the late nineties, as did the only woman I've ever loved."

Liam let the silence hang over the room a moment as he thought about what he wanted to share. He wanted the transcript to tell others who he was. More than just the bad things about his life.

"We had one son, Colt. I believe you all heard from him already today."

Several heads in the gallery nodded along, clearly listening.

"Colt's mother—Marlene—loved him very much. I did a poor job raising him after she passed, but he's all I have left when it comes to family."

"And your son recently got out of prison?" Maggie asked.

"That's right. Colt served close to five years on a trafficking conviction. He's out on parole now."

"And he's now serving as a confidential informant for the Blake County Sheriff's Office?"

Liam nodded again. "That's right. The BCSO's narcotics squad plucked him out of prison to come after me."

Liam and his son discussed what needed to be said to the grand jury the night before. Liam knew that everything about Colt's work over the last few months had been put on the table for the grand jurors. They knew everything Colt knew—but they didn't know the whole story.

"How'd that come to be, Mr. Hudson?"

"I sent a stack of photos to a man by the name of Tim Dawson—"

"My husband," Maggie added, obviously for transparency. "Now the commander of the BCSO's narcotics squad."

"That's right," Liam replied, "and those photos were taken the night my son was arrested."

"What could you see in those images, specifically?"

"Me, along with two boys from Detroit, putting a delivery into the back of my son's car. One that ended up costing him a chunk of his life, and that of a girlfriend he loved quite a lot."

"Did you know the BCSO planned to use your son as a CI?"

Liam shook his head. "No, but I knew they'd try to do something. They had to."

"Why's that?"

"Because I decided to get out of the dope game."

"You decided to retire from drug dealing?"

"That's right," Liam said as he scanned a few of the faces in the gallery. "That's how I've made my living for almost thirty years. I've maintained one of the largest networks in the South for at least half that time."

Maggie turned to the group and explained that he'd been offered immunity, in exchange for his testimony that day. When she finished her short briefing on the issue, a hand went up in the gallery. A woman by the name of Angela Carter stood to ask a question.

"You're saying that Mr. Hudson can admit to all of this on the record, and he won't be prosecuted?"

"Not here in Georgia, at least. The US Attorney's Office won't take it, either."

"Why?" she asked.

"We'll get to that, Ms. Carter."

Maggie turned back to Liam. She walked him through his operations. His office at Hudson Auto. His land holdings and other unique aspects of his organization. Then, she got to protection.

"Mr. Hudson, you would agree that you're quite a bit older than most large-scale dealers, right?"

Liam smiled. "That's a nice way to say that I've gotten a bit long in the tooth."

Several people chuckled in the gallery. Liam hoped they recognized this self-deprecating humility wasn't something he was usually able to tap into.

"How have you accomplished this?"

"I've not taken a very unique approach. Protection is paid for, usually at the varying levels of local law enforcement."

"People like our sheriff?" Maggie asked.

Liam paused a long moment. "Along with some of the people that work for him."

Several murmurs could be heard throughout the room. The beginnings of an argument that would no doubt ignite once the jurors entered any deliberations. Liam felt the need to again defend the local sheriff.

"I'll have you all know, that it wasn't until very recently that Charlie decided to receive support from my organization."

"How'd you convince him?" Maggie asked.

"It wasn't me this time."

Maggie took a few steps closer to him. She leaned in for her next question.

"Who was it, then?"

"A man I've known for quite a long time—Senator Bill Collins."

The murmurs grew to outright exclamations as everyone reacted to the testimony. An older man in the front row seemed especially troubled by the news. He tried to stand from his seat, citing an unwillingness to listen any longer, but another lady seated behind him encouraged him to sit back down.

"How do you know the senator?" Maggie asked.

"I've known him since the early years. He needed some support to run his campaigns. I needed to get some help when local law enforcement pushed things up the chain to the feds. It was a symbiotic relationship from the beginning."

"So, you're here to offer evidence against him and the sheriff?"

"Bill is the root of it all," Liam said, a serious tone to his voice. "If it wasn't for his influence, half the terrible things that've happened in this county would've never taken place."

"Like what?" Maggie asked.

"The corruption of our sheriff, for one. Along with his office."

Liam noticed that the man in the front row had his eyes squarely on him. "You don't know Senator Collins," the man said. "You're lying."

While Liam let the man's accusation sit with them all for a moment, he felt for the recording device in his pocket. The same one that Tim Dawson provided his son with to take *him* down.

"I met with the senator at his home a little more than a week ago," Liam said as he produced the device. He showed it to Maggie, and she stepped to the stand to take it from her witness. The recording on it was his insurance —the only reason anyone would believe him. "Bill and I've always had our meetings at the main house on Kelley Hill Plantation. Always in his office there because it kept us out of sight, and that's where he hid all of our records. Records that burned up a few days ago..."

"What happened at that meeting?" Maggie asked.

"Bill admitted to paying for the hit on John Deese."

The man on the front row piped up again. "I don't believe that! Not for a second."

Liam kept his voice even as he pointed toward the courtroom's main door. "There's a young, impressionable deputy in the hallway out there that needs to be questioned about all of this. Go ahead and ask him about Trevor Meredith, too."

"That's on this tape?" the man asked, arms crossed.

Liam nodded. "Listen for yourself."

Maggie made her way over to a small speaker nearby. She plugged the recording device into it and turned back to her witness. Liam could tell that everyone in the gallery wanted her to play it, but she had her eyes trained on his. She wanted something more.

"Before we listen to the recording," Maggie said, "do you know if the senator has been involved in any other killings?"

"We only discussed the murders of Meredith and Deese on that recording."

"I don't mean just what's on the recording, Mr. Hudson. I'm asking about any others you may know about."

He paused another second. This was the first question asked by the lawyer that hadn't already been discussed beforehand. He suspected that Maggie had an angle. "Which one in particular?" Liam asked.

"How about his wife?"

Liam stared at Maggie for a long moment. He understood what she wanted. He turned back to the group of grand jurors seated before him and leaned forward, placing his elbows on the edge of the witness stand. Everyone in the gallery seemed to lean forward in their own seats to hear what he had to say. He knew that Maggie Reynolds would prosecute the senator to the fullest extent of the law. He just hoped that he'd be around to see the old politician get what he deserved. Liam paused as he took a deep breath in, then asked the group the question that they needed to answer.

"What do y'all think?"

THE BURDEN OF POWER

A beloved senator. An unspeakable crime. A new face for the prosecution. Welcome to the trial of the century.

In the heart of Blake County, an unprecedented legal storm is brewing. A long-time US senator, Bill Collins, is at the epicenter of this maelstrom. A man of power and influence, he now stands indicted, accused of an unthinkable crime—conspiring in the region's most recent unsolved murders.

Enter Maggie Reynolds: a top-notch trial lawyer, famous for handling high-profile criminal defense cases. In a surprise twist, she crosses the aisle to stand on an unfamiliar side of the courtroom. Tapped as a special prosecutor, Maggie finds herself leading the State's case against the senator, an assignment that carries as much scrutiny as it does prestige.

Maggie knows the stakes are high as she builds out her trial strategy. The task is formidable; the history of several well-known families weaves a complex and thick web. Yet, despite the heavy smoke around the senator's deeds, she seeks more. She needs solid, irrefutable evidence to convince her jury. Evidence she finds on the eve of trial, in an unexpected place that will leave readers breathless.

ABOUT THE AUTHOR

Joe lives in Thomasville, Georgia. When he is not writing in the early morning hours, he devotes his attention to his family and law practice. The love he has for travel, sports, and the practice of law play a large part in shaping his stories. If the sun is shining, you may find him holding tight to his Triumph's handlebars.

Sign up for Joe Cargile's newsletter at
severnriverbooks.com/authors/joe-cargile